AF525436

Introduction

A once rich, powerful, and influential man throws everything away for a woman he loves—a woman whose mother's name is Naamah from the ancient book of Enoch. Naamah is a demon who fell in love with a man, producing a being known as a cambion they named Grace. Sounds like a familiar love story—right? Well, except for the demon part.

Have you ever thought of what your life would have been like if you chose to turn left instead of right? You are not human if the thought never occurred to you, at least occasionally or several times in your life. Think about your choices to arrive at your current place in life. What if I went to college instead of trade school or neither? What if you mustered the courage to ask that pretty girl out and watched someone else beat you to it? Life is a computer program, a series of yes or no choices, in binary code zero or one, but the same results. I don't think there is a person on earth who has not lived their life with some, or maybe many, regrets. Regret can be a powerful catalyst to change yourself if you can take advantage of an opportunity to move in a direction with your life. According to a USA TODAY Blueprint Loans report, nearly one in four college graduates

(25%) wish they had pursued a different educational path or skipped college altogether.[1] This report tells us what many may have already guessed: that a good percentage of people with a higher degree don't value it as much as they did when they pursued it. I suspect the actual rate could be much higher; that is my feeling, not based on any data I can cite.

Is there a solution to this social dilemma? I am afraid I am still figuring things out for myself, too. I have a degree in nuclear medicine, which has helped me raise a family and pay the bills for many years. I confess I enjoyed the challenges of solving problems and helping people, but like anything, the 'shine' wore off. The pride that came with the title of Nuclear Medicine Technologist and all the associated letters behind my name did wane over the years. I have always been drawn to writing at a young age but had little discipline or desire to take it as a serious career choice. Like my character, Brother Greg, who loved the fame and adoration of his flock, not to mention the money of being the head pastor of a megachurch, I liked the comments from others that said things like, "Wow, you must be smart..." etc. My childhood was nowhere near as tragic as Brother Greg's character, but I think most of us can understand the need to be *seen,* at least to ourselves, as a person of value. Greg compensated for a crappy early life by being famous and wanted to be in control instead of it instead of at the whims of fallen angels.

In this third and maybe last? In this installment of the Brother Greg series, Greg is now a humble groundskeeper for St. Rita's Catholic Church, mainly to keep watch over the remains of Bezalel and Azâzêl. He no longer desires to be the center of attention and has never been happier as he navigates the next phase of his life. His former assistant is now his wife, who gives him the love and security he never had. Greg is overjoyed when Grace, his wife, is pregnant with

1. https://www.insidehighered.com/news/quick-takes/2024/10/11/report-quarter-grads-say-they-regret-going-college

twins. However, expanding his new family presents new complications that the couple did not anticipate. Allies of the fallen angels have decided to keep watch over the couple not only to exact revenge for losing their allies, the fallen angels, but simply because a demon-human hybrid should not live by their laws.

Grace finds new allies from another older realm across the sea. They promise to defend her and the unborn twins, whom they believe are the fulfillment of a prophecy.

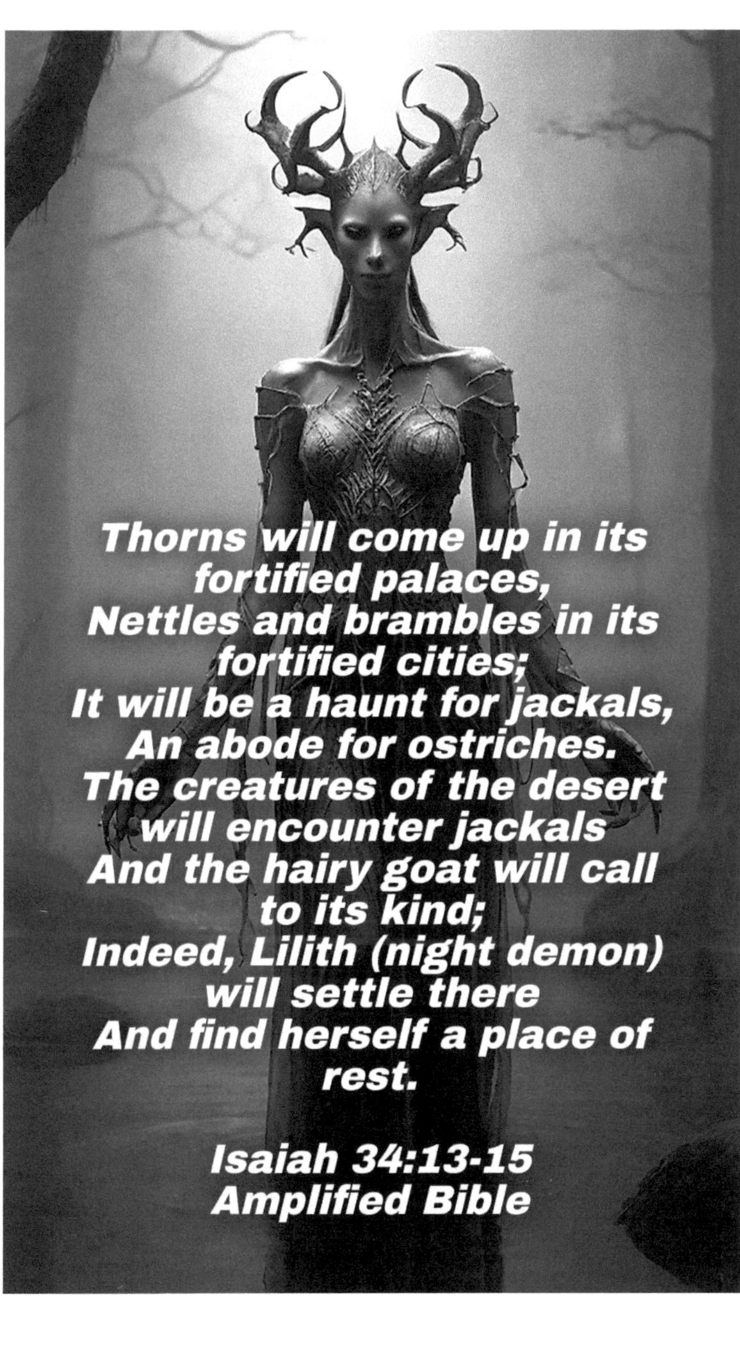
Thorns will come up in its
fortified palaces,
Nettles and brambles in its
fortified cities;
It will be a haunt for jackals,
An abode for ostriches.
The creatures of the desert
will encounter jackals
And the hairy goat will call
to its kind;
Indeed, Lilith (night demon)
will settle there
And find herself a place of
rest.

Isaiah 34:13-15
Amplified Bible

Contents

Chapter 1

Governor Tan

Ash S. Tan, the former Governor of Virginia, was lying prone on a massage table. A small towel covered him as a young, attractive woman dressed in a short, snug bathrobe massaged his shoulders and neck. For an older man, he still had a muscular body and looked much younger than his peers. The press had once inquired about why he looked so young and fit; he waved them off and said he did nothing special; he was naturally this way. He had had an exhausting evening the previous day with an old friend who was one of the few in his world who could keep up with his appetites, and he was a little sore this morning.

"Don't be afraid to use more pressure, Janice; I won't break."

"Yes, sir."

Since leaving Office, he has been one of Janice's regular customers. According to his bio, he was fifty-six and stood at just over six foot five and about two hundred pounds. He was often seen outside his home running or swimming in his large personal indoor pool. Ash Tan was considered a handsome man, according to the latest People magazine, with olive skin and jet-black hair; his eyes were golden brown, and he had a smooth-shaven face. He made his fortune in the computer tech industry, owning a patent for groundbreaking computer chips for today's market—an AI chip with properties that even his fiercest rivals could not duplicate. The design was radically different from other AI chips; when his competitors inspected them under a microscope, they could see unusual letters or symbols etched on his chips, without any identifiable functions.

James, Mr. Tan's assistant was also in the room, reading emails that had come in from the Party office. Most were about the catastrophic loss they suffered to Nicole Cooper in the gubernatorial race. He had been with the former governor the longest of his political associates. James was also hiding a secret like his boss, Mr. Tan: they—were not human. But that is where the similarity ended; Tan was a more powerful being, and James was... something else. He knew his employer hid what he was from everyone except close associates. He read off the last email from a political PAC that wanted his blessing to start saturating the media with ads against the new Virginia Governor.

"Sir. I wouldn't worry much about Governor Cooper; she is not a threat—at least not yet. What about that former Brother Greg? Do you think he will cause us trouble, James?" Mr. Tan said.

"Mr. Cassidy is a concern, but I don't think it is an immediate one, sir. We should focus on rebuilding the party first. The former pastor and his mongrel wife can wait," his assistant offered.

"As you wish, James. Your instincts have not been wrong yet. Especially trusting those damned angels. Before you go, James, if the second masseuse is here, please send her in."

"Of course, sir."

Mr. Tan pushed himself up on his elbows, "And one last thing, clear my schedule today. I need to take care of some personal business."

James bowed and closed the door. A few moments later, a second young woman dressed just like the first stepped into the room.

"You require my services, sir?" She said.

"Yes, my dear, over here. You can work on my legs while Janice continues working my arms and neck."

"Of course, sir." She rubbed massage oil in her hands and began to work on Mr. Tan's legs.

Outside the office, at his desk, James began replying to the emails he reviewed with his boss. The former Brother Greg is a potential problem, Mr. Tan was unsure how Mr. Kanker became free of Azâzêl, and James was unable to contact him. There is also the troubling problem of Bezale's disappearance; he, too, is missing. The carefully laid out plans for political power have run into an obstacle; for the moment, no alternate plan was apparent to James. Maybe his boss, Mr. Tan was working on other ideas.

"James, there is a call for Mr. Tan. Should I route it to his Office?" Gloria Cope screened all calls coming to the office, routing them to James before she could send them to Mr. Tan. She made the mistake of routing a call from a supporter during the previous political season and was punished with one day in Mr. Tan's 'resort' for retraining. She never made that mistake again.

"Who is it, Gloria?"

"A Ms. Rebekah Lot. She says it's important and must speak to Mr. Tan directly."

James sighed audibly and didn't care if Gloria heard it.

"Let me talk to her first, Gloria."

"Yes, sir." She connected the call.

"Hello, Rebekah. How are you doing today?"

"Oh, I thought she would connect me directly to Mr. Tan, James." She said with irritation in her voice.

"I am afraid he left strict instructions with me not to be disturbed. I'm deeply sorry." James was glad this was not a video call, or she could have seen his sneering face.

“Well, please connect me anyway, James. It is vital!”

“Sorry, I cannot. If you have anything important to say, you can tell me. Otherwise, call back later.” He sounded calm and professional, but underneath, his patience was running thin.

“You listen to me, you overpaid...” Rebekah couldn’t finish because she suddenly found it hard to breathe. James smiled hearing the gurgling noises and her audibly struggling to inhale.

“What is that, Rebekah? I can’t hear you.” He taunted.

Rebeckah felt invisible hands around her neck, and the pressure was growing. James put his phone on speaker while walking from his desk to the coffee pot across the room. James smiled, hearing the gurgling noises and her audible struggle to inhale.

“Are you still there, Rebekah? If you are, give me a sign,” he spoke up from across the room.

“Mmmmm...”

“Oh good, I am glad you can hear me, my dear.”

There was a loud gasp, and then coughing could be heard.

“Are you still there, my dear?”

“Yes, I am.” She said with a hoarse voice.

“I am glad. Where were we? Oh yes... You were about to give me a message for Mr. Tan. Is that correct?” James sipped his coffee and sat back down at his desk.

“It is about the party finances,” she said softly with no hint of her defiance earlier. “Donors are becoming hesitant to give to our party now, especially considering the defeat of Mr. Kanker. We will have trouble competing in future races if we don’t find new revenue streams,”

“And what is your suggestion for Mr. Tan?”

“Well.” Rebekah said in a meek tone, “Mr. Tan should consider making more public appearances to show that we are not like Mr. Kanker and care about the country and its people.”

"Are you saying he doesn't care?"

"Oh no... no, that is not what I am saying, but several of our biggest donors threaten to pull their money and support."

James could hear the panic in her voice. But he had to admit she was usually right about these things. People have short memories if Mr. Tan has been out of the public eye for too long, the public will forget about him and move on to someone else. That cannot happen.

"Ok, Ms. Lot, I will talk to him when he is available and forward your concerns."

"Thank you, sir."

James hung up the phone, irritated. In this world, money is power and sometimes more formidable than any of the deadliest weapons devised by man. Man excels at ways to inflict harm on themselves and others. It is no wonder they are so much fun to play with. It's time to make a phone call. But who? James had an idea and smiled; he picked up his phone.

"Mr. Laban. I have a job for you... Yes, it's been a long time. You did an excellent job as Mr. Tan's chief of staff when he was governor. Here is what I need you to do for us."

Chapter 2

Handyman

It was midday. The blazing Sun scorched the parched earth, where scattered scrub brush and grasses clung to life. The air was dry and hot, much like the inside of an oven. Dust devils spun lazily in the shimmering air. Far in the distance, he could see rolling hills and, further out—are those mountains?

Where am I? This place feels familiar.

He heard shouting from behind him in a strange yet strangely, not an unfamiliar language. What he initially thought was scrub brush, he now recognized as pine and Cyprus trees. Confused, he reached out a hand and plucked one of the trees as if it were a weed.

This is crazy. My hand is as large as this tree.

Then he felt pain from something hard striking his head and then another on his body. Behind him were people with crude slings. Were those swords they were holding? But the people were impossibly small, and they looked angry and scared. He ran away from the confusing situation, the wind in his ears rushing past as if he were in a speeding car.

Greg woke up.

What the fuck was that? Maybe, too much of a good time last night?

He had a "boy's night" out with a childhood friend. A little too much to drink?

Greg stepped out of the shower feeling refreshed. Yesterday, he completed installing vinyl siding on the Pastor's cottage outside vinyl trim. It took him over a week to replace the siding and paint the new front door. His hands were still full of blisters and cuts, but it was worth it, doing an honest day's work. He offered to be the church handyman, at least for now, until he and Grace knew what the next stage of their lives would be. Greg never had a *real* job in his life before. So, he didn't know what to do after being the Pastor of the now much-diminished church an hour away from here. Greg and his new wife, Grace, lived in an RV on church property while their new house was under construction. They hoped it was scheduled to be finished by the end of summer. One morning, soon after they married, Grace felt nauseous, and her coffee tasted horrible. An at-home test confirmed what she thought: she was pregnant. She saw her doctor and estimated she was four weeks into her pregnancy. At first, she resisted seeing a doctor at all. She was scared primarily because of her mixed heritage. Her mother is a succubus, and her late father was human. Outwardly, she looked more or less normal as a human woman, but Greg had Nephilim blood; he was not entirely *normal,* either. The prospect of the unknown scared her. In the past, Grace had given no thought to having children; she never thought she would fall in love— until Greg. His best friend's grandmother congratulated them when Grace told her the news and Grace's belief, she would ever have kids and said, 'Life happens.'

The pregnancy was progressing normally, and she was due to deliver about a month after they were scheduled to move into the new house...they hoped. The couple still has not gotten over what the ultrasound tech told them: She thought she had heard two heartbeats, but it was not conclusive yet. It was still early, and they still did not know the sex, or sexes, of the new little one or ones in their lives.

"Grace. Where are the clean towels?" Greg stood on the bathmat, dripping wet. He thought there was a towel hanging up next to the shower.

"It was hanging up on the hook," she yelled, sitting at the small table in the middle of the RV. She had been finding it hard to move quickly lately because sometimes she was hit with a wave of nausea. Right now, she was in no mood to get up and help him find a towel, even if he looked sexy standing there.

"Found it!" Greg grinned, quickly dried himself off, and wrapped the towel around his waist. He approached her and kissed her on the top of the head. She was nibbling on a piece of toast at the small table. She looked a little better this morning than in the past week.

"How are you feeling, babe?"

"A little better. I think the toast is helping," she waved a half-eaten piece. A coffee cup was in her other hand; the tea bag string hung off the side.

"What time is your doctor's appointment?" Greg asked, pulling on his clothes and taking the towel back to the shower.

"10 am. Are you still able to come?"

"Yes, of course. I can convince the boss to let me go for a few hours. After all, it is for the health of his future godchildren." Greg winked. He referred to Father Ortiz, the Pastor of St. Rita's, who was recently happy when the couple asked him to be their children's godfather.

At that moment, there was a knock on the door.

"You guys up yet?" Father Ortiz said through the door.

"Yes, Father, please come in," Grace said.

The RV's door opened, and St. Rita's Pastor stepped in, holding a cup of coffee. "Good morning."

"Good morning, Father," Grace said, not very convincingly. She was not feeling the 'good' part this morning.

"Oh, my child, you look green. My mother always advised toast with honey and lemon ginger tea for morning sickness. Just plain toast only goes so far."

"We don't have any honey here, Father."

Father Ortiz waved, "Can you come over to the cottage? I have honey and ginger tea. My mother swore by them when she had my sister."

Greg shrugged, "Let's go, Grace. I hate to see you like this."

Grace sat at the cottage's kitchen table, which felt more spacious than the RV one. She already felt better, maybe because this kitchen was less claustrophobic. Father Ortiz made toast and spread honey on it; next to it was a fresh cup of hot ginger tea. Grace had to admit that his mother's remedy did make her feel better.

"Thank you, Father; your mother was right about the tea and honey toast for morning sickness." Grace managed to give a weak smile.

"I am sure my mother would say you are welcome." He turned his attention to Greg, "The new siding looks good. Thank you for all your hard work. I wish you would accept payment."

"That's all right, Father. It keeps me busy, and I feel great doing manual labor for a change. It's good for the body and soul," he smiled, "Grace and I don't need anything. We have plenty from my investments and the sale of my old home. We are still unsure what our next chapter will be besides, of course, being parents." Greg looked lovingly at his wife, holding her tea in one hand while the other rested on her expanding tummy.

"Well, for myself and Fr. O'Brian, we are happy for the company and look forward to greeting the little ones when they are here." Father Ortiz grinning like a proud grandfather.

Chapter 3

Warning

Robert found himself walking on a tropical beach, its soft, powdery white sand massaging the soles of his feet. The gentle ebb and flow of the waves and the warm sun on his face filled his heart with a peaceful feeling. He walked without pain in his hip and with a cane. It was perfect—too perfect. He sighed and shook his head.

"Hello Raphael, what's up, my friend?"

"I guess it's pointless to surprise you, Robert." A man in a simple t-shirt and jeans materialized, walking beside him.

"We know each other too well after all these years."

They walked on an idyllic sandy beach—one that could be anywhere in the world, and it may be an actual beach somewhere, for all Robert knew. The sun was high in the sky, and a warm breeze skimmed off the ocean waves. Birds were chattering in the distance.

"So where are we, and why have you brought me to this paradise?" Robert said, filling his lungs with the clean sea air.

The angel spread his arms out, "Don't you like your Lola's home island?"

"You brought me to the Philippines?" Robert looked around and wondered why anyone would leave such a beautiful place. But she told him she moved with his grandfather to find work in the capital. "I'll have to tell her it's beautiful."

"Yes, it is an unspoiled part of this world. But I am sure you are wondering why we are here."

"That's an understatement, my friend. You wanted more words of wisdom from this simple human?" Robert teased.

Raphael looked puzzled. No matter how long they had known each other, he still struggled with human sarcasm and humor. Robert laughed and slapped Raphael's back.

"I see you are 'messing with me,.'" the angel said, "one day, I'll understand you, my friend."

"I am happy to see you again. But seeing you usually means you have a warning for me or something serious I need to know about," he said, his voice now grim.

"Sadly, you are correct."

A person slowly materialized a few steps away from them. At first, all Robert could make up was a general human form that gradually coalesced into a tall woman... no, a man? His hair was black, and his wings were like Raphael's, except they were golden with black tips at the ends. An ornate sword hung on his back. He was wearing a T-shirt and jeans, much like Raphael.

"Robert, let me introduce you to Michael."

"Nice to meet you, Michael," Robert said, trying not to sound nervous. After all this time and all the things Robert had seen and done, he thought he lost the capacity to feel surprised by his interactions with Raphael until now.

Michael extended his hand. "I am glad to meet the man who has done so much to keep Bezalel and Azâzêl 'on ice,' as you humans say."

"It was not just me, you know."

"Yes, of course, Robert." Michael smiled, "How is your friend Greg doing these days? I hope you know that we value your privacy as much as you do and only interfere if the situation calls for it."

Robert was not entirely convinced angels watched people only, when necessary, but he kept that to himself. "Greg is finally getting the life he always wished for."

"What do you mean?" Micheal said.

"When we were kids, he didn't have a loving home life. I know his mother loved him, but she had her own issues to deal with, and so he was left most of the time lacking her love and support. He didn't have confidence in himself or his future. The events caused by Bezaliel only made things worse for him. I am sure he became 'Brother Greg' to give his life value, with adoration and money. Also, I believe he had some resentment about his younger days. As the saying goes, the best revenge is being successful, so Greg thought being rich and adored was a success. He was remarkably successful for a time, even when it made him miserable. Today, he lives simply as a church caretaker with the love of his life, Grace."

"Ahh, yes, the cambion, and you trust her?"

"Yes, I do. You know we can't choose who our parents are."

Michael nodded. "How is her pregnancy going?"

"I thought you did not keep tabs on humans unless it was important?" Robert felt a little irritated; he didn't know this angel as well as Raphael, so he didn't understand his motivations.

"Sorry if I was not clear. We don't generally, as you would say, 'keep tabs' on humans in their daily lives. But Grace is not an ordinary being."

"Yes, I know. So does that mean that Grace is easier for angels to find and monitor?" Robert didn't like where this was going.

"Yes."

"Ok. So, the reason you are here has to do with Grace?"

"Not entirely, Robert. She is only one small piece of what Raphael, and I are concerned about. The real concern is the former governor of your home state. Mr. Ash S. Tan. You see, he is not what he appears to be. Much like, Mr. Kanker was."

"Another fallen angel?" Robert stopped walking, bowed his head, and sighed.

"Not exactly," Michael said.

"What is wrong, my friend?" Raphael asked.

Robert didn't know how to express what was swirling in his head and heart. A heaviness appeared inside his chest.

"How do I say this to two immortal beings who would have a limited understanding of my feelings? My life is finite; like all humans, I don't get many chances to start over when things go wrong. Some people never get a second chance. I lost so many years of my own life because of one of those—things. I got my chance with my wife to have a happy life and, hopefully, a family. I missed so many opportunities that only come around when you are younger. I am grateful AM stayed with me, and I don't know what I would have done if she had given up and left. What you are saying to me now is that our lives are in danger again because of one of *them*."

"I'm sorry, Robert, but I would not be much of a friend if I didn't warn you." Raphael rested his hand on Robert's shoulder.

Robert didn't look at the Angels; he closed his eyes and took a few deep breaths.

"Robert, did we say something wrong?" Michael said.

"No, Michael, you said nothing wrong. You need to tell me everything you know about Mr. Tan and what you think he is up to so we can devise a strategy to defeat him. I am tired of those bastards interfering with my life and my friends."

"Of course. Let me tell you what we know so far..."

Robert raised his hand, "I think we need to have this conversation with my wife, Greg, and Grace. Also, let's involve Father Ortiz; he has been a big part of this fight."

The two Archangels exchanged glances, and Raphael said, "Agreed."

"I will contact you, Raphael, when I set things up," Robert said.

"Please don't take too long, my friend," Raphael said.

There was a moment of disorientation, and Robert was back home.

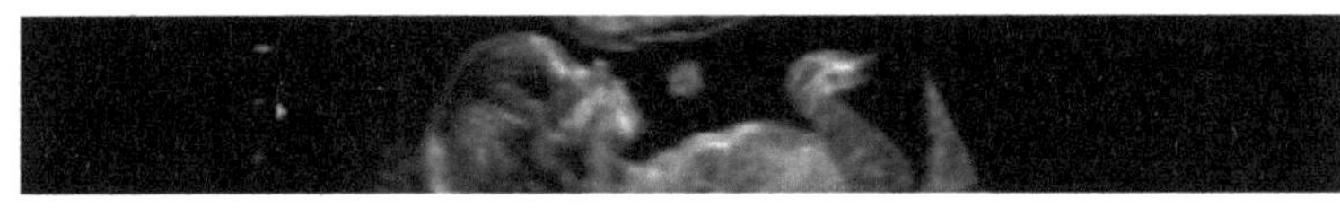

Chapter 4

Prenatal Surprise

"This way, Ms. Cassidy, we are ready for you. My name is Angela, and I will perform your exam today." The ultrasound tech directed them into the exam room. Greg's heart skipped a beat when he heard her name; no time for dredging up old memories. He wanted to be with Grace at her ultrasound appointment.

This was the first appointment since she confirmed the pregnancy two months ago. She held Greg's hand tight; to say she was nervous was an understatement. She had yet to tell her mother about her condition, and she wondered how she would take the news of being a grandmother. Naamah was still very protective of Grace even after she married Greg, so there was no doubt in her mind that her mother would be equally protective of any of Grace's children.

"It will be OK, babe," Greg said, gently squeezing her hand.

"It's OK to be nervous, Ms. Cassidy. This is your first pregnancy, and your partner is here, which is an important first step," the tech said.

"I do have a good partner," Grace said, squeezing her husband's hand back.

Once in the exam room, Grace was instructed to change into a gown and empty her bladder in the adjoining restroom. The technologist said she would return once Grace was ready. Grace did what was instructed and sat next to Greg. Greg could tell by her posture that she was anxious.

"Don't be nervous, babe. It's just a routine exam." Greg said.

She flashed a nervous smile, "I know."

"So, what is bothering you?"

She looked straight ahead, opened her mouth as if to say something, and closed it again.

Greg squeezed her hand gently and whispered in her ear, "Remember, we are in this together. It was scary leaving our old lives and starting again. Maybe not as scary as facing fallen angels, but this is more *personal* for both of us. We took a chance on each other. Wedding vows are just words spoken in a moment and are not as important as the unspoken words that bind us each day. I can say to you that I am here for you with words. But Grace, I am here with you in heart, mind, and body. I intend to be with you always, in good times and bad."

A tear ran down her cheek, "Thank you."

"So, tell me, what is bothering you?"

"I am nervous about the babies and if they will be 'normal.' I am not normal, and the people of my mother's world tried to kill me. I fear getting you caught up in my family—issues."

"*Our* family issues. When I married you, I joined your family too... willingly."

A knock on the door broke the somber mood. "Are you ready, Ms. Cassidy?"

"Yes."

Angela came in and sat at the ultrasound console. "Please lay down on the table here, Mr. Cassidy. You can sit in the chair next to her."

Grace laid down, and Angela confirmed Grace's patient identification with her. "To recap our phone conversation last week. The ultrasound is performed transvaginaly. Did you empty your bladder?"

"Yes."

"OK, let's begin. If you feel any discomfort or pain, please tell me."

"OK," Grace nodded her head.

The tech began the exam. The ultrasound probe, called a transducer, was kept in a holder with warm ultrasound gel, which, when used, did not 'shock' the patient because it was the same as body temperature.

Grace was bracing for the exam, but it was not as uncomfortable as she first feared. She relaxed a little.

"Better than room temperature, right? It makes things a little more comfortable during the exam." She moved the transducer very little, and Grace felt the tech's other hand press lightly on her abdomen. The exam, for the most part, was comfortable.

"Relax, Ms. Cassidy: we are almost done."

"You can tell I'm nervous?"

Angela smiled and moved the transducer a little to one side.

"There we are..."

She was momentarily quiet as Grace could feel the probe move around more. Grace and Greg looked at the screen but did not know what they were looking at. The tech leaned in to look at the screen closer, moving the probe slightly. It was like she was searching for something.

"Is everything OK, Angela?" Greg asked.

"Yes, things are good. I just wanted to confirm what I saw before saying anything."

"What do you see?" Grace said.

"Well, to put it simply. Twins."

The couple returned home with a mixture of emotions. Because it was confirmed that Grace was pregnant with twins, she had to schedule another ultrasound exam in a month and one each month during the pregnancy.

"What is on your mind, honey?" Not known for her sense of humor, Grace said teasingly to her husband, who barely spoke a word on the drive home.

"Huh?' Greg was sitting down now, just staring in a daze outside one of the windows.

Grace, this time, was the one to needle him instead of the other way around. She snickered. "You have been a zombie ever since you were told you are the father of not one child but twins."

"Zombie? That is a good description. I am happy, but I am still processing all the changes in our plans for just one little rug rat. Now, two rug rats."

"Honey, you worry too much. We are not the first parents to ever have twins. I know you will make a great father. But we do have one slight problem."

"Problem?" Greg snapped to attention. "What is it, babe?"

Grace laughed. "You need to settle down, Greg, or you will age ten years before the babies are born."

He looked at his running shoes at the door and said, "Sorry. Ah maybe, maybe... I should go for a run to clear my head. So, what problem are you talking about?" Greg was babbling.

"Who should we tell first about the change in our family... size?" She rubbed her hands on her abdomen.

"Yes, we have to tell everyone. But when we learn the sexes, I am not a fan of that silly gender reveal crap." Greg paused, his thoughts swirling. "We know we are having twins, but we don't know if they are identical or fraternal twins... at least not yet."

"Maybe we should tell your friend Raphael?"

"Why him?" He said in surprise.

"Well, I always wondered how much those guys knew before the rest of us. Can they see the future?" Grace said her face looked serious. She had never interacted with the archangels and had only heard about them secondhand from Greg and Robert. Secretly, she wondered if they had something against what she was: a cambion, half-human, and demon.

"Our earthly friends deserve to know first; they put more on the line than some immortal beings. The question is how and when." Greg said.

"How about telling Father Ortiz, Robert, and AM that we want to treat them to dinner tonight?"

"Why tonight?"

Grace tried crossing her arms across her chest, but she discovered it was getting harder to do that these days and then gave up. "Do you honestly think we can keep this a secret for long? Everyone knows that my ultrasound was today, and there will be questions that any person would ask."

"You got a point. Any ideas where we should go?"

"How about that nice seafood restaurant in Williamsburg? The Colonial Seaman." Grace said.

"What about your mom?"

"I will have to tell her soon. She will be upset if she is left out. I will have to tell her before dinner with our friends. I don't think she would take it well if they had known before, she did. After all, she is the grandmother and has the right to know."

"You know she can't come to us here because the RV is parked on holy ground. What do you want to do?"

Grace stood up and picked up the car keys. "I will go to a neutral place like the Walmart in town. People are strange there anyway, so no one will give her a second look and tell her then." she smirked, "I'll be back soon."

"Are you sure it's safe?"

"I am still wearing the pendant that came with the Ring of Solomon. I will be OK. You go ahead and make the restaurant reservations so we can tell our friends," she said, kissing him while reaching for her car keys.

"OK, babe, see you soon."

Grace left, and Greg picked up his phone.

"Robert, how about we all have a nice seafood dinner tonight? My treat."

Chapter 5

Invisible

Naamah was waiting to meet Grace at one of those awful shopping centers that seem so popular these days; how she missed the old open-air bazaars that represented the local city culture. Of course, that was a few millennia ago when she and her kind easily blended into the crowds. Early in Naamah's life, humans lived a short and passionate existence. Today, their lifespans are much longer, but they still have the same passions that are magnified with the extra years they live. Despite her critique of human nature, she is grateful that humans have not changed because she would have no means of sustaining herself. The raw emotions of vise and lust provide her with sustenance.

Where is that girl?

"Hello, Mother," Grace said as she approached from behind.

How did she sneak up on me? Grace could never have surprised her mother like that before.

"Hello, child, how are you?" Naamah reached out to hug her daughter and stopped in her tracks. "Something is different with you, Grace; what is it?"

"That is what I wanted to talk to you about. Would you like to have some coffee with me? There is a Starbucks next door."

"Lead the way."

Mother and daughter sat at a small table. Naamah had coffee and Grace tea.

"So what is it you wish to talk about, dear?" Her mother said, holding her cup to her lips. "You hardly ever use the stone to call me. The last time you did was when you were away at college." Naamah had given her daughter a round stone that looked like a small piece of jade. If Grace ever needed her mother urgently, she would use it, and her mother would be at with her immediately. This time, Grace left a kind of non-urgent voicemail asking her mother to meet at the usual place, a Walmart.

"Well, this is important, but not an emergency?" Grace hesitated on the best way to tell her mother the news of her pregnancy. Never mind, it was also twins.

"Oh?" Naamah put her cup down and reached across the table, putting a hand on Grace's arm. Something was different.

Grace could tell by her mother's expression that she sensed something about her. "I wanted you to be the first to know mother. I am pregnant with twins."

That felt good to let it out.

Naamah did not react; her face was unreadable sometimes, even to Grace.

"Mother?"

Naamah stood up. Grace thought she was going to leave and stood up, too. Naamah reached out and took her daughter's hand, and the Starbucks disappeared around them. Grace could see that they were in a well-furnished apartment. On one wall was a large floor-to-ceiling window that overlooked a familiar cityscape. It was Naamah's apartment in San Francisco. Grace had only been there once before, a long time ago; she could see the Golden Gate Bridge on one side of the window.

"Why did you bring me here, Mother? I'm in no mood for games. I only wanted you to know first because I love you, and you have a right to know." Grace felt a tiny seed of pain at her mother's silence and an unscheduled cross-country trip.

Naamah embraced Grace. "I am so happy for you." Naamah let her go, and Grace could see a tear in one of her mother's eyes.

"Thank you, Mom. But why am I here now? Please explain why you are acting this way."

"Please sit. I want you to know I am happy for you and Greg. But when I touched you, something was...*off*."

"Is there something wrong with me or the babies?"

"No, nothing like that... I think." Naamah seemed to reach for words. "How many times had you been able to sneak up on me without my knowing first?"

Grace thought back to her childhood. Her mother always knew if someone was close. No one had ever been able to 'sneak up' on her because she could always sense any human nearby, even Grace. "I don't think I have ever been able to sneak up on you. Why?"

"You did it for the first time today in that store, and you are not wearing the pendant Greg gave you that protects you from beings that would want to harm you." Her mother said.

Grace reflexively reached for her neck, where the pendant usually would be. She had taken it off when she showered this morning and forgot to put it back on because she didn't want to be late for her ultrasound appointment. She was still on her mom's radar when she wore the pendant, but not as strongly as without it.

"I don't know what to say, Mother; you can still sense me when I wear the pendant. But now you can't?"

"I wanted to come to *my* safe space to feel your presence. Right now, you are blank, as if no one is standing in this room with me, "Naamah said flatly.

"The babies?" Grace touched her abdomen.

"Yes, I think so, dear." Naamah hugged her again, "but your medical exam was normal, right?"

"Yes, mother."

"Then we should consider this a good thing for the safety of you, the twins...and my grandchildren," she said with a smile.

Grace looked at her watch, "I need to call Greg."

"Why?"

"We agreed to tell our friends the news, but we wanted to tell you first. I want to find out if he had made arrangements to meet with them today and what time." She looked at her smartwatch; it had already adjusted to Pacific time. "It's 12:30 here, so I assume dinner with our friends will be in a few hours. I would love to spend more time with you, but can you take me back to my car, please?"

"Child, you will not be able to keep me away from my grandchildren. Take my hand, I'll get you home."

Naamah and Grace faded away, and the apartment was empty again.

Naamah watched Grace leave the parking lot to join her husband and friends for dinner. It was then they planned to break the news about the twins. She was happy for her daughter, considering last year's events. Naamah's biggest fear then was that she would not have survived the wrath of fallen angels and their ambitions. When Grace was young, Naamah taught her to stay under their 'radar' and not interfere with their plans, but things got complicated when she fell in love with that human. In all her long life, she never truly knew fear until her daughter was in danger of losing her life by defying Bezaliel and Azâzêl.

"How are you, sister?" A voice from behind her said.

Naamah closed her eyes. "I am unchanged, sister." She turned to face the woman standing behind her. "And so are you."

The woman standing behind Naamah appeared to be in her twenties. She was about six feet tall and had long, silky brown hair and almond-shaped grey eyes. She wore a loose T-shirt, jeans, and a white baseball cap. Her figure was one most women would envy, and straight men could not help but notice.

"The blessing of immortality." She grinned.

"What do you want from me, Lilith? I thought we parted as friends as long as we didn't see each other anymore." Naamah gritted her teeth at the word *friends.*

"But that was such a long time ago, sister. Can't you forgive me? It's only been what, twenty years?" Lilith made a pouty face. One corner of her mouth curled up as if to smile.

"Try thirty years."

"That's a mere clock tick for beings like us, sister. Can't I miss you and want to chat after all this time?"

"I do miss you, sister. I miss what we used to mean to each other as family. But I just can't trust you after you exposed me to... what does he go by these days? Oh, Mr. Tan, who divulged my true nature to the man I loved—Grace's father. I did not have the courage to tell him myself at that time. Even after Tan told him the truth about me, he still accepted me and loved me. I was not at home with him when the fallen angels attacked." With a catch in her voice mixed with anger," I lost someone good and—cared about me for me. That man was one of the rare humans immune to a succubus' influance." The thought of that incident still caused Naamah pain. "Then, when Grace was born, you betrayed me again by letting others in our world know of her existence. She was almost killed soon after she was born."

"I'm sorry you feel that way, sister. I don't make apologies for wanting our race to remain pure."

"If you still feel that way, why do you waste my time? We have nothing left to talk about." Naamah growled.

"Oh, but we do, dear sister. Some members of our circle have gone missing, and I was hoping you may know something about it." Lilith's grey eyes darkened.

"That is your problem, not mine. I have no contact with *your* circle of friends anymore. My only concern is my daughter and seeing that she has a good life."

"How long will that be, Naamah? Her human blood is a weakness. She has no power over mortals and will have a short lifespan like all of them." Lilith said in a disgusted tone.

I can't be if sure Grace has any powers, or how long she will live. Just today, I was unable to sense her, which is something she has never had before.

"Lilith, if you come here to insult my daughter or me, I will be going now." Naamah was about to leave when Lilith blurted out.

"I know you were working with Bezaliel before he disappeared, Mr. Tan told me so."

Naamah froze. She didn't know anyone else knew about their arrangement. Of course, she could be bluffing. "What are you talking about, sister?" She spat the word sister.

"I don't know much, but everyone knows that he offered protection to your migás (half-breed) child in exchange for working for him on some project. I never learned what that work was, sister." Lilith spat the last word back.

Naamah moved quicker than anyone in the parking lot would have been able to see if anyone were looking at two women conversing in a Walmart parking lot. She put her hands around Lilith's neck, but she wiggled free just as fast.

"I hit a nerve, didn't I?"

"Leave my daughter out of your filthy mouth!" Naamah's angelic face twisted in rage. "I'm going now. Leave Grace alone, or you will deal with me, and you don't have your old lover to save you again."

"I don't need saving, dear sister."

Naamah melted away, leaving Lilith alone.

Chapter 6

Julius Laban

The convention center was buzzing with men and women from all over the state and country dressed in expensive gowns and tailored suits. People who were old hands at these events mentored a new generation of political operatives for a price; of course, some were there because they had the money, and others had more personal currency. It all appeared to be a well-choreographed event, with each attendee there for a shared political agenda. Still, Mr. Laban saw it for what it was: political predators circling each other, waiting for the right time to strike.

Humans think so highly of themselves. They believe they are the most dangerous creatures, but they are so naive.

Julius Laban was here on the orders of the former governor, Mr. Tan. After what happened to Mr. Kanker, Party support for him was soft. He was here to shore up flagging support and remind some of the people who championed their causes and lined their pockets. There were many familiar faces and some new ones he did not recognize. All the attendees were just as they appeared—human, at least in his immediate vicinity. There were no non-humans in the crowd he stood among.

"Mr. Laban, it has been too long, sir. How have you been?" said a man's voice behind him.

Julius turned around to see a short, portly man in his fifties leaning on a cane.

He is? Oh yes, Mr. Fredrick Holt. A senior partner at a prestigious law firm outside Fredericksburg.

Julius put on his best political smile, "Good to see you again, Mr. Holt." Next to Holt was a young woman, whom he guessed was in her mid-twenties. She had auburn hair tied up in a bun on her head. She had light blue eyes framed with dark lashes and eyebrows. The woman wore a conservative pantsuit strategically cut to accentuate her slim and toned figure. "Who is this lovely woman beside you? Your daughter?"

Mr. Holt laughed, "Oh no, she is just one of my trusted associates at the firm. Let me introduce you to Miss. Georgia Cassidy."

She extended her hand, "I'm pleased to meet you, Mr. Laban." The two shook hands, and she lost her balance for a moment but quickly recovered. The moment they touched each other, she felt weak.

Julius pretended not to notice. "Cassidy? By chance, are you related to Greg Cassidy? You know the one that used to run that church in Franklin?"

"Not that I know of, and if I was, I would not have wanted to be associated with him... especially after his crazy talk about Senator Kanker and fallen angels."

"That's smart, Georgia. I would not want it known that I had any connection to that unfortunate soul either."

Georgia smiled demurely, "Thank you."

"So, what brings you here, Julius? Mr. Tan has not retired, I assume. I don't see him slipping away into a quiet retirement." Mr. Holt said.

"I have nothing to share at the moment, Fredrick. But don't count Governor Tan's absence for so long; you could say he is reassessing the political environment and his options." Julius said with a broad smile.

"Yes, I can understand. It may be best to wait until the memory of Senator Kanker has faded from public memory."

"Well, if you will excuse me, I am on my way to get a seat inside the main hall." Julius turned to go, but Georgia quickly grabbed his arm.

"Why don't we all find a table together." She said breathlessly, "After all, that is where Fredrick... I mean, Mr. Holt and I were going to find one anyway. Right, Mr. Holt?"

"Ah, yes, we were. I guess we can go now if you wish, Georgia." He touched her back, gently nudging her away from Julius. *Damn, he always had this effect on women. Trying to talk to him in the first place was a bad idea.*

"Well, of course, lead the way," Julius said.

They entered the main hall. A raised stage was positioned at one end of the room, with the party logo and a banner high above it.

Welcome to the Annual Leadership Summit!

There were round tables arranged across the room, each with a small tea light and settings for four or six people, depending on the distance to the podium. They found one near the middle and sat down.

"Good choice, Julius; we should be able to see each of the speakers very well here." Mr. Holt commented, helping Georgia to her seat; he chose in an attempt to keep her and Julius apart.

"I can't see the stage very well from here, Fredrick." She stood up and moved beside Julius. "There, that's better." She smiled.

Mr. Holt's face darkened, "Very well, my dear," and he sat down.

One of the servers stopped by and took their drink and food orders. Mr. Holt ordered a dirty martini, Georgia ordered a Moscow mule, and Julius had an absinthe. The first speaker would come on the stage in a few minutes, and the presentations were scheduled to end around 4 pm. The first group of speakers were from the local area party members, thanking everyone for attending the convention and delivering optimistic predictions for the future of the local, state, and national organizations.

"Funny how no one has even touched the subject of the disastrous elections. It's as if they are afraid to admit the Senator Kanker debacle ever happened." Georgia said, her voice was a little slurred. She was on her third drink, and her face was flushed. When she talked, her hand kept touching Julius' arm beside her.

Mr. Holt was becoming visibly agitated. Julius sighed. *I don't have the energy to deal with jealousy right now.*

Julius moved behind him and touched his shoulder; with a slight squeeze, he whispered, "I think you should order yourself another drink, and when you feel the need to urinate, you should use one of the potted plants in the lobby."

"Excellent idea, Mr. Laban."

"Now, excuse me," Julius said to Georgia.

"OK," she whispered, her eyes locked on him.

Julius walked toward the stage, waited while the person speaking wrapped things up, and walked away. Another person went to the microphone and said, "Our last speaker is the Chief of Staff for Governor Tan, Mr. Julius Laban." The room, which had been a little sleepy, seemed to wake up at the mention of Governor Tan. The room erupted into loud applause. Julius walked across the stage, a picture of confidence and power.

"Thank you, everyone, for your kind applause. It is good to see that the party is alive and well, at least in this room." Mr. Laban paused to a smattering of laughter, "But outside this room? Outside this room, Mr. Tan believes that you all here are **cowards**." His voice boomed, and the attendees became silent, and the clinking of utensils and quiet chatter stopped. Julius raised a hand to shield his eyes, trying to get a better look at the members gathered. "Can you turn up the house lights and take the spotlight off me?"

The house lights went up, and the spotlight was turned off. Confused attendants looked around at themselves, mumbling in confusion.

"Take a good look at yourselves. **No, Take a Good Look!**" he shouted the last few words. "What do you see? Do you know what Mr. Tan sees? He would see many lazy, self-serving people who have become too comfortable with how things are and how the party is today!" The attendees' voices went from mumbles to scattered shouts directed at Julius.

"I hear many of you now denying it but don't have the balls to say it loud enough to tell me to my face!" The crowd was suddenly quieter, still with a few muted protests being heard in the room. "So, what does Mr. Tan thinks we can do about it. I am here to announce that he will be making a major speech in a few days about what he wants us to do to win again. If you are not on board, I suggest you get out of the way, or we will toss you aside like the trash you are. That is all I have to say. Enjoy your last meal as a party member because if you don't work to advance the agenda, you are no more than a parasite needing to be excised from the body. Good night!"

Julius stepped off the stage to shout and protest. There were many angry faces, but no one dared confront him, just like he thought. When he returned to his table, Mr. Holt was gone, and Georgia took a sip from her drink. "That made quite an impression with these parasites." She snickered a little too loudly. She was plastered.

"Come with me," He took her hand roughly, and they left the room.

Julius never intended to stay at the hotel, so he never booked a room for himself; they went to Georgia's room. Mr. Holt had openly booked two rooms to keep up appearances at the law firm. One was for him, and the other for his young assistant. Holt had no plans for her to stay in a separate room; he planned for them to share the king-sized bed in his room.

"I wonder where Fredrick went?" she said, still slurring her words.

"Does it matter?" Julius said

"No," she began, removing her clothing, and Julius saw confirmation of what a good figure he thought she had.

The following morning, Julius stepped out of the shower and got dressed. The TV was on, tuned to the local news. The anchor gave a synopsis of yesterday's convention when a reporter interrupted him with an urgent update.

"Mr. Fredrick Holt from Fredericksburg was arrested yesterday in the lobby of the hotel for indecent exposure because he was urinating on one of the potted plants. Witnesses said..."

Julius could not repress a smile. *What a fool. He was too easy.*

He glanced over at Georgia lying naked on the bed; her chest rose and fell slowly with each breath, her eyes wide open, but no one was home.

"I'm truly sorry, my dear. I got carried away last night. You see, I had not fed in so long that I could not help myself; I was just too hungry. Young energy is so tasty. I do hope you recover someday." He kissed her on the forehead and left the room, knowing she would never recover.

Chapter 7

Celebration & Warning

"A toast to the new parents!" Robert said, raising his glass to his friends, Grace and Greg.

Glasses clinked across and around the table at the Colonial Seaman Fish House. The expecting parents invited their friends to dinner to give them the news about the ultrasound results. Greg booked a small private room for dinner. Fathers Ortiz and O'Brian were there, as well as AM and Robert. The couple also invited Robert's mother and Lola (his grandmother) to dinner, but Robert's mother was not feeling well. Lola would not leave her alone while she was sick. Greg thought he and Grace should stop by later to give them the news personally. That is if AM or Robert hadn't spilled the beans before then,

"So, Grace, how did your ultrasound go?" AM was sitting beside her, grabbing her arm, maybe too excitedly. Grace was still not accustomed to having friends and blushed. Because of what her mother is, she never strayed too long in one place to make friends, never mind close friends like Robert and AM.

"It was good," Grace looked at Greg, and he nodded. "The babies are doing well."

Everyone stopped talking, and the room fell silent. Then it exploded with excited congratulations and hugs.

"Identical or fraternal? boy or girl, or both?" AM was excitedly firing off questions, and Grace just sat there, unsure what to say.

Greg laughed at his wife's discomfort until a kick from under the table stopped him.

"AM, slow down. We don't know much yet, and it is still too early." Greg said in a calming voice.

AM sat back in her chair, "Yes, of course, it's early. But it's still exciting!"

"I agree, my dear. Our new parents are still processing all of this. Besides, I am sure we could all agree that no matter the sex or whether they are identical or not, those are merely details. The important thing is, as their friends and family, we are all happy for you, Greg and Grace, and I am sure you know we will do all in our power to make this change in your lives as easy as possible." Fr. Ortiz said.

"Amen." chimed in Fr. O'Brian.

"Yes, of course. Sorry if I got a little carried away, guys." AM smiled, "But you can't blame an auntie for being excited."

"It's okay, AM; your enthusiasm caught me off guard." Grace smiled. I know my children will have a good auntie in you."

"Greg, do you know if your house will be finished before the babies arrive?" Robert asked.

"The contractor assures me that construction should be completed in early September."

"That's cutting it close. Isn't Grace due by late October? You won't have much time to move in and get things settled. Grace will not be in much shape to help move and set up the house."

"That's true, but we can count on Uncle Robert." Greg slapped his friend's shoulder.

"Sure, but hire some movers, anyway." Robert laughed.

Grace woke up the next morning feeling sick. Last night at the celebration dinner, she had only had tea, water, and chicken salad, nothing to upset her stomach.

This is not fair. When will this morning sickness end? This sucks.

Greg, on the other hand, was snoring loudly beside her. Listening to him did not help with her nausea, forcing her out of bed. After she left the bathroom, her phone rang.

"Hello? Yes, mother. I am glad you finally got the hang of using these things.... Ok, see you in an hour."

Grace agreed to meet her mother at a local pancake shop for breakfast, hoping she would have an appetite by then. Because her mother could not set foot on holy ground, they had to meet outside the church. Grace got dressed, left Greg a note, and drove away.

Once inside the pancake place, she saw her mother sitting at a table.

"Good morning, Mother."

"Good morning, child. How are my grandchildren?" She smiled.

"Making me hate mornings."

"I'm sorry. I wish you could have inherited a resistance to sickness from me. Sigh, you have inherited some of your father's human weaknesses."

"I am happy to be at least half human, but I don't regret being your daughter, mother." Grace reached over and grasped her mother's hands.

If Naamah could cry, she would have. At times like this, she felt a strong protective emotion. "Thank you."

The restaurant server came up to the table and took their order. Like everyone else who saw them together, they thought Grace and her mother were sisters. Naamah's immortality gave her the appearance of a young woman.

"I am glad we got you that cell phone," Grace said.

"I hope to see you more when your house is completed. At least it will not be on holy ground. Also, I look forward to watching my grandchildren grow up there with you."

"I would love that, mother." Grace shifted in her seat. Are you still unable to 'sense' me?

"Yes. All these years, the one thing I could do was feel where you were and if you were in trouble. When you walked inside here, I did not know it until I saw you in front of me. It is almost like you have been invisible to me since your pregnancy." Her mother said, with a mix of confusion and fear, that this was another first Grace had seen in her mother. "This must be what it is like to be human and not know what is around the corner—I don't like it."

Grace reached across the table again and squeezed her hand. "Maybe it's good that you understand me a little better."

Naamah managed a weak smile.

"Maybe it is a good defense for them to shield their presence from undesirable attention?"

"I hope so, child. I can't die, but it would be worse than death for me to lose you just like your father."

"You won't, mother."

Naamah was unconvinced, "I see you don't wear that protection amulet anymore. Why?"

"The danger has passed; Mother, Azâzyêl, and Bezale are gone. What else is there to worry about?" Grace smiled.

"Ash-Shaytān."

"Who?" Grace said, then opened her eyes wide in recognition, "Wait, I've heard that name before, Mother. Where?"

Naamah frowned, "I thought you were too young to remember it."

"Remember what?"

"After I rescued you from that awful family when you were five, I took you to an old temple in Cyprus. I had asked you to wait behind one of the columns with a crowd of schoolchildren visiting that day." Naamah paused. She seemed to struggle to tell the story.

"What is it, mother? Please tell me."

"I was summoned at the worst time to meet with the leader of my kind. He is at the top of the food chain... so to speak."

Grace knew who the top of the food chain was in her mother's people. "Ash-Shaytān?"

"Yes. Tan told me that some fallen angels had escaped their prison, and we were not to have anything to do with them. At least for now... Only he is to have any contact with them. He instructed me to look out for them because I had known them in the past and may come looking for me."

"How well did you know them, mother?"

"I knew them well enough to know they had shed all remaining traits that made them angels." She said flatly and turned her back on her daughter.

Grace knew her mother well enough that she would not get anything more from her on this subject. "What should I know about Ash-Shaytān?"

"He goes by the name Ash Tan today."

"The previous governor?" Grace is not easily shocked. "I would have never guessed it was *him*, mother."

"That is what makes him so good at what he is, child—deception."

"Why tell me this now? What has changed?"

"Everything has changed. I believe Tan was working with Bezale and Azâzyêl. He now knows that Greg was responsible for their disappearances, just not how."

"What should we do?" Grace asked.

"Wear the pendant and tell Greg to keep the Ring close. I will do my best to protect all of you, but I am only one demon against many. If I hear anything new, I will let you know." Naamah said.

"Thank you, Mother; I will always wear the pendant from now on."

Grace embraced her mother, and Naamah dissolved away.

Chapter 8

Spy

"I saw your speech, Julius," Mr. Tan said as he hung up the phone. He just ended a call with some of his party officials who were unhappy with Julius Luban's 'attitude.' Many wanted him fired and publicly rebuked by the former governor.

"How well do you think it was received, Julius?" Tan asked.

Julius Luban shrugged, pouring himself a drink from the bar on the other side of the room.

"Does it matter if I hurt their feelings? They are all weak and lower creatures anyway."

Tan sat back in his desk chair. "True, but things these days call for a little finesse."

Julius sat down, swirling the ice in his glass, and let out an audible sigh. "I am sure you are right about that, but I don't have your patience."

Tan stood up, gazing out of the office window. He often did that when deciding what to do and say next. The view out the office window was a small private beach along the Atlantic Ocean. Located in the Sandbridge section of

Virginia Beach, his home was along a row of expensive beach houses, costing more than most of his former constituents could afford.

"Julius, you know I value your work, and you can do things publicly that I cannot do... at least not yet. So, you will have to be my lightning rod for all the fake outrage from the press and the opposition. I will put out a statement that you and I talked about it, and you agreed to be less; how should I say it? Abrasive."

Julius bowed, "Yes, sir, as you wish."

"Good; next thing I need to address is the former Brother Greg and his half-breed wife. Lilith has been keeping tabs on them through that traitor Naamah."

Julius sniffed in disgust, his face not hiding his disapproval.

"I understand your feelings about her, and we should not tolerate any of our kind aligning themselves with humans. But for now, we must watch them and only act when it is in *our* interest." Mr. Tan turned to face Julius again, "Are we in agreement?" His tone did not leave room for any disagreement.

"Yes, my lord," Julius sat up and bowed, confused by this restraint. *Something was off about him; he never cared about Naamah's affairs.*

"Good. Tell James to come here in ten minutes."

Julius closed the door behind him as he left the office. Mr. Tan's assistant, James Dolus, was sitting at his desk, busy with whatever was on his computer.

"The boss wants me to tell you that he needs you inside in ten minutes," he said over his shoulder.

James did not look up as he moved the computer mouse, "thank you for telling me. I will be in once I finish this."

Julius heard a series of clicks as James appeared to concentrate on his work—this annoyed Julius, for some reason, who rarely showed emotion to underlings. Julius spun the unfazed assistant in his chair to face him. "How long will you pretend that the boss is not himself?"

"What do you mean, incubus?" James said with a hint of disrespect in his question.

Julius grabed him the front of James' shirt lapels, glaring at him. "Your attitude toward me lately is annoying. It would be best to show me more respect—you are a lesser being. I don't know why the boss would want someone of your rank working for him."

James stood up, freeing himself from the incubus' grip, his face flushed angrily. The two beings stared at each other, waiting for one to make the next move.

"James, I need you now!" It was Mr. Tan, calling him through the door.

"Yes, sir. Right away!"

James never broke eye contact with Julius. "We can continue this next time εφιάλτης (efiáltis, incubus) when we will not be interrupted." He turned and walked into Mr. Tan's office, leaving Julius fuming.

The incubus left the office, closing the door hard behind him and cracking one of the windowpanes in the door.

How did that low-ranking creature become so smug lately?

"Sir, are you Julius Luban?"

Julius nearly ran over a small woman in athletic clothing at his boss's home entrance. The woman looked as if she had just returned from a run. She was in her early twenties, with short blond hair and light blue eyes. He could tell she was one of his kind, a demon, specifically a succubus.

"Who is asking?"

"I'm Hannah; I'm glad to meet you, sir." She extended her hand. "Mr. Tan asked me to find you when I have news regarding the former Brother Greg."

"I wasn't aware that he assigned someone to watch them?" He ignored her hand. *Things are getting more irritating.*

Hannah put her hands behind her back, unintentionally, or maybe not, thrusting out her chest. "Mr. Tan wants to know if the former Brother Greg has done anything of interest since leaving his church. The boss asked me to pose as a neighbor so I would not draw any suspicion. My story, if asked, is that I am a student at the local community college. They see me occasionally, and I wave to them to be 'neighborly.' you know, so I don't look out of place there."

"I see very well. What do you have to tell me about your quarry?" Julius said.

"Huh?" She looked puzzled.

"The people you are watching. What do you have to tell me about them?" He said with irritation.

"Oh, yes. I never get too close to my target because of the whole 'holy ground' thing—they live on the church grounds. But my boyfriend and I can see them almost daily." She said, seemingly proud of herself.

Julius was nearly out of patience, "So all you do is wave at them and have no new information for the boss?"

Hannah's smile evaporated, "No sir, that is not all..."

"Then get on with it, girl; what do you know! Do you have anything useful?"

She stepped back, and her face blanched. "Yes, yes. Well, there is something about Brother Greg's wife, Grace."

"You mean the cambion?"

"Yes. When I first began to watch the... cambion, it was easy to sense her presence and aura because of what she is, but now it is like she is not there. Also, she seems pale and walks slower when she goes between where she lives and the priest's home or the church."

Julius's eyebrows arched. "Interesting. Let's get closer and see what is happening."

"You mean at her house?" she shook her head, "They live on church grounds. You know I cannot set foot on holy ground, etc."

Idiot. He sighed. "What about using a human male as a boyfriend?"

Hannah perked up, "Yes, but I already have one!"

She is not very bright; she is a stereotypical airhead blond. He sighed.

"You have a human boyfriend? Does the boss know of that?"

"Yes," she smiled, "he is okay with it because Jack, my boyfriend, doesn't know what I am, and he is my *meal* ticket." She grinned and licked her lips.

"What?"

"Meal ticket. You know I am a succubus, right?"

"You must be young because you are not very bright." his face flushed, "I don't detect any old power from you." Julius looked closer at Hannah. She blinked at the intensity of his gaze.

"I am sorry, sir. I should have known you are an Original. I mean no disrespect, sir." Hannah was trembling now.

An Original is a powerful demon that has existed since the world's creation. They are genuinely immortal and cannot be killed; they are only contained in prisons constructed by one of two primary entities on each side. Beings like Hannah are born from Originals and considered lesser demons. Because of that status, they can be destroyed permanently. After the millennia of conflict, only a handful of Originals were not imprisoned, and they remained free. And even some of them have depleted their essence or life force to the point they are unrecoverable; what they were is spread out across the ocean of time to a state of non-existence.

"I hope that Jack is unaware of your true nature. If so, you know what you must do." Julus cautioned.

"No, he doesn't." Hannah giggled, "I tell him he is always so tired because he is a great lover, not because I am draining his life force."

Hannah crouched over, trying to get some leverage on the tire wrench to remove a stubborn lug nut. She pushed hard to no avail; the lug nut was not budging. Next, she stood on it and bounced up and down with the same results: the nut was not moving. All she got for her efforts was a sweaty T-shirt and a few scrapped knuckles. *I hate the human world!*

"Need any help?"

Still angry, she glared at the voice behind her, and a man in his thirties approached from the other side of the street. He was wearing old jeans and a T-shirt. Her face softened, "Yes, please. I need to change this tire and put on the spare, I need to get it fixed, but I can't get this fucker off," she said in frustration, kicking the deflated tire.

"Let's see," the man said. "Where is your spare?"

"It should be in the back... I never looked." She blushed.

He opened the trunk, but there was no spare inside. He looked under the car, thinking it might be mounted there, but he had no luck.

"Sorry, I don't think you have one."

Hannah leaned back against the car, looking agitated. "My boyfriend was supposed to take care of this yesterday."

"Where is he now?"

"At work. My boyfriend left an hour ago and won't be back until after dark, and the tire shop will be closed by then."

"I can spare some time to help you get the tire repaired."

"Could you?" Hannah brightened. "That would be great, but I don't want to take you away from what you are doing now."

"It's ok. By the way, my name is Greg. My wife and I live across the street at St. Rita's." He extended his hand.

"My name is Hannah. Are you the minister there?" They shook hands. Greg felt a warm, pleasant, floating sensation pass through his body. He pulled his hand away more forcefully than intended and shook off the feeling. Greg managed to pass it off with a smile.

"No, I am not any sort of priest or minister." *Not anymore.* Greg broke out of that thought, "We live in the Winnebago behind the church while our house is under construction on the lot behind it."

"Oh, that's your house! Nice, is it part of the church?"

"No. My wife and I decided it was a good place to settle." Greg knew that if he told anyone the real reason, they were building a house near the church was to keep an eye on two fallen angels' ashes in the graveyard, they would sound crazy. "Here, let me get the tire off first, and I will take it down to the tire shop for you and bring it back when it is ready."

"You don't have to do that, Greg. Let me come with you at least." She moved closer to him, her sweaty T-shirt practically transparent.

Greg coughed. "It's no problem, Hannah. I'll drop it off and come back when it's done. I'm sure you have things to do here anyway." He didn't realize he was stammering a little.

"No, not at all!" She said, rocking on her heels and drawing Greg's eyes back to her sweaty T-shirt.

"Hannah, it's ok. Let me get to work and take off the tire first, and then we can talk about it," Greg said, forcing himself to the task.

He managed to get the wheel off and carried it to his truck across the street. Greg touched his chest and felt the ring underneath his shirt. After the last of the fallen angels was put to rest, Grace suggested that he keep it on a chain around his neck. He did not want to wear it constantly because of the intense overload it gave his senses. Also, Robert warned him that it may not be wise to keep it on his finger because it could change him. It was also Raphael's advice for Robert to pass it on to Greg. Good advice or not, he always kept it with him. Greg got into his car, and Hannah sat in the passenger seat.

"You don't have to come, Hannah." He said it a little louder than he intended.

"But I can't let you do this for me alone. Besides, I must pay for it; it is my car." She buckled up, and Greg knew he would not win.

"Ok. Let's go."

At the tire shop, they dropped the tire off for repair. The owner assured Hannah that it was repairable and should be ready in less than an hour. He suggested they stay in the waiting room, or there was a coffee shop next door where many of his customers waited instead.

"Let's wait at the coffee shop, Greg. I didn't eat breakfast anyway."

"Ok, sure, I don't mind having coffee with a new neighbor."

They found a table and sat down; Greg chose a chair furthest away from her and ordered himself a cup of coffee and breakfast. Hannah said she was not hungry (she was still full from last night's meal), so she just had black coffee.

I am coming on a little too strong with him. The boss would not be happy with me if I blew my 'cover.'

She shivered at the thought. It was hard for her to hold back her true nature with men since coming to the mortal world. It was like letting loose in a candy store, and the owner was not watching. It was such a psychological rush, but the mission was critical. Maybe, another time, she could have some of Greg's forbidden fruit. For now, she would tone down her 'gifts.'

"So, tell me about yourself, Hannah; where are you from?" Greg said between bites.

"I am from Las Vegas, believe it or not. My mother worked there for many years, and I grew up there."

"What brings you out here? Las Vegas is far from this place, physically and culturally."

"True, but maybe you know the old story of a girl who meets a boy and follows that boy around the country, and then she dumps him when he turns out to be a scumbag. But the good news is I found a new boyfriend who is good to me, and now I am enrolled at the community college hoping to get into the nursing program." She said in between sips of coffee, trying to look casual.

Greg kept his thoughts to himself. He felt that nursing would not be a good fit for her.

"So what do you do, Mr. Greg, if you are not a minister at St. Rita's?"

"Just call me Greg, Hannah. I am the church groundskeeper, and my wife does the bookkeeping. We have a nice, quiet life that suits us well." He was unsure why he added that last part, but he meant it.

"Oh, I see. My boyfriend says he has seen you cutting the grass since spring."

"I will be outside more as things get warmer, and that's ok with me." He smiled. "What about your boyfriend?"

"What?"

"I mean, what does he do?" Greg said.

"Oh, Jack works at the paper mill in Franklin but wants to be a chef, so he takes classes between shifts."

"He must be a good cook then; I am sure whatever he makes is tasty."

"Oh yes, he is. I know he will do well when he finally finishes school." Hannah finished her coffee.

Greg snickered at what she said and glanced at his watch. "It's been over an hour now. Should we check on the tire?"

"Ok."

The tire was ready, and they returned to Hannah's place in a few minutes. He quickly put the tire back on her car.

"Thank you, Greg. I wish there were a way I could repay you." She slipped again, her voice a little more seductive than it should have.

Damn, back off, Hannah! She shook her head.

Greg stepped back. "Maybe I can introduce you to my wife next time. I need to go now. It was nice meeting you, Hannah. Good luck with school."

Greg hurried across the street and back to the church; he saw Grace stepping out of her car.

"How was your visit with your mother?" He said and kissed her passionately.

After she caught her breath, she said, "Good, who is that girl across the street?" She looked at him strangely. "Are you okay?"

"I'm fine. That is our neighbor across the street, Hannah. She had a flat tire, and I helped her get it repaired. Her boyfriend is at work, so I offered to help." He spoke a little faster than he intended to.

"Did you?" She brushed her hand on his cheek, teasing him.

"Yes, I did."

Grace smiled and looked him in the eyes, "I am glad you were able to help. So help me now with some of the bags in the back. I got a few groceries."

Across the street, Hannah entered the bedroom. Jack lay motionless on the bed. His breathing was shallow, and his face gaunt. She did not think he would live much longer.

I must learn to savor my meals and not drain them so quickly. Oh well, I can always find another one like Jack.

Jack could barely move his eyes, but he saw Hannah approaching the bed and straddling him. A tear escaped one of his eyes.

"I'm sorry, Jack, but I am so hungry. Our handsome neighbor across the street is to blame for increasing my appetite." Hannah's angelic face moved closer to his face. "If it is any consolation, love, you lasted longer than anyone I have known—so far." Hannah could see Jack's car in the backyard through the bedroom window as she savored the last of her now-former boyfriend. She would have to get rid of that tonight, along with Jack's shell of a body.

Chapter 9

Gender Reveal

"How are you feeling, Ms. Cassidy?" The ultrasound technologist asked as the exam was underway.

"A little pressure but not painful." Grace squeezed her husband's hand.

The machine clicked, and the tech put the probe away. "They're all done," she said. "You can get dressed now. The report should be at your obstetrician's office by the time you visit this afternoon."

The technologist left the room, and Grace got dressed. This was her second ultrasound exam; her doctor scheduled one exam a month until Grace delivered the twins sometime in late October.

"How are you feeling, babe?"

She squinted, "Pregnant, silly." She buttoned her shirt, "I'm hungry; let's get some breakfast."

"Yes, milady," Greg bowed.

Grace slapped him on the back of his head while it was still bowed. "Jerk."

"Sorry, sweetheart." He rubbed his head, "What do you feel like eating?"

She looked at him with a slight smirk, then shook her head. "No, not now."

"What?"

"We would get in trouble if caught here." With a naughty smile, Grace said, "Let's go to that pancake shop."

"Well, there's always lunchtime."

By afternoon, the couple was at her obstetrician's office. After a twenty-minute wait, they were inside to review her ultrasound results.

"Ms. Cassidy, the twins look good on the ultrasound. They have separate umbilical cords. Your blood work is normal. How are you feeling overall?" Dr. Sato asked.

"Besides the obvious feeling that things are starting to get crowded here," Grace said, placing her hand on her belly, "overall, it's good."

"Good to hear."

"Doctor, can you tell the sex of the twins?" Greg asked.

"Do you want to know? Some couples choose not to know, though it is not so uncommon these days," Dr. Sato said.

"Greg and I talked about it, and we agreed that knowing now is fine," Grace answered. "I would like to know."

"So, it does not matter to you if it's boys or girls?"

Grace smiled, "Our children are part of us regardless of what they are, Dr. Sato." Grace never shared, even with Greg, her fear that, because of her background, she did not know what to expect from this pregnancy regarding the children. It was especially concerning when her mother told her she could not 'sense' Grace anymore since she got pregnant.

"That's good to hear, Grace.' She turned her monitor around so they could see it. "I think you are in for a treat then."

"How so?" Greg said, studying the screen. He could see the general images but not much else.

"The ultrasound shows that this one," she pointed at the screen, "is a girl, and this one is a boy."

They both were silent as the news sank in.

"Fraternal twins?" Grace whispered, breaking the silence.

"Yes," Dr. Sato smiled. "If you were hoping for a boy or girl, you got your wish."

Greg had recovered and was talking nonstop on the drive home.

"This changes everything. We will have to change the nursery's color and size. We should go shopping for a second crib and additional furniture." He kept babbling, "I need to talk to the contractor about some changes to the house. I wonder if it is too late."

Grace burst out laughing. She laughed so hard that she began to cry.

Greg's face flushed. "I guess I'm talking too much. Sorry, babe. I am excited and nervous at the same time."

"Me too... a little, but it seems not as much as you are." She laughed.

Greg deliberately took a few deep breaths to slow down his excitement. Grace reached across and rubbed his shoulder.

"I love you, honey, very much. You don't know how much it means to me that you are excited about the kids, too." She paused a moment when she said kids. "It will take a little getting used to the notion that we will have a little boy and girl in the house."

"I love you back, sexy momma. Yes, it will take some time to get used to the idea of a boy and girl."

Grace tapped him lightly on the head. She would have hit harder, but he was driving. "Don't start calling me that now."

"Too late."

"Well, now we need to tell our family and friends," Grace said.

"I'll leave your mother to you, babe." Greg laughed. "How do you think she will take the news?"

"About the same as she took the news about me being pregnant in the first place, I guess."

"You should tell her sooner rather than later. I think we were right to let her know first." Greg squeezed her hand, then put it back on the wheel.

"I was thinking about that. Can we go ahead and tell Mother now?" She said, rubbing his shoulder again.

Their car was about to pass the town's Walmart store when Greg turned it into the parking lot and stopped it.

"What's wrong, honey?" Grace said, concerned clearly heard in her voice.

Greg turned to her and took both of her hands. "Sweetheart let's talk with her together. I know I said that you should do it, but the more I think about it, the more it occurs to me that she is and will always be in our lives, and now the children's lives, for years to come. I can't avoid not interacting with her. I don't want to explain to our children why their father avoids their grandmother. So can we talk to her now before we get home?"

"Are you sure you want to do it now? I agree with you about the children, and it would make me happy to see you and my mother get along, not because you have that Ring." She touched his chest and felt it underneath his shirt. Grace now wore the protection pendant, and even with that on, she could feel the power of the Ring through the fabric of his shirt.

"We are one now, my *γυναίκα* (gynaíka, wife), and I am better for it." He kissed her, "Let's tell her together."

Grace reached out with the stone her mother had given her years ago. Its surface had engraved old Greek lettering and felt heavier than it looked. Grace put the stone between her hands, and they waited.

"Okay, it's done."

"Yes, child?" Naamah said she was sitting in the backseat of their car.

"Hello, mother," Grace smiled.

Naamah smiled at her daughter and then turned her attention to Greg. "I was not expecting to see you again so soon, my son-in-law."

"Hello, Naamah," Greg said. He still was not used to seeing and feeling a full-blood succubus so close to him. It's nice to see you."

Naamah arched an eyebrow, "That was so kind of you to say. Has my daughter taught you etiquette lessons when talking to me?"

"Mother!"

"It's okay, Grace," Greg said, "that's fair. Naamah. I want to call a truce between us for the sake of Grace and the children."

"I see. That is wise." She said flatly.

"Mother, please, he wants to have a normal relationship with you."

"There's nothing normal about this relationship," Greg interjected. "But I knew that going into this marriage with you, Grace." He looked over to his mother-in-law. Naamah, "I know that Grace loves you very much, and I will never do anything to get in the way of you two. So, starting today, I promise never to use the Ring to force you to do what I want as long as you promise to respect my wishes as Grace's husband and the father of your grandchildren."

Naamah studied his face. She had been around long enough to be good at reading a man's intentions simply by reading at his face. She stayed silent a little longer and determined that Greg was being sincere.

"Very well, Greg. I accept your terms for this truce. It is good we had this understanding before the children were born. For that, I am grateful. When Grace was born, caring for her wasn't as easy as I would have liked. I missed too many of her firsts because I could not keep her near me. First words, first steps, first time she spoke..." Naamah paused momentarily, and Greg was unsure if she would cry, but her face was as stoic as ever. Grace knew her best and reached out and touched her mother's shoulder; Naamah smiled and kissed her daughter's hand. She turned her attention back to Greg.

"Greg, you are now part of my family, and I will protect you as fiercely as I will protect my own. You have my word."

"Thank you, and I will do all I can to protect you as well, if needed, from others of your 'kind,'" he said.

"Mother, we want to tell you more about the twins."

"Good news, I trust?"

"Yes," Grace said, reaching for her hand. We are having a boy and a girl—fraternal twins."

"That is wonderful, my dear. You both will have your hands full in a few months. You must promise me again to take care of yourself and always wear that protection pendant."

"Yes, Mother, I promise."

"Shall we celebrate with a meal somewhere?" Naamah said.

Chapter 10

The Morrigan & Betrayal

Naamah wore a coat and scarf to avoid drawing attention to herself while along Bishop Street in Derry. She didn't need to dress in heavier clothing because, to a succubus, the weather did not affect her like humans. She was here to meet with an old friend about a nagging concern about Grace or, more specifically, her future grandchildren.

Where is she? I don't like the games she plays. Damn Celts.

A little girl, maybe eight years old, was a few homes ahead of her. The girl was wearing a school uniform and skipping toward her, singing a song in a language Naamah did not recognize. The girl stopped, looked at Naamah, and smiled.

"Looking for the Morrigan?"

"Yes, I am. Are you whom I am looking for?" Something *felt* wrong with the child because it was not a little girl and not the person she was looking for.

"Oh no, I am nothing like her but walk through the pedestrian side of the gate when you reach the city wall. She will be waiting for you." At that moment, the girl dissolved, and a black crow took her place. It cawed and then flew away.

If Naamah had been human, she would have been surprised. "Still always one for drama and mystery," she said at the departing crow.

Bishop's gate is an opening in the old city walls. The gate had two openings, one large to accommodate vehicles and a smaller one for foot traffic. Naamah stepped through the pedestrian opening and instantly found herself in a grassy field that had to be outside the city. In the distance was a small hill where a lone oak tree stood. Its leaves were a deep green and moved in the light breeze. It was still early spring in Ireland, too early in the year for an oak tree full of leaves. Naamah reached the foot of the hill and stood admiring the oak.

"Hello, my friend. Thank you for inviting me to your home." Naamah spoke out loud to the tree. A large crow cawed from within one of the branches as a response. Naamah knew this was not a bird at all. "Lovely black feathers, my compliments."

The crow jumped off the branch and glided down to the foot of the tree. Once on the ground, a swirling cloud enveloped the crow and grew in size. When it dissipated, a tall woman with braided red hair and a flowing jade-colored dress stood in its place.

"What brings you to see me here after so long, my friend?" the Morrigan said in her musical voice.

"Can't I just visit an old friend?" Naamah smiled.

The Morrigan shook her head, "You and I were never friends. We are more like acquaintances; the only thing we both have in common is that we are not human." Her eyes bore into Naamah's. Behind her, the grass grew taller and thicker until it solidified into an oversized ornate chair. The Morrigan sat down. "I know you are not here for the craic (conversation), so please don't insult me with excuses to talk to me."

"You are right. We are not friends, but we are also not enemies. I am here with a problem that I believe that only you are capable of helping me with. I don't lightly ask for help from other beings outside my realm. Truthfully, I cannot trust anyone in that realm with what I want to ask you about."

"Ok, you have my attention, Naamah." The Morrigan sat up in her chair.

Naamah closed her eyes, bowed, and got down on one knee. "I need your help with my daughter," she said in a low voice.

The Morrigan's eyes widened with surprise, "I had heard you had a daughter, but I never confirmed that to be true. I try to stay out of the affairs of angels and demons. Who is her father, another demon?"

"No, he was human."

"Was? I see... So, your daughter, she is not like you?"

"Grace, my daughter, shares some of my 'traits,' but they are not as strong as if she were a demon. She is a person I am proud of and has excelled in the human world in many things. She has no desire for riches like most humans. Maybe a trait from her father? I know it is something you never thought you would hear from a demon, but she means everything to me." Naamah said, still on one knee.

The Morrigan stood up and put her hand on Naamah's shoulder. "I once had a daughter, too, so I understand your feelings about our children. You and I are not human, but we do have something like human emotions, I guess. Maybe we spend too much time around them. Who knows?" She leaned over. "Stand up and face me, mother to mother."

Naamah stood up; her eyes were moist, but no tears flowed.

"What is it you ask of me is one mother to another?" The Morrigan said.

"I want my daughter to have a good life. She may not be immortal like us, but I still wish her happiness."

The Morrigan nodded knowingly.

"She is married to a human man who has Nephilim blood and is pregnant with twins," Naamah said.

"Twins?"

"Yes. My daughter having twins is the least of my concerns. Ever since my daughter was born, I could sense her presence, her life force, if you will. As you know, my nature is intimately associated with the life force, mostly of men. Ever since her pregnancy, I have been unable to sense her. It is like she is not there."

"Are you implying the twins are blocking you from sensing Grace?" The Morrigan said.

"Yes, that has to be the only explanation. Because even when Grace wears an ancient amulet that protects her from my kind, I can still sense my daughter's life force."

"What is it you need from me then? I have no power in your realm, just as you have none in mine."

"You are known for your powers of prophecy and even predicting the future. I hope you can tell me if I am not being overly cautious with this.... My blind spot when it comes to Grace is that I hope this is a good thing for her and the safety of the children. Am I just being a nervous mother and grandmother?"

"I am only gifted with that when it comes to humans, not so much with beings like ourselves." The Morrigan paused; she appeared to be thinking over something. "But your daughter is half human. Maybe I can do some small service for you because she has human blood."

"Thank you. I will never forget this." Naamah said.

"Good to hear, my friend. Now to business. Do you have something personal from her?"

"I thought you may ask that. Here is a lock of her hair." Naamah smiled.

Lilith had never been to this part of the world before. The air was thin and cold, and a few snowflakes drifted around her. Small huts lined the frozen earth under her feet. She was dressed in native clothing: a hooded coat made of skins and leather boots that covered her entirely but not much else underneath. She never felt the cold anyway; clothing was needed to blend in with the local population.

"Our informant told us to meet the dealer in the hut with a red trim on the door flap, "her companion said. The woman walking with Lilith was one of Mr. Tan's closest confidants tasked her with searching for the item he sought. Eisheth was a succubus like Lilith and just as old. She was Mr. Tan's favorite for longer than Lilith liked. Eisheth had considerable influence on the boss, which secretly irritated Lilith.

"How can we be sure that the information is correct? We have been down too many blind alleys searching for this treasure." Lilith said dismissively.

"It comes from a source that Mr. Tan and I have confidence in my love. Don't jinx it now with doubt." Eisheth purred confidently.

Eisheth pushed aside the flap and walked in with Lilith behind her. The hut's center had a wood fire that warmed the air. Smoke escaped out a hole at the shelter's apex. Lilith saw a human and another being sitting by the fire. The human stood up and made his way to them.

"Welcome Eisheth! Welcome to my home, and who did you bring with you?" the man said.

"She is of no consequence, Wangchuk. Do you have a thing we discussed or not?" Eisheth demanded.

Wangchuk did not flinch at her tone; he smiled at her. "Very well, then, right to business." He turned to the figure opposite the fire, with whom he had been sitting when the succubus came in. "This is my friend, Jiangshi. He has the item you requested, but you cannot handle it... That is why you brought your friend."

Jiangshi extended his arm and opened his hand. In his palm was a small circular object with a small ruby in the middle and a silver chain attached. The 'person' had no expression on its pale, almost white face. Lilith could tell it was not human but something else. What it was, she did not know.

"Yes," Eisheth smiled, "Lilith, take it from him."

Lilith backed away, "What is this about?"

"Like he said, Lilith. I cannot handle the item, but you can. Remember, we are under orders from our master to bring it to him."

"And if I refuse?"

Eisheth laughed, "Do I have to tell you? Or do you want to guess how many millennia he will imprison you? Maybe before the earth ends, he will let you out to watch the final days."

Lilith's face was red with anger. "What will happen if I touch it?"

"Nothing, my dear," Wangchuk said, "the charm simply needs to imprint itself on your nature. I promise it will not harm you at all."

Lilith knew she could not disobey her master, so she went to the creature holding the charm. Jiangshi did not move and only looked at her with expressionless eyes as she picked up the charm. Lilith felt a slight tingle in her fingers when she took it from him and brought it to Eisheth, who extended her hand.

"Thank you, dear; now give it to me."

Lilith placed the charm in her hand, "as you wish," then smiled.

The charm sizzled in Eisheth's hand, burning a hole where the silver disc portion sat; the chain wrapped itself snake-like around her wrist. Eisheth screamed. The ruby in the center glowed brightly. Lilith stood still and smiled; while Eisheth franticly clawed at the chain, she briefly phased into her full demon form and then screamed so loud that the human in the hut had to cover his ears; Lilith barely flinched. Jiangshi did not show any emotion still. Then, it was over, and the chain fell to the ground. Eisheth collapsed to her knees, her energy drained. There were blisters in the palm of her hand and a nasty circular one around her wrist where the chain had been. Breathing heavily and confused, she looked at Lilith, "What the hell did you do to me?"

Lilith stood in front of Eisheth, looking at her with disdain, and slapped her across the face, and she fell to the ground. "I have made you human." She picked up the talisman only by the chain, holding it before her. It spun while dangling from her fingers, and the ruby glowed. Wangchuk brought her a small leather bag, which she put the medallion and chain inside. "Thank you." She looked back at Elisheth lying on the floor, staring back in disbelief at what happened. There were new scratches on her face, bleeding, where Lilith had struck her. "Now for your payment. Wangchuk, she is yours now do as you please."

Eisheth tried to stand up, but she was still too weak, "what the fuck, Lilith! What do you mean I am his?" She felt weak; her senses were duller than earlier. The slap from Lilith drew blood! That is impossible; Eisheth is an Original!

Lilith laughed, "I am enjoying this so much, but I have a schedule to keep now that I have this." She held up the leather pouch. "Enjoy your life as a human, Eisheth. It may be brief, but I hope it is painful. Goodbye." She melted out of the hut.

Jiangshi walked around the fire and stood in front of a terrified Eisheth.

"Eat, my friend. It is not often you get to eat such a rare meal," Wangchuk said.

Outside the hut, screams traveled far in the freezing, snowy air.

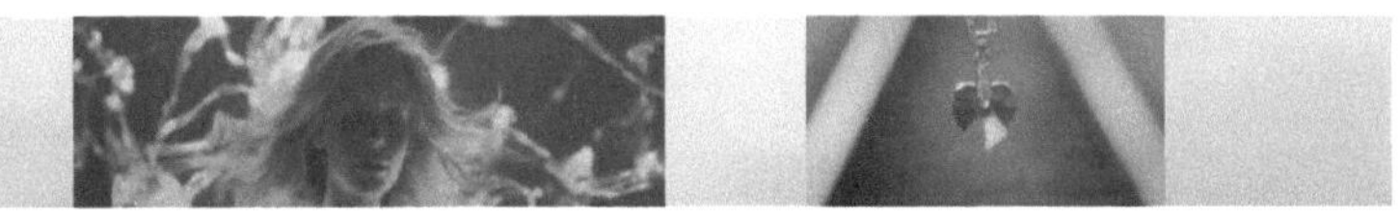

Chapter 11

Hannah's Medallion

Hannah saw Greg outside working on the church grounds again. It looked like he was going into the maintenance building, but even with her keen eyesight, she could not tell what he was up to.

Watching him is hard; this would be much easier if he were not on holy ground.

A few moments later, he brought a rake, a large trash can, and a riding lawnmower. Impatience was gnawing at the young succubus and a different kind of hunger for food that only this kind of demon could experience. That peculiar kind of hunger was growing again. Since she 'broke up' with her boyfriend, she lost her food source. Typically, if someone asked what happened to her boyfriend, she said they broke up, which always ended with some more questions. Humans were so gullible. They would have never guessed that she drained her male companions of their life force. Hannah thought she could leave her post and satisfy her succubus appetite while Greg cut the lawn. She had gathered her things to go when she heard the doorbell ring.

Who could that be?

She looked through the peephole and saw two young men in a white shirt, black pants, and tie standing at the door. Bicycles were behind them on the sidewalk. They looked like they were in the prime of their lives. *Yummy.* Despite her eagerness to feed, she opened the door slowly. She didn't want to seem too friendly at first.

"Yes, may I help you?"

"Good morning, Miss. I am Gideon, and this is my friend Oliver. We are missionaries from the Church of Latter-day Saints and would like to share our message with you," the older one said, holding out a pamphlet.

Hannah reached for the pamphlet and deliberately touched Gideon's hand. He felt an electric shock coursing up his arm from her touch, ending in his toes. Gideon inhaled sharply, and an embarrassing bulge appeared in his pants. She pulled him inside the door, catching Oliver off guard and still standing on the porch.

"You stay here, love; I'll be back," she whispered in Gideon's ear. The dazed boy could not move. Hannah opened the door and turned her attention to Oliver, "Please come in love." Moving faster than the boy could see, he found himself standing beside the frozen Gideon. The succubus had a hand on Oliver and Gideon.

"I am so glad you came over to see me. I am soooo hungry. You guys are better than Uber Eats..." She licked her lips, unable to decide first who to feed off. She didn't hesitate too long and kissed Oliver. The boy wanted to scream as he felt his life draining away, then finally falling to the floor. All that was left of the missionary was a husk. Hannah luxuriously licked her lips, moaning with the pleasure of the meal she ingested, like a cat that enjoyed a meal.

"That was delicious, Oliver, thank you, dear. Don't worry, Gideon. My hunger is under control—for now." She walked behind him, reached around, and grabbed his crotch. "I have other ways of feeding myself, extending your life maybe a little bit longer. You may even enjoy it, love." She kissed his ear and gave it a little nibble. "Follow me. I have a place you can stay until I need you, my love." She led him to the bedroom where, not long ago, her last 'boyfriend' had died. Gideon, powerless to refuse, was instructed to lie on the same bed.

"I'll be back later; you sleep now until I wake you up. Sweet dreams." She left the room. A single tear escaped, running down his cheek as she shut the door. She stepped over the body of Oliver.

I need to clean up after myself. There's still room in the woods out behind the house. It would have been easier if I hadn't had to look at that church.

She resumed watching Greg, still outside, on the riding mower cutting grass.

He's so boring. I wish Mr. Tan would tell me how long I had to be here.

"Good morning, Hannah; anything new to report?"

She almost jumped when she heard a voice from behind. It was Mr. Tan.

He can't know what I was thinking about him. Can he?

"Good morning, boss. It is nice to see you again." She bowed slightly from her waist. "I am surprised to see you here in person."

"I like to get out from time to time to, as the humans say, 'stretch my legs,'" he said, stepping over Oliver's body and toward the window where she was watching the former pastor still on his riding mower going up and down the church lawn. It seems like a dull existence for someone who defeated two fallen angels." Mr. Tan turned his attention back to Hannah; she squirmed slightly under his gaze. So, to repeat myself, do you have anything to report?"

"Well, sir, what I see is much as you see it now. He occupies himself with mundane tasks around the church. The same every day. If he is not working on the grounds, he is inside one of the buildings. But what he does, I can't tell you because of the whole 'holy ground' stuff. If I knew what to look for, I could serve you better."

"I want to know how he defeated the angels," he said with annoyance. "But I think I have a way of helping you with that 'holy ground' stuff, as you put it. Come over here, and let's talk." He motioned to the chairs in the sparse living room, if it could be called that, to sit down. Mr. Tan reached into his jacket pockets and pulled out a small leather pouch.

"What is that, sir?"

"Something that will allow you to enter the church and its grounds. But at a price," he said. Opening it, he turned it upside down, and a small object fell onto his open palm. Hannah could have sworn she heard a sizzling noise. The object was a silver medallion on a chain with a red stone in its center.

"What is it?"

"Nothing of any real value except to a demon, my dear, because it is a passport of sorts. And I am handing it to you to assist in your mission. It took me a long time and significant effort to acquire this. Tan picked it up between his fingers and held it to the light. The silver medallion looked ordinary except for a small red ruby in the center that sparkled in the filtered light through the dirty window. A ruby?

"How do I use it?" Hannah asked, mesmerized by the red ruby.

Mr. Tan shrugged, "simply wear it around your neck, my dear."

Mr. Tan watched her stare at the object in his hand.

She was not the brightest, but she was expendable.

He smiled and said, "So what do you think?"

"So, I put it around my neck, and I can walk on holy ground, even inside the church?"

"Yes. You do not have to worry too much about supplying a weak report to Julius. Because you can give him first-hand accounts of what the pastor is doing." Mr. Tan said, dangling it off his fingers as it reflected the light.

"That sounds good to me, sir." She reached out her hand, "may I?"

"Very well, my dear. I am glad you have accepted the assignment and this new tool." He handed it to Hannah.

The moment she touched it, there was an immediate stinging sensation. "Kinda burns a little," she said.

"It will at first, but that goes away," he assured her.

Hannah looked at the ruby again. The chain had no clasp, so she brought it over her head and around her neck. The effect was immediate; Hannah screamed; the pain was one she had never experienced before in her whole life.

A fire was coursing throughout her entire body as if it was ablaze. She fell to her knees and opened her mouth, but no sound came out. The pain was so intense that she could not form a coherent thought. Then, just as quickly, the pain vanished. She felt weak but alive.

Mr. Tan touched her shoulder, "How are you, my dear?"

"Better. What the hell was that?"

"The medallion's power is to mask your succubus nature, so you won't be discovered. But the initial shock is quite intense. For that, I'm sorry."

Hannah finally caught her breath. "That's okay, sir, as long as I can help you. I am always concerned Julius will get upset with me about my reports, so if I can give him first-hand information, I am sure he will be happier."

"Good, but one warning: I didn't tell you about it." His face was solemn.

"Yes?" she said, suddenly nervous.

"Don't try to take it off your neck unless I am with you. You see it takes someone of my status to take it off, if you did it yourself or someone took it off by force you will die."

Hannah's face blanched, her hand shakily touching the foreign object around her neck. "Sir..."

Mr. Tan put his hands on her shoulders, "Don't worry, my dear. I will not let that happen to you. After all, you are a valuable spy."

"How long am I to wear this?" she said meekly.

"It's not long, maybe a few months, until the job is done. When that happens, I will reward you handsomely." He smiled and squeezed her shoulders.

"Thank you, sir." she swallowed, though not entirely convinced.

"I think you should take advantage of this and introduce yourself to Greg's wife and the pastors at St. Rita's. Find a pretense to visit more often... maybe volunteer. Stuff like that." He shrugged. You are an intelligent girl. To coin a phrase: I have faith in you."

Hannah smiled, "Thank you, sir. I will walk over to the church now."

"Not yet, my dear. Get used to it around your neck first. You will find you are weak like a human, so do not injure yourself. Some of your powers will be diminished, but that should improve soon."

"Oh, I don't like the idea of being weak!" She protested.

"It's only temporary, my dear, and you want to please me, right?" He stroked her cheek.

"Yes, sir."

"Good. I will go now; I have more things that need my attention today. I have great plans for you, Hannah. Don't let me down." Tan dissolved away, leaving her alone. Hannah felt the medallion resting on her chest.

I hope this is worth it.

Back at Tan's office, Julius sat waiting for his boss. When Mr. Tan dissolved into the room; he stood up.

"Does she, have it?" He asked.

"Yes, and I hope the cost of acquiring that medallion was worth it, Julius," Tan said.

"Hannah is not very bright, but she is eager to please. She will not fail. But even if she fails, we have others who would be willing to take her place."

Chapter 12

The Crow

Grace ate lunch with Greg before he needed to go to the hardware store to get a part for the old riding lawnmower. The couple had plenty of money, so Greg offered to buy a new one for the church, but Father Ortiz refused. The pastor explained that the church could not afford a new mower yet. Grace washed the dirty dishes in the sink before resuming her work on the church's utility bills.

She put the last glass into the dish drainer when she heard a rapid pecking noise behind her. A large crow was perched on the narrow window ledge in front of the sink. Its large, dark eyes seemed focused on Grace. Then, it resumed pecking at the window. Afraid the bird would break the window if it kept it up, she grabbed a dish towel and waved it at the window.

"Go away."

The crow cackled back in a manner that almost sounded like it was laughing at her. Grace tried again, waving the towel at the window. As she got closer, she brushed the towel against the inside of the window. The crow still didn't flinch.

"Stupid bird..." Grace stopped trying to shoo it away. Something was off about this bird looking at her through the window. She stared into the bird's eyes, and it was staring back. She went outside. The crow was still perched on the windowsill, still watching Grace. It cawed once and jumped to the ground.

"Who are you? I don't recognize what you are, but you are no crow."

The bird continued staring but remained silent.

"Did my mother or someone else send you?" She said as forcefully as she could, unconsciously placing her hands over her still-growing abdomen.

The crow cawed again, and a swirling grey cloud gathered around it, growing taller. Strangely, the ground around the whirling cloud was undisturbed. The cloud dissipated, and a woman with long brown hair was dressed in what looked like a robe. Or a dress? Her clothing seemed to be moving as if it were alive. The woman bowed slightly at the waist. She looked normal otherwise, except her eyes looked more prominent than usual for a person, and Grace could have sworn they were a light red color.

"Good morning, Lady Grace." The woman's voice had a strange, lilting tone.

"Good morning. Can you tell me who you are and why you are here?" Grace still had her hands on her tummy and kept her distance.

"My apologies, Lady Grace. I have forgotten my manners. It must be because of the long trip to get here." The woman did seem sincere. "My name is Fiadh, but you can call me Fia." Fia noticed the picnic table outside of the RV. "Do you mind if we sit there and have a chat? I mean no harm. My master sent me to find your mother, Naamah."

That statement got Grace's attention, "yes, please sit."

They sat facing each other at the table. Grace was distracted and a little nauseous by the motion of Fia's dress and looked away. Fia realized the waving motion was making Grace uncomfortable. She looked down at her dress, and it solidified.

"Thank you for that," Grace said.

"Of course, I understand pregnancy can make a human's stomach sensitive, but I thought that you would be immune because you are not human."

"I am half human, Fia." she said as the nausea subsided, "Please tell me, what is your business with my mother?"

"It's not my business but my master's. The Morrigan." Fia said with reverence.

"I have heard that name before," Grace said, puzzled.

"She is the goddess of Iverio or, known in this era, Ireland and Britain."

"I see, but what business would the Morrigan have with my mother? They are from two different realms."

"I am not privileged to know that, Lady Grace. I was instructed to deliver my master's message personally and told to contact you first because I could not find Naamah."

"It makes sense, I guess." Grace thought it over and decided that her mother would not cross realms unless necessary. "Okay, please give me a few moments to contact my mother. I will be back soon; please stay here."

"As you wish." Fia nodded.

Grace returned to the RV and called her mother. When Grace exited the RV, Fia was exploring the church grounds. She seemed interested in the nearby graveyard, and Grace thought she heard the strange 'person' talking. But to whom?

"My mother has agreed to meet you. In fact, she seemed eager. We can leave now if you like." Grace said, holding her car keys.

"You want me to sit with you inside that?" Fia pointed at the car.

"Yes."

"That sounds lovely. I have always seen humans in those things but never rode inside one myself. Thank you, Lady Grace." Fia smiled.

"You are welcome, Fia. Please call me Grace."

Ten minutes later, the two pulled into the Walmart parking lot. Grace could see her mother standing in the same section of the lot where they had always met.

She did not waste time getting here.

"Hello, Mother. I have someone here who wants to talk to you. This is Fia. She tells me she has a message for you from The Morrigan."

Fia stepped out of the car, approached Naamah, and bowed low. "I'm pleased to meet you, Lady Naamah."

Naamah nodded, "I am happy to meet you as well, Fia."

"As I told Lady Grace, I mean Grace. I come with a message from my master, The Morrigan." Fia looked at Grace and then back to Naamah. "I know she is your daughter, but I have to ask. Are you okay with her being here when I deliver the message?" Fia glanced back at Grace. "I mean no offense."

"None taken, Fia." Grace turned to her mother and said, "I am very interested in this message, too."

"You can tell my daughter what you have to say to me. It affects her and her family; she has the right to know." Naamah said.

"As you wish, Lady Naamah..."

"Wait, one moment, Fia." Naamah interpreted, quickly extending both arms and touching Grace and Fia. Grace experienced a moment of vertigo that she was too familiar with, and then the trio stood in Naamah's apartment in San Francisco.

Fia jumped back away from Naamah, frightened.

"It's okay, Fia," Grace said. I think my mother took us here to talk in private."

"I didn't mean to frighten you, Fia, but my daughter is right. We can talk freely here; no being can eavesdrop on us here," Naamah said and sat on the couch. "Please, everyone, sit."

"Thank you, that is very kind of you, Lady Naamah. The Morrigan asked me to inform you that she has an answer to your question."

"What question, Mother?" Grace asked.

"I asked The Morrigan to find out why I cannot sense you now that you are pregnant. You must understand that it is concerning to me that my powers of perception have been limited toward you lately. I wanted to be sure that no external source was the culprit. I can't keep you safe if something or someone can block my ability to find you."

"Yes, I understand," Grace said. "Go on, Fia, please tell us what your master said."

"As you wish. The reason Lady Naamah is unable to sense Lady Grace's presence is not from an external source or being. The source of the interference, as it were, is the twins themselves."

Grace reflexively touched her belly, "I don't understand. How can they interfere with their grandmother? They are mostly human—right? I am half human, and Greg is human."

The pooka said, "Sorry to disagree with you, Lady Grace. But your husband is not fully human, either. He has Nephilim blood. The Morrigan thinks that the combination of you and your husband has created two unique individuals. She believes they are divine twins, which are powerful, protective beings in my realm."

"I see; what is the significance of twins according to your master?" Grace said.

"She did not say, but twins are important in my world. Suppose they are divine twins; then they are even more important. Divine twins have been known to have opposite traits, such as healer and warrior; they have complementary gifts. I am afraid there is no way of knowing at this time."

"In your experience, Fia, what is the significance of my twins?" Grace said.

Fia seemed to hesitate, looking at Naamah first and then back at Grace. "My lady understands. I am a humble servant of The Morrigan, and my opinion is insignificant compared to my master."

"I understand, but for someone like me who has lived a relatively short life compared to my mother and yourself, you have seen things that I have not or may never see because of my humanity. I only want to know your best guess, or as we say in this day and age, what does your 'gut' tell you?" Grace said in a voice that had a slight quiver of fear.

Fia smiled, "I forget you are only a child compared to beings like us. Very well. As you say, my gut tells me your twins have immense potential and could give their grandmother... I heard this term recently from some mortals. A run for her money, if I understand the meaning correctly."

"Thank you, Fia, for your honesty." Grace smiled, unconsciously holding her belly.

"I am grateful for your master's assistance, Fia. Please give her our thanks, and if she learns anything new, I would be very appreciative." Naamah stood up. "I can get you home now, Fia and Grace."

"Mother..."

Naamah raised her hand, "We can talk about this again soon, daughter. I promise."

Grace relented; she knew her mother was true to her word. In a few moments, they were back in the parking lot. Grace got back in her car and drove home; Greg was back, too, he met her in her car.

"Out for an errand as well, babe?" Greg said.

"Not exactly. Let's go inside. We have something to discuss."

Chapter 13

About the Twins

"She told you *what* about the twins?" Greg did not know how to process this new information about their unborn twins.

"I am still not sure what to think myself, either. But I know deep inside the children are not dangerous, honey."

"Are you sure about that? After last year, I hoped you and I could have a nice, boring, but wonderful life together. I could have lost you last year from many threats, some we knew about and others we could not have seen." Greg said in frustration, sitting next to her.

She put her hand on his, "I was more afraid of losing you, too, because you were always a target. Until Robert gave you that Ring, you had no protection. I at least had my mother."

"We learned all of this is because of your mother's inability to 'sense' you anymore, or at least since you became pregnant."

"Yes."

Greg closed his eyes, trying to control his swirling thoughts.

"Who is this 'Morrigan'? Should we even trust her information? I mean, she seems like someone from a different— circle. I don't know how to classify her other than your mother, who comes from different realms." Greg was agitated, unsure where to direct his frustration.

"They are from different realms, yes. I don't know much about The Morrigan because I have only dealt with beings in my mother's realm. What I do know is that she may be older than my mother and possibly more powerful. I guess she has to be more powerful because my mother does not talk about someone else with that degree of deference. I think she is a Celtic goddess with talents that my mother cannot rely on with others in her realm without raising questions and inviting suspicions toward her and us. She knows that as long as we live here and you hold the Ring, you and I are safe. But now she is concerned for her grandchildren and understandably wants as much information about them as possible for their protection." Grace rested a hand on his lap.

"I am grateful for that. So, what is the game plan? Does your mother have any advice?" Greg said.

"She is checking into that, honey. She knows people— seers with 'gifts' of divination that she can trust. Most of them are mortal and have no allegiance to demons. She wants us to stay close to the church for now and for me to keep on wearing the protection pendant." She unconsciously placed her hand on it.

Greg stood up and walked to the door, staring outside. Since childhood, it has been his habit to stare out a window when troubled. Unfortunately for Greg, his life had given him plenty of opportunities to process his problems in this manner. Grace learned to wait until he was done; he would not quickly answer any questions until he was ready. Besides, she was tired and had no words of comfort or wisdom to give him. Greg took a deep breath, then turned to Grace as if he had decided something.

"I love you, babe; that will never change. I love our growing family," he shrugged, "who knows what, but they are our kids and *our* responsibility. I have faith in you, your mother, and my partner. We will take on any threat to this family together."

Grace stood up and hugged him from behind, saying, "You are my all, *αγάπη μου*" (agápi mou = my love).

Greg noticed a few things about his wife lately and chuckled.

"Something funny in what I said?" she playfully tapped him on his head.

"Not at all, babe. I love you too."

"So, what made you laugh?"

"Nothing."

Another hard tap on his head.

"What?" she whispered seductively in his ear.

"Ok, ok. I have always enjoyed you hugging me when I am troubled, and it is a little sexy when you hug me from behind. But I could not help but notice something different."

"If you mean my tummy genius, I think you know the reason behind that body change." she playfully slapped his butt this time.

"I was not talking about that." he snickered again.

Grace was getting curious and unsure if she should be mad. "Explain yourself, Brother Greg!"

"Well, I have one question that maybe only you can answer, and it is about other beings, maybe like your mom."

"Huh?"

Grace hugged tighter.

"Ok, I am just going to say it. Is there such a thing as boobie fairies? Because if they exist, they are overachieving with you."

It took Grace a moment to comprehend what he said, and her eyes opened wide. She let Greg go, stepped over to the sink, and pulled a wooden spatula out of the dish drainer. The next thing Greg knew was a sharp pain on one side of his butt.

"Ouch!!"

Chapter 14

New Friend

It was darker inside than expected, even with the abundant stained-glass windows and overhead lights. She marveled at the smoothness of the wooden pews arranged from the back to the front. Hannah knew some of the basics about what was inside a church but had never been within its walls until now. Hanging on the interior walls were pictures of a man subjected to various forms of humiliation and torture.

What a strange way to depict a mighty God. She knew the basics of the story behind the images.

She moved closer to the focus of the interior: a raised table dressed in fine linens with unlit candles placed at each end. On one side was a golden-looking—*What is that?* A candle was burning inside a red glass dome. The closer she looked, the more questions she had.

At two hundred years old, she was still considered a baby of her kind, and her education in the mortal world was sparse at best. Most of what she knew of this world was through the lens of being a succubus, the carnal side of men and women, not the spiritual side. She previously had no desire to learn anything about this side of mortals.

"Can I help you, child?" a voice from one side of the table—she would later learn that it was called the Altar—startled her.

"Oh no, I am just exploring, sir." She replied softly, and her low tone seemed oddly appropriate in this place, but she didn't know why.

The man smiled back at her. His face was kind, but she knew enough about humans to know that a kind face often meant little. The man was dressed in an old polo shirt and jeans. He had an accent she could not place from where, but he was not from this part of Virginia, maybe five foot six. Dark skin with wrinkles and grey hair; otherwise, he looked in good health, at least by Hannah's standards. But she was never really concerned with her prey's health when she was hungry.

"Oh my, it's been a while since someone called me, sir." he chuckled.

"Was that inappropriate? I am sorry I didn't mean to offend you," she babbled nervously.

The old man laughed, "Not at all, Miss..."

"Oh, my name is Hannah."

"I am Father Ortiz, the pastor of this church." he extended his hand.

Hannah was not sure to accept the handshake. Something inside her was afraid that he would know what she was, but that shouldn't be possible for just a mortal. But he is a priest; she is much older than the pastor but, in many ways, younger socially, having only recently been allowed into the mortal world a few years ago. She had a sheltered existence until she was allowed to enter the world of mortals; her knowledge was incomplete. She reached out and shook the Pastor's offered hand.

Wow!

"You seemed surprised, Hannah. Is everything ok?"

"Oh no, sorry, Father, my mind was elsewhere."

The old priest smiled, "Did you have any questions since you are just exploring?"

"Oh no, not really. This is my first time inside a church, so I was just curious."

"Really? So, you did not grow up in a home that knew God?"

Well, yes, I did, but not in that way.

"No, I grew up in an ordinary home. I didn't get out much, but I am now free to explore; I thought, why not start here." She said.

"I see. Are you from around here?"

"Oh no, no, not at all. You can say I am far from home."

"So, what brings you here to this town?"

"Well, I had a boyfriend... but he is gone now, so now I'm looking for work while I attend classes at the community college." Hannah rambled on, trying to make a convincing story. Most of it was true; she had a boyfriend who was no longer alive because she drained his life force. So yes, he is gone. Looking for a job while attending college was Julius' idea for a cover story if anyone asked.

He offered, "I have some friends I can talk to about finding work for you if you like. "

"That would be great, Father!" She jumped up and hugged him.

Father Ortiz gently pushed her away. "You are welcome, Hannah. Would you like to come with me and talk to someone here who may be able to help you find a job? She is quite a wizard with financial affairs and knows a few local business owners who may help you."

"Yes, please,"

They left the church and went to the church offices behind the sacristy. It looked large for such a small church, a long hallway with a few doors on either side. One was labeled "Records," and one said "Storage." Hannah could hear a woman's voice talking to someone at the very end of the hall. It sounded like she was disputing something with another person on the phone.

"Is the City still disputing the damage to our sign outside?" Father Ortiz asked as they walked into the office.

"Yes, but I told them to check their email for the security video, and they can clearly see that their truck had backed into it," the young woman said. "Who is your friend?"

She stood up. Hannah noted that she was beautiful and very pregnant but still seemed energetic.

"Please sit, Grace, and this is Hannah. We met inside the church; she was 'exploring.' She is a student in community college and mentioned that she was interested in finding work while at school. Would you know anyone who could use someone like her part-time?"

"Nice to meet you, Hannah. I help this nice old man here with the books." She smiled warmly at the priest. "You are in school? What are you studying?"

Hannah froze. She never thought about someone asking her that question. "Studying? Well, I just started, so..."

"Oh, still undecided. I can understand that. Not everyone knows what to major in at first." Grace sat down, suddenly feeling nauseous.

Hannah looked puzzled; Grace saw it on her face.

"Being pregnant is not all that glamorous at times; it comes with a cost in your comfort and energy. I may know someone looking for someone to help in their shop with things like stocking and the occasional cash register duties. Do you think that may work for you?"

"Yes, I think that will be great!"

"Excellent. I can make a call for you. Where do you live?" Grace opened a small notebook and thumbed through some of the pages.

"I live in a house just across the street."

Grace and Father Ortiz exchanged puzzled looks. "How long have you been there, Hannah?" He asked.

"A few months, why?" she smiled, not understanding the concern in his voice.

After a short pause, he replied, "Nothing, Hannah. That house had been abandoned for quite a while now. I'm just curious."

"Well, at least you live close by. Do you have a phone number you can give me in case my friend wants to talk to you?" Grace said, holding a pencil to the notebook.

"Sure, it's 867-5309."

"Same area code as here?" Grace said.

"Oh, sorry," Hannah giggled, "it's 442."

"Where is that?" Father Ortiz asked.

"Death Valley, California. Well, near it anyway." Hannah said.

"You are a long way from home. What about your parents?" Grace wrote down the area code.

"They died long ago; my uncle, Julius, took care of me, who sometimes comes to visit me."

"Ok. Maybe, you can introduce your uncle to us one day?" the priest smiled.

I doubt either of you would survive the introduction.

"Ah, yeah, sure," Hannah said in a softer tone than she meant to. She envisioned the priest and Grace meeting her 'uncle' and how such a meeting would be disastrous for them.

"Sorry, what, my dear?" the priest put a hand to his ear.

"I mean, yes, sure, Father!" Hannah looked behind her. "I should be going now. I should get ready for class soon. I don't want to be late."

"Yes, of course. I can walk you out," the pastor said, leading her to the exit.

Grace stood up quickly and said, "Father, when you finish, I have more to discuss with you, please."

The priest waved and led Hannah out of the office.

"Stop kicking me, you two!" she said to her stomach. As if the twins heard her, they stopped kicking when Father Ortiz and Hannah were out of sight. "Thank you. Yes, something feels off about her, but we shouldn't be prejudging people."

A few moments later, Father Ortiz appeared back in the doorway. "Strange girl. But I hope your friend can help her, Grace. She seems lost and a little naive. Do you think she is a little *slow*, or is it just because, maybe, because she came from a cloistered environment?"

"I don't know, Father, but she is different. She reminds me of someone I met in college who escaped one of those religious cults, a smart girl who is inexperienced with our society. I don't think Hannah is slow; maybe something else."

"I didn't mean to denigrate the young woman, Grace." Father Ortiz said, holding up his hands.

"I know, you weren't the only one who got that impression, but I think she is naive, like you said," Grace said, holding her stomach.

Father looked at Grace, "You feeling, ok?"

"I'm good now. The twins seemed stimulated when the three of us were talking. They have settled down now," Grace said, rubbing her belly.

Robert opened his eyes and quickly shut them. The light was so bright, almost blinding—like when you walk into daylight straight out of a dark room. He blinked a few more times as his eyes gradually adjusted. Before him was a familiar sight: a sandy beach with brilliant blue waters lapping gently on the shore.

"It took you long enough to get back to me, Raphael. I almost called out to you several times yesterday." Robert said in a normal tone.

"Sorry, my friend. A lot is going on in this realm that we try to take care of without you. We know you have a life and a wife who deserves your undivided attention."

Robert chuckled, "Yes, I know she hoped we were done with you and could have a *normal* life together."

The angel drifted down, standing beside Robert, "That is understandable, and you both have earned some peace, my friend. You and your wife have done more to maintain the balance between us and the other side than other humans have in many years. Well, of course, your friend Greg and his wife Grace also."

Robert spotted a large conch shell at his feet. He picked it up; the shell was perfect, like everything in this place. It was large, thick, heavy, and darker than the white sand. It was about the size of his hand; it had spines in a circular pattern that ended in a point. It had a flared lip with an iridescent pink hue that melted into the interior. Robert wondered if he could take items from here back with him.

"So, what do you want to talk to me about," Robert said.

"There was a meeting between Grace and someone outside our circle."

"I don't understand."

"A being from the lands of Keltai, or what is known today as Ireland and Britain, met with Grace, and she left to see her mother, and then we lost track of her," Raphael said.

"How do you know about this meeting? Are you watching her?" Robert was getting concerned about his friend's privacy. "Those two have done as much as anyone to help defeat the fallen angels."

The angel raised his hands and said, "Agreed. I am not spying on them, my friend, but when a nonhuman being walks onto holy ground, a kind of alert is triggered, and we look into it."

Robert sighed, "I guess that makes sense. Do you know what this other wants to discuss with Grace and her mother?"

"No, we don't. It may be nothing to be concerned about, but I think you know I am naturally cautious. A Mr. Tan has also been on our 'radar,' as you would say, and has been very active lately. He may run for higher political office, and there is a good chance he could win."

"That would not be good. From what I know about Tan, he talks a big game like Kanker did last year, and they are from the same political party. Do you think he is one of 'them'?" Robert said.

"If by 'them' you mean fallen angel, I think so, but I have no idea which one. Of course, they don't advertise their presence to the world and, of course, to us. I am afraid I need to ask you to look into it for me. I hope the being from Keltai is not working with Tan because that would not be good. They live by different rules than you, and I understand."

Robert's attention went back to the shell in his hand. Spines poked his fingers and palms. It felt real and solid, more real than the prospect of another confrontation with, yet again, another fallen angel.

"I'll talk to AM first. Then Grace and Greg talk about this. I have come to trust Grace regarding her mother, and I am sure she has a good reason to meet with this being you are talking about. Thank you, Raphael, for alerting me about Tan, too. My friends need to be aware of any possible threats to them and their growing family."

"Of course."

"I'll ask them what their visitor had to say about Mr. Tan," he said, absently rubbing his thumb over the spines of the shell.

Robert's vision clouded briefly, and he found himself standing in front of AM. She yelped in surprise.

"Where did you come from? And where did you get that shell?"

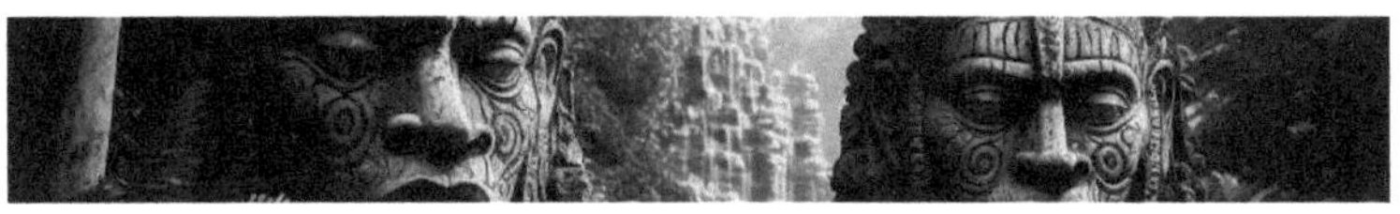

Chapter 15

Father

Naamah was at the usual meeting place, waiting for Grace. They both agreed to meet once a month at a coffee shop. Because Grace lived on holy ground, she could not 'pop' in at any time; this irritated her and gave Greg a sense of relief. Grace never wanted to know all the details of what her mother was doing in her spare time; after all, she grew up with what a demon like her did to survive. Naamah tried to shield her daughter from the worst of it when possible. These days, she wants to spend time with her mother. Grace knew that maybe she was asking a lot because of her mother's nature, but she never stopped loving her.

Naamah sipped her coffee but barely touched the cinnamon roll she had purchased earlier. It looked so tasty inside the glass case, and the young man who sold it to her looked even more tasty. But she couldn't risk drawing attention to herself before Grace arrived. What a shame.

Where is that girl? I told her it was urgent. Sometimes she is more of a bitch than a real succubus. Naamah smiled. *I guess, I raised her well.*

“Sorry, mother, for being so late.” It was Grace. Her gait slowed down at this point in her pregnancy, and she spoke slightly out of breath.

“Oh, my dear, you should have let me help you instead of driving here to talk with me. You look awful!”

“I love you too, Mother,” Grace said sarcastically. Grace had grown up accustomed to her mother’s blunt nature, so it usually didn’t bother her too much, even if it is true the pregnancy was wearing her down these last few weeks. “I don’t look that awful, do I?” she pulled a makeup mirror from her purse.

Naamah reached across the table for her daughter’s hand. “It’s a good thing you are my daughter because otherwise, as a normal human female, you would look worse.” She winked.

It was true that Naamah’s vision was keener than the average human’s, making her capable of seeing things in people that most humans could not. Grace remembered a time when her mother, after meeting one of her high school teachers, flatly said she was sick with cancer even before it was publicly announced to the students at large, and only then when that teacher was away for extended periods for treatment.

“I guess I should thank you for the good genes, mother,” she smirked

“Let’s hope my grandchildren inherit them, too, sweetheart.”

Grace squeezed her mother’s hand, “I would like that.”

Naamah pulled her hand back and sat up in her chair. “So, what is new, my dear? How are my grandchildren doing?”

“Good mother, they have sometimes been naughty, kicking and moving.”

“Oh, that’s nothing. You were quite active if I remember correctly. Maybe, that is a good thing, and you turned out well.” Naamah smiled.

“I guess so. Most of the time, it is just a mild annoyance, but once, I thought one of the twins would kick through my stomach.”

“Really? Too much coffee or strange food?”

“No. At least, I don’t think so; it is because I have twins that things are getting crowded?” Grace shrugged.

"Well, you do look larger this month, my dear. I'm afraid you will only get larger until you give birth. But don't worry, your man will always stick with you no matter what."

"What do you mean by that?"

"Well, your body is changing, and what if you don't return to your old sexy shape?"

"Greg is not like that mother!" Grace said indignantly.

Grace wished her mother knew it was not a good idea to mess with a pregnant woman's self-image. Her mother had the advantage of not being human and retained her shape even after having a child. Grace was hopeful she would inherit that trait, yet it bothered her. But that was a worry for another time.

"I'm sorry Μωρό μου (Moró mou, 'my baby'). I forget myself sometimes. I still should be more considerate of your human emotions." Naamah glanced downward, sadness flashing across her face briefly. "I have been out of practice since you have been out on your own and... your father."

Grace reached across the table, bumping her tummy on the edge. She stretched a little more to touch her mother's hand. "It's okay, Mother. Sometimes, I expect too much of you and forget myself too." She squeezed Naamah's hand.

"You are much like your father in that way. Thank you."

"I still wish I could have known him. You never talk too much about him, even today."

Naamah was silent, her eyes still downcast.

"Mother, will you ever tell me about him? Where is he from, or what was he like other than being exceptional as a human?" Grace pleaded.

Naamah stayed silent, looking into a past her daughter could not see. Grace hoped she would give Grace some clue about what her mother was thinking.

Grace sighed and said, "It was nice seeing you again, Mother, but I should return to work. I hope you will be able to answer my questions one day. See you again soon. I love you."

Back in the car, Grace tried to suppress a familiar emptiness in her chest when she mentioned her father. Over the years, Naamah had always deflected questions about her lover, closing discussions with a simple declaration: 'Your father was an exceptional man.' When her mother melted into the passenger seat, Grace was about to start the car.

"I'm sorry, child. You deserve to know everything about your father." Naamah reached across and took hold of her daughter's hand. "Do you have time for a short trip with me?"

"I have until lunchtime or as much time as we need," Grace said, her eyes welling with joyful tears. One finally escaped and ran down her cheek. *Why am I so emotional today*? She looked down at her swelling abdomen. *It's gotta be you guys' fault.*

"Yes, I am sure the babies have made you more emotional these days. I am not reading your thoughts but your face, child." Naamah said.

"Mother, I wish you would stop reading my mind!" Grace was irritated but happy that her mother finally relented in her request to know more about her father.

"Ready?"

"Yes, Mother, let's go."

"Here we go."

The car melted away, and Grace felt a familiar sense of vertigo as her mother took her along in a demon's unique traveling style. She closed her eyes, fighting the dizziness until she felt solid ground under her feet. When Grace opened her eyes again, she saw the nighttime sky; the numerous stars were bright and stunning. Living in urban areas most of her life, she had forgotten how the open sky full of stars was such a wonderful sight, an almost religious feeling of awe seeing the Milky Way stretch across the sky.

"So beautiful here, Mother. But where is it here?"

"New Mexico, just outside of a place called Red Rock."

"Father was from here?"

"Yes, and so was his family, dear." Naamah's voice was hesitant. Grace detected a catch in her voice when she said the word family.

"Was? So, none of his family is around anymore?" Grace said.

"Correct. Your father's family lived an ordinary life and now are buried over there," she pointed at a dim light in a small graveyard in the distance. "I can't go there, but if you wish, you go. Your father had one living relative when we met, his grandmother. Her name was Ataltonin Quinn. Your father's name was Yolotli Quinn, and he is next to his mother." Grace heard a catch in her voice when she spoke her father's name.

"Yolotli Quinn," Grace said her father's name out loud. She wanted to say his name and hear it coming from her own voice.

"Your father went by his middle name, Connor, because when he was in the service, they had difficulty pronouncing his Aztec name."

Grace blinked, "He was Aztec?"

"On his mother's side, Antonin Quinn married a man with Irish ancestry, hence the Quinn last name.

"I see; thank you, Mother."

"I didn't meet your grandmother when I was with your father. She had already passed away. We met in New York City a year before you were born. He was one of my targets at first, but there was something about him that prevented me from draining his life— killing him. He had an unusual aura for a human that attracted and was so intriguing. I think he may have known all along what I am but still 'courted' me. We had a wonderful year together, and when you were born, he was so happy. A man like him does not easily cry, but I saw tears in his eyes when he held you. It was at that point I knew I loved him. But Uzza, another fallen Angel, somehow found out about him and your birth. It was he who told my sister Lilith about us. She confronted me and wanted me to kill you, and they would spare Conner's life, but I refused. To keep you both safe, I tried to hide you and your father, but they found us each time. Ultimately, a month after you were born, he was dead, and I was desperate to find a safe place for you." Naamah couldn't cry, but the look of pain was crystal clear.

"Mother," Grace hugged her tight.

The two hugged for a long time. Grace shed tears for herself and her mother, but Naamah pushed her back.

"You should go and pay your respects." I will wait here for you. Naamah bent down, plucked one of the wildflowers, and handed it to her daughter. "Place this on his grave and tell him I miss him."

"I will."

Grace went inside the small cemetery as the sun rose over the distant desert mountains. It didn't take long for her to find her grandmother's and then her father's markers, which were side by side.

"Hello, grandmother. I am Grace, your granddaughter. I am happy to meet you finally. I just learned about you, and I hope to make more trips here in the future to pay my respects." She turned her head and looked at her father's marker. "Hello, Father. Long time no see..."

Grace remained inside the cemetery until the sun cleared the tops of the mountains. She then rejoined her mother off holy ground, tears in her eyes. Grace felt like a small child once again, hugging her mother tightly. Naamah returned the embrace, and after a few moments, they melted away from Yolotli Connor Quinn's final resting place and returned home.

Chapter 16

Death and Threats

"Hannah, don't forget to clock out tonight before you leave." Mr. Henderson called out over his shoulder at the front of the store as he closed and locked the front door.

"Yes, sir!" Hannah turned her eyes back at the young man in the office chair. He was in high school and had been hitting on Hannah since he walked into the store minutes before closing. She loved a meal that delivered itself.

"I guess you have me all to yourself—stud."

The young man was pale and breathing rapidly; he felt cold, so cold. He couldn't form a coherent thought in his muddled brain. Instinct took over, and he wanted to run and scream for help. Help is not coming because the last chance for help just locked the store door, and he was left alone with a monster. He tried begging with his eyes at the thing now, straddling his lap with pants and underwear bunched up around his ankles.

"Now, where were we, my love? Oh yes, you were helping me with my hunger." She looked down. I see you are having a little 'performance issue' right now. Not to worry; I can keep you going a little longer." She reached down between his legs, and he felt an electric jolt. The blond monster smiled, "There's my big boy."

She pulled up her skirt a little and settled on him with a satisfied moan, "I love young boys; they almost fill up my hunger...almost."

An hour later, there was a knock on the back door. Hannah opened it.

"Hello, James. Thank you for helping with my leftovers." Hannah said as James Dolus closed the car trunk.

James Dolus, Mr. Tan's assistant was tasked with helping Hannah dispose of her 'leftovers' so she did not have to while still on assignment watching the former Brother Greg.

"You should not feed on humans while you work; if you are caught, the boss will not be pleased." James pulled off his rubber gloves. "Now to edit the security records."

He logged in to the security system computer in the store's office. "This should only take a few moments to erase any images of your *meal* coming into the store. When do you think, you will need to feed again? "He said in an almost disapproving tone.

Hannah missed the sarcasm: "I think I will be okay for a few days. He was yummy, though. I wish I could have more before he gave out." She licked her lips, savoring the memory.

James ignored the commentary. "Done. Next time, call me; you will not have to wait too long for me to assist you. The longer you are in one place, the higher the chance of being caught with leftovers," James said.

"Yes, of course, sorry."

"Very well. I will go now, but Julius asked me to get a progress report from you first." James stood, hands crossed, waiting for a reply.

Crap! There is not much to report. Has it already been two weeks since Julius gave me this medallion?

"Well?" James sounded impatient.

Suddenly, she remembered, "I have made friends with the pastor at St. Rita's. Then, I met Brother Greg's wife. She is a strange one. I got a funny sensation just being in the same room with her, and she is pregnant."

"Pregnant?" His face twitched.

"Yes, maybe a few months along. The cambion was a few months along and did not look very comfortable. I understand pregnancy is sometimes not easy for a mortal woman."

"I think you should find out how far along she is, and you can text me the answer when you get it. Do you think that you can get close to her again?"

"Maybe, but you know I can talk to the pastor, and he should be able to tell me." She smiled.

"Remember, even though the medallion allows you entrance to holy ground, you can't use all of your 'talents' there."

"Why?"

"I am not privileged to know the reason; I am only reminding you not to attempt using them, or it will be bad for you and Mr. Tan," James said with a deadly tone.

Hannah gulped, "I understand. You can assure the boss that I will stick to the rules."

"Excellent. Then, until next time."

James left, and Hannah clocked out.

James returned to Mr. Tan's office shortly after leaving the young succubus.

"I see you are back, James. That took a little longer than I expected. Are there any problems with the 'leftovers?" Mr. Tan asked from behind his massive desk. His eyes focused on his tablet, reading something that intrigued him.

"No problems, sir; I handed over the 'leftovers' to our contractor, who ensures the proper disposal with no questions. The contractor does have a family to feed after all, and I cautioned it not to get greedy and don't eat it all at once."

Mr. Tan nodded, "Hannah, what was her report?"

James quietly put his hands behind his back. "Something is interesting to report. Well, maybe two things to report."

"Oh, a bonus in the report? And I was losing faith in that girl. A little longer with nothing useful, I would have to find another low-ranking demon to entrust the medallion to."

James knew what passing the ring off from Hannah to another demon would do to Hannah. It would kill her. "That would be unfortunate for her, sir."

"And a pain in the ass for me, James. So, what is the report?" Mr. Tan sat back in his chair.

"It seems that Hannah has made friends with the pastor of St. Rita's. She plans to visit often to build trust. But the best bit of information may be on Naamah's daughter."

"Oh? You have my attention."

"She is pregnant."

Mr. Tan's eyebrows arched. "That is interesting. I remember discussions we had in the past about the cambion, that she should be unable to have children because of her, how should I say, muddled heritage." He stood up and walked over to his assistant. "You have done well, but I want confirmation."

"I understand, sir. How should I proceed?"

"Thank you, James, but I will handle it from here."

"Sir?"

"You can go now, and I will call you when I need you again." Mr. Tan walked with him to the door and showed him out.

Naamah watched Grace drive away when she felt a familiar presence again.

"Are you following me, sister?"

"I still miss you, my sister, and will always wish we could bury the hatchet, as the saying goes," Lilith said.

"If only I could use a hatchet and be rid of you."

"Such harsh words for me, your dear sister." Lilith watched Grace's car; it was almost out of sight. "I see I missed my niece again. That's a shame."

Naamah's face flushed. "Save it, traitor! You never had her welfare in mind! I'm going."

She was about to melt away when Lilith said, "I hear she is pregnant."

Naamah froze.

"Yes, I know about that. How far along is Grace in her pregnancy? Is it a boy or a girl? You understand I have many questions about my new family members, right?" Lilith's voice was kind, but her eyes were icy cold.

"Let's not do this here, sister. Shall we go somewhere where mortals or other distractions will not hinder us? I think we have much to discuss." Naamah's skin turned darker, almost red, and her fingernails looked like claws. Dark translucent wings briefly appeared behind her back.

Lilith smiled, "I hit a sore spot, it seems. But I got a few answers I was looking for just by your reaction." Like her sister, her skin turned red with large wings and claws for her hands. "I don't care where we do this; unlike you, I don't care about the mortals here if they see us or get hurt. They are just food for beings like us, am I right, sister? That's all they are—cattle."

Naamah, still seething, "What have I done to hurt you that makes you feel this way about me?"

"It's not you, dear sister; it's that migás (half-breed) of yours. I am offended by her very existence." Lilith lifted a few inches off the ground; her feet resembled an eagle's claws.

"Be warned that if you ever come near my daughter, you will regret it." Naamah spat. She was in full demon mode, just like her sister. Anger had clouded her judgment, and she no longer cared if anyone nearby saw them.

"You are only one, dear sister; your threats have no bite," Lilith snapped, her mouth full of razor-sharp teeth snapping shut.

"Just ask Bezale and Azazyel that question."

Lilith settled on the ground, "What do you know about what happened to them?" She didn't hide the surprise in her face.

"Just know that my daughter has more than me for her protection, and if you are not careful, you may disappear like those two have. So back off bitch, or you will have more than a mother's wrath to deal with."

Naamah took advantage of Lilith's confusion and melted away, leaving Lilith in the Walmart parking lot with an angry and puzzled expression. The air was heavy with the scent of sulfur.

Chapter 17

The Helper

"Good morning, Hannah. It's nice to see you again," Father Ortiz said, opening the church doors. "I was happy to hear from you yesterday."

"Good morning, Father. I should follow up on my promise to come by more often and help my new friends, you, and Grace."

Hannah called Father Ortiz earlier, asking if there was anything she could do to thank him and Ms. Grace for getting her that job. The pastor assured her it was their pleasure, but Hannah insisted she do something in return. He suggested she could help with light cleaning since the regular cleaners took time off at the beginning of summer break. They agreed to meet at 9 a.m. when he opened the church doors.

"Thank you for agreeing to help with this, Hannah. The work is not terribly hard, but much appreciated," he said.

"It is the least I can do to return your help finding me a job, Father."

Hannah went inside, still marveling at her ability to enter holy ground again without consequences. She felt the medallion around her neck and, for the first time, wondered who made it and where it came from.

It's too late to ask that kind of question, I guess.

"So, what will you have me do first?" She said.

"Let me show you where the janitor's closet is, and we can start vacuuming first."

Father Ortiz was amazed that she seemed unfamiliar with basic cleaning equipment. It wasn't that she did not know what they were, but it was as if she never had to clean a room before. He watched her as she went in between the pews and decided she was good to leave alone.

"I have to attend to some work in the parish office, Hannah, but I will return soon. Will you be ok if I go now?"

"Sure, leave everything to me. I think I've gotten the hang of it now," she shouted over the vacuum.

"Ok."

When she finished with the carpets, she grabbed the duster and dusted some tables and the lectern. The last thing to do was to clean the sacristy behind the altar. There was a small opening concealed behind a wall where a large crucifix hung, which led to it. She looked up at the figure of a man hanging up on a cross. It gave her an anxious feeling of dread as if he was going to leap off the wall and attack her because he knew her secret. She quickly moved past it and into the sacristy. The room was not large, so it took her no time to vacuum and dust exposed surfaces. Hannah finished and then put the cleaning supplies away.

What now?

Through one of the windows behind the church, she saw the utility building where they stored the groundskeeping equipment. Greg was there, opened the large garage door, and went inside.

Greg was inspecting the riding mower and checking the oil and gas when he felt a tap on his shoulder. Startled, he turned around to see a young blond woman with striking blue eyes standing there, her hair in a ponytail. She was wearing leggings and a baggy T-shirt. It took him a moment to realize who she was. Greg took out one of his earphones and smiled.

"Hannah? Right?"

She flashed a brilliant smile that made his heart skip a beat for a moment. "Have you heard of me, Greg?"

"Yes. What are you doing here?"

"I was helping Father Ortiz with some of the cleaning inside the church."

"Oh, that's nice of you," Greg said, scrunching his face as if thinking of something. Grace told me that you were looking for a job, and they were able to help you find one while you were in school."

"Yes."

"I see."

"Well, I wanted to return the favor. It's the least I can do, don't you think?" She flashed that smile again, which made Greg feel uncomfortable.

"I'm sure Father didn't expect you to return the favor, Hannah. But I know he appreciates the help since the regular cleaning people are on vacation."

Hannah was in Greg's personal bubble. He felt uncomfortable again and backed away, "Well, I need to get to work. The grass is not getting shorter, so..."

Hannah nodded, "Ok. I'll see you again another time, Greg."

"Sure."

She turned to walk out the door and fell on the ground, letting out a yelp of pain. "Ouch."

Greg was at her side, "What happened?'

"I'm not sure. I must have tripped on something," Hannah tried to stand and let out another yelp of pain, falling back on the ground.

She grabbed her ankle. "Let me look at that," Greg said. She was wearing tennis shoes that seemed one size too large for her feet. He saw some gravel on the driveway where she fell, and she might have rolled her ankle on one of the large rocks. His hand touched her ankle and squeezed, feeling any sign of swelling or any other damage.

"Ouch!"

"Hurts there?" he said, touching the outside part of her ankle.

"Yes."

"I don't see any swelling yet. Let's get you off the ground first." A workbench was behind them, and Greg picked her up and sat her down on top of it. "I'm going to take your shoe off, ok?"

Hannah nodded yes; her face flushed.

Greg took off her sneakers and socks. Her feet were tiny and delicate, with black-painted toenails. He did not see any swelling or bruising around her foot and ankle. When he moved her ankle, she grimaced a little but did not cry out.

"I think you will be ok, Hannah. The first aid kit has an ACE wrap that I can put on your ankle to keep it from moving too much. Will that be, ok?"

"Yes, thank you. I'm sorry I feel so stupid, Greg."

"It's not stupid, just bad luck," he smiled, retrieving the ACE wrap in the first aid kit and wrapped her ankle. "There, try and stand on it now."

With Greg's help, she scooted off the table, stood on the uninjured foot, and tried putting weight on the other.

"It's a little better, but I can't walk too far right now."

"You live across the street, right?" He asked.

"Yes."

"Lean on the table a moment; I'll be right back." Greg walked to the back of the room and returned with a folding chair. "Sit here. I will bring my car to the front and take you home."

"I don't want to be in a lot of trouble." Hannah looked embarrassed and stood up, "Ouch." She sat back down.

"You are no trouble." He grabbed the toolbox he had been using a few moments ago and placed her injured foot on top of it. Hannah put her hands on his shoulders. Greg felt something like a small electric charge that momentarily caused him to catch his breath.

"Did you shock me? That's a lot of static you have, Hannah." Greg cleared his head, "I'll be back with the car." Greg stood up, turned around, and saw Grace at the garage door.

"Hi babe, what's up?" His voice was a little louder when he saw his wife.

Grace looked uncomfortable, holding her stomach. "I was coming by to ask what you would like for lunch. Besides, the doctor ordered me not to sit too much at my desk." Greg looked strange; his pupils dilated, and his face pale. "Are you ok, honey?"

Greg shook his head, "Yeah, just feeling a little weird. Maybe I should have eaten breakfast."

Grace noticed Hannah's ankle with the ACE wrap on it. "What happened?"

"I tripped on one of those rocks over there." Hannah pointed to several at Grace's feet, "Please be careful."

Grace tried to smile, but it looked like a grimace, "Thank you, I will."

"You ok, babe, you look a little green." He said, grabbing her hand,

"I was ok until I got here. Maybe I should move around more, and the babies may settle down."

Greg put his hand on her stomach. "I can feel them. What are they doing? Jumping jacks?"

"Making their mom sick."

Greg was conflicted for a moment. On the one hand, he had a pregnant and sick wife; on the other hand, he was a person who could not walk home. At that moment, Father Ortiz appeared and stood next to Grace.

Greg was relieved, "Father, I'm glad you are here."

"What can I do?"

"Father, do you mind helping Hannah get home? She twisted her ankle." Greg said.

"Of course." Father Ortiz looked at the girl. I'm sorry you hurt yourself when you volunteered your time. Give me a moment, and I'll get the car." He paused. Do you want me to take you to see a doctor?"

"Oh no, Father. If I rest it a little, it will be ok." She slid off the table and began walking. "See, it's much better now." Hannah had no noticeable limp as she began to leave.

"Are you sure? It is no trouble, and I feel bad you got injured only helping out today," the priest said.

"Yes, Father, thank you. Thanks for taking care of my ankle, Greg. I hope you feel better, Grace. See you all later," Hannah said.

"I can at least walk you to the road." Father Ortiz said, catching up to her.

"You don't have to, but thanks."

Father Ortiz left the shed following Hannah, still insisting that he help her, leaving Grace and Greg alone.

Greg turned his attention back to his wife. "Here, sweetheart, have a seat." He indicated a stool next to the workbench.

Grace batted his hand away. "I'm ok now. The twins seemed to have settled down."

"You sure?"

"Yes, Mr. Overprotective, I'm fine.

"Those guys seem to pick the oddest times to act up," Greg said, touching her belly.

"They move around, but normally, it does not bother me too much. This time, it was like they were fighting or running."

"Has this happened before?"

"No." Grace said, squinting as if trying to remember something, "Wait. Yes, it has."

"When? Something you ate or did?"

"No," She grasped her husband's hand and squeezed tight.

"It has only happened once before. The first time I met Hannah, the twins were doing somersaults, and I thought I would throw up."

Greg turned his gaze back toward Hannaha and Fr. Ortiz was already across the street; they were almost at her house. "She seems like an ordinary girl—a little ditzy but nothing out of the ordinary that I can see."

"She can stand on holy ground, which rules out her being a demon." Grace moved over and sat on the stool. "I'll talk to my mother about this and see if she can shed light on it." She rubbed her tummy again.

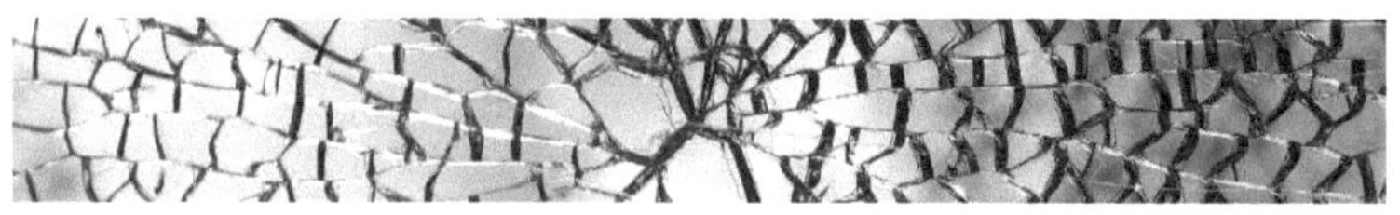

Chapter 18

Breach of Privacy

James sat behind his desk, busy with emails from party supporters, all trying to schedule time with the former governor. A few were from local civic groups in various parts of the state. There were only a select few that Mr. Tan would agree to meet with, mainly the ones with deep pockets. The rest generally received canned thank-you responses and vague promises of revisiting their requests at a future date. He was in the middle of sending a response when his phone rang. The caller ID on the phone screen said 'Private'; James knew who it was.

"Good morning. I hope you are calling because you have the information I requested?"

James had a pen and wrote down a few words on a pad.

"Is this accurate?... I see. Thank you." He ended the call and knocked on his boss's door.

"Come in."

"I have that information you requested," he handed the slip of paper to Mr. Tan.

Mr. Tan looked at the paper, "so we have names and addresses."

"Yes, sir."

"Good. I'll attend to it myself."

"Sir? But we have others who can handle this for you. Do you think it would be wise to be directly involved? I fear you would be recognized if you went there in person." James rarely voices his concerns to his boss. He is the perfect assistant and carries out his orders. But he never knew that Mr. Tan would actively participate in problems. Mr Tan delegated action to subordinates, especially if they were unseemly. It was easier to deny involvement when no one could trace his involvement—plausible deniability.

"Don't worry, James. I will be discreet. I know someone who can handle *this* delicately."

"I see, sir, if that is what you wish, but I hope you can still trust that I handle the situation. I hope you have not lost faith in me, sir."

"It has nothing to do with that, James. Don't worry. I know you could handle this; however, it is more personal. Please finish those email messages. We need to schedule meetings with some of our donors."

"Yes, sir." James closed the door.

Mr. Tan reread the note. "This requires a personal touch." He closed his eyes.

"It sure does, and it is very *personal* to me, "Lilith said from across the room. "Since I am going to be a great aunt, I should check up on the health of my new family members."

Lilith melted away out of the office.

Sandy tidied up in the lobby before going home after a long day. She was the receptionist at Dr. Sato's OB office, and everyone else had gone home. Ordinarily, an obstetrician's office does not have messy patients; pregnant women rarely make a mess alone. Unless they bring kids with them, then all bets are off, especially when the 'little darlings' do not behave. Today, one of their patients brought her two younger children and a less-than-attentive— husband. He spent most of his time staring at the screen on his phone while the children ran all over the waiting room, scattering magazines to the floor and dropping cookie crumbs on the carpet. She did not have to vacuum, but he could at least pick up the magazines, some of which she had to throw out because the 'little darlings' destroyed them.

"Some people should not reproduce," she mumbled to herself; she was sure no one else was in the room.

"I agree with you, Sandy." said a soft voice at the waiting room door.

Sandy jumped, startled, "I'm sorry the office is closed."

"It's okay. I will be only a moment." said a young woman. "I just have a few questions for you. I promise not to take too much of your time."

"I thought I locked the door. How did you get in?" Sandy said.

The woman pushed on the door, confirming she did lock it.

"Don't worry about the door, Sandy. I need your help, please." The woman whispered in her ear, 'Please.' Sandy felt like she was suddenly thrown into a warm bath, losing her inhibitions. She felt a powerful need to help this gorgeous woman. Her almond-shaped grey eyes bore into her eyes, and Sandy felt drunk; her will was not hers anymore.

"What can I do to you; I mean for you?" Sandy said haltingly.

The woman reached out a hand and brushed her cheek. Sandy almost collapsed onto the carpet. The young woman grabbed her by each arm to steady her. "Easy, my love, not yet. First, you must give me some information you have here on a patient."

Sandy blinked, "it is against the law." she said in a brief moment of clarity.

The woman smiled and ran her fingers across her head, "against human law, not mine."

"Yes."

"I have questions about a woman, and her name is Grace Cassidy."

"Oh, the twins?"

"Twins? Is that what she is having?" The woman showed surprise on her face.

"Yes, we see a few cases a year, and she already knows the sexes of the babies," Sandy remembered Grace because she used to go to her husband's church until just last year. She left after the tragedy and never came back; as far as she knows, the church is still struggling with the aftermath of that day when so many parishioners died in a horrible accident.

"Enlighten me."

Sandy told her everything she knew about Grace and all the information from the practice computer systems.

"So she is pregnant with fraternal twins, and this is her sixth month?" the woman said.

"Yes." Sandy breathed.

"That would make her due date near the end of October. Thank you, my dear. You have been very accommodating." She leaned over and kissed Sandy on the lips. Sandy closed her eyes and never opened them again.

The woman left the office, leaving the practice with a lifeless employee sitting at her desk the following day.

Chapter 19

Cookout

"Tonight sounds great. Grace and I haven't made any plans. She would love an excuse to leave the RV for a little while." Greg ended the call.

"Who was that, honey?" Grace asked, rubbing her eyes. She had just woken up from a nap and sat beside him.

"It was Robert. He wants us to get together for dinner at their place tonight. I told him we could go if that's alright with you."

"Sure, honey. It's been too long since we have seen our friends, and you are right. I want to get out before it gets harder for me to get around anyway." Grace said as she shifted in her chair, trying vainly to get comfortable.

Greg had finished his work for the day and began stripping off his clothes to take a shower. "Then I'll get cleaned up first, babe."

Grace allowed her eyes to roam over his body. "Physical work suits you." She noticed lately more definition in the muscles of his arms and legs. He was never fat, but before they resigned from the Christian Fellowship Center, Greg had a slight muffin top. That was all gone, and his torso was more defined and toned.

"Yum." She grinned.

Greg turned around with a devilish smile on his face. “Do you like what you see, Ms. Cassidy?”

“Very much so, Mr. Cassidy.”

Greg moved closer, and Grace held up her hand. “But shower first. I love you, but eww, gross. You smell of sweat and grass.”

“I thought you would love me as I am, baby?”

She picked up a pillow and threw it at him, “Be gone, you foul beast, and shower.” Grace giggled.

Greg caught the pillow and faked a frown. “Ok, but ok, be ready for me when I’m squeaky clean.”

“I hope you guys are hungry. We have burgers, pancit, lumpia, and corn on the cob.” Robert’s mom, Lisa Diaz, opened the front door for Greg and Grace. “Oh, Grace, I have not seen you in so long,” she said, putting her hand on Grace’s belly. “Don’t worry; I will keep the best seat in the house for you.”

Grace blushed and put her hand on Lisa’s. “Please, Mrs. Diaz, any chair is fine, and yes, I am hungry. Everything sounds so good right now.”

“Please, call me Lisa. Don’t worry; we will feed you well.” She led them to the backyard patio, where Robert stood before a smoky grill.

“Hi guys, I’m glad you could come.” Robert waved with a spatula in his hand. Just then, a large flare erupted.

“Robert! Pay attention!” AM yelled, admonishing him from the patio table.

“Hey, little momma and Greg.” She went to Grace and hugged her first, then Greg.

“Hi AM, it has been too long since we have been over.” Greg said, “What can I do to help?”

“Well, everything is done out here. Maybe you can check Lola in the kitchen to see if she needs help.”

Greg went inside the house, and AM sat with Grace at the patio table.

“So, how are you feeling?” AM asked.

"Like a beach ball, but otherwise good."

"Still living in the RV?"

Grace grunted, "Yes, the contractor does not think he can finish the house until late August or early September."

"I'm sorry if RV living becomes too much. You can stay here. We have an extra room," AM said.

Grace squeezed AM's hand. "I'll survive a little bit longer. Besides, I think Father Ortiz would miss us too much. He acts more like an expectant grandfather than a godfather, but that's ok with me. He is part of the family now."

"Speaking of Fr. Ortiz, he should be here after dinner. We invited him, but he said that he was running late. Something about a Zoom meeting with the bishop."

"Oh, about what?"

"I don't know, but it sounded routine. Robert and I invited him because we have some things we need to discuss regarding our mutual friend, you know, the one with wings." AM pointed up at the sky.

Grace sighed, "We have some things we need to tell you, too."

"I'd offer you a beer to smooth things out, but you are still on a restricted diet." AM touched Grace's expanding belly.

"That is a shame; sometimes, I need a drink to take the rough edges off the day."

Greg was back with Lola, holding a large plate of pancit.

"I think you guys cooked too much. Are you expecting more people?" Greg said, putting the noodles on the table.

"Just Fr. Ortiz and Fr. O'Brian." AM said, "Come on, momma, let's go to the table and eat."

Frs. Ortiz and O'Brian arrived twenty minutes later to join the meal. Greg was hungrier than he realized. He ate two burgers and a plate of pancit with a handful of lumpia and washed it down with a few beers.

Physical labor is good for the body and appetite. Greg rubbed his belly.

"Thank you for the invitation to your home, Ellan and Lisa. The food was wonderful." Fr. O'Brien said, pushing back from the table.

"You are welcome." Lisa smiled. Does anyone care for dessert?"

"Maybe later, thank you," Fr. Ortiz said.

Lisa and Ellen began clearing the trays from the table to take inside.

"Let me help you with that," Fr. O'Brian stood up and grabbed the plate of uneaten burgers.

"Thank you, Father," Ellen said as he followed her to the house.

"So I talked with Raphael not too ago," Robert blurted out.

For a moment, everyone was silent. Somehow, that news was not a shock to anyone.

"What did he have to say, Robert?" Fr. Ortiz said.

Robert put down his beer, "What do you guys know about former Governor Tan?"

"Other than that, he has some of the same slimy people around him as Kanker had. Why?" Greg said, then his eyes widened, "Are you implying what I think you are?"

"What am I implying, Greg?"

"That he is another fallen angel? "

"Raphael thinks so, though he also admits that he is not 100% certain what he is. With Kanker, he was more certain, but Tan is a mystery to him." Robert sipped his beer, "There's also something else for you and Grace."

"Me?" Grace said.

"Yes. Raphael is not saying anything bad, but he is concerned about a visitor you had recently. A being from Ireland." Robert said.

"Wait! Is he spying on us?" Greg said, with irritation in his voice.

"No, no. Understand that when something that is not human enters the holy ground, a kind of alarm is triggered." Robert explained.

"That sense, Greg," Grace said, touching Greg's hand. "Yes, I had a visitor from a being known as a pooka named Fia. She is quite harmless to me. She traveled here to deliver a message from her mistress. I've already told Greg about it."

"We were going to tell you about it next time we got together, but I never thought that the church grounds had a kind of alarm system for the supernatural." Greg shrugged.

"No worries, so tell us about your Irish visitor?"

"And what is a Pooka?" AM blurted out.

Grace giggled, "fair question. I didn't even know about them until I met one." Grace shifted in her chair, trying to get more comfortable. Lately, a comfortable position was becoming more elusive the larger she got.

AM could see Grace getting increasingly uncomfortable. "Grace, come sit in Lola's chair. I'm sure she will not mind considering your condition."

"Ah, that's much better, thanks. So, how do I start?" Grace glanced over to Greg. "Guess I will start with my mother. She was concerned when she could not 'sense' my presence."

"What do you mean?" Fr. Ortiz said. Grace almost forgotten the priest was there; he was not the type to interrupt conversations unless asked.

"Well, one of the things my mother can do since I can remember is she didn't have to see me to find out where I was in a crowded room or a building. It is a kind of radar only for me, her only child. She couldn't do that with anyone else. It was comforting when I was young that she always watched over me. But ever since I became pregnant, she cannot 'sense' my presence even if she looks right at me."

"Wow. That is interesting and a little scary." AM said.

"It is not, AM. My mother is a lot of things, but she loves me and would do anything for me and now her grandchildren. She didn't know why she had lost her ability to sense my presence, so she asked for help outside her circle of 'people.' She is acquainted with.' a powerful being from northern Europe called

The Morrigan. They are not friends but not enemies either. They respect each other as long as they don't interfere in the other's affairs. Mother went to her asking for advice about her problem because if word got out that I was pregnant, it might cause issues for her and maybe me."

"What does this have to do with the creature, the pooka?"

"The pooka, Fia, is a shapeshifter who works for The Morrigan. Fia was directed to deliver an answer to my mother about why she was having trouble sensing me. It seems that the twin's unique genetic heritage of Greg and me have made them 'special.'"

"I don't understand."

"The Morrgian called them divine twins; at least, that is what she believes. There is no way of knowing at this stage, but if they can shield themselves from demons and maybe angels, which would concern both parties." Grace said.

"What are divine twins?" Fr. Ortiz said.

"In The Morrigan's tradition, one could be a healer and the other a warrior."

"For what purpose?"

"I don't know, Father. I know in my heart that the twins are not malevolent, and I hope all of you will not prejudge them because of what I have told you." Grace appeared nervous and vulnerable.

AM grasped her hands, "We don't, Grace. We are your friends and family, who have been through literally hell and back; I know we are not giving up on you guys."

Robert and Fr. Ortiz nodded in agreement.

"Thank you, guys," Greg said, holding his wife's other hand.

"Well, one thing AM, and I can say about being your friends, Greg," Robert said.

"What is that?"

"You guys are not boring."

Chapter 20

Wet T-Shirt

When Hannah entered the church on Monday morning to help with the cleaning, the floors were dirtier than usual. It had rained all day yesterday, so parishioners had tracked mud up and down the aisles. They placed extra mats at the entrance, but they only held so much mud and water before they were useless. Hannah sighed and got to work, wondering how much longer she would have to pretend to care about the people here in this church and the target humans she was watching. The usual people who did this work were due by the middle of the week, so she would no longer have a good excuse to come to the church.

First, she dragged all the soiled mats to the front of the church. She would rinse off after she mopped the church floors. An hour later, she was done with the floors and started to drag the soiled mats behind the church, where she could use the garden hose to remove the caked-in mud. It was hard and hot work in the July sun. By the time she hosed off the last of the mats, Hannah had gotten her sweatpants and t-shirt covered with dirt and soaking wet.

I hope Mr. Tan appreciates how hard I am working to gain the trust of these humans.

She left the wet mats in the parking lot to dry in the sun but realized that they would not dry very fast this way. She was planning to find Fr. Ortiz to help her when a car pulled up behind her; it was Greg.

"Hi, Hannah," he said, getting out of the car. "Can I help you with that?"

Greg saw that she was soaked, and when she turned around, it looked like she was a participant in a wet t-shirt contest, leaving nothing to the imagination. Her shirt clung to her torso in a way that was not appropriate in most public places, especially on church grounds. Hannah sensed that Greg was interested, so she walked closer to him and touched his arm. An electric shock ran through him, and his body reacted. Greg's mouth went dry, and he was very conscious of a physical reaction in his pants. Hannah smiled, happy with his response to her touch.

"Thank you, Greg. Yes, I do need a little help with these wet mats."

Greg swallowed and closed his eyes, forcing himself to calm down. "There is a chain-link fence behind the garage, and we can drape the mats over it so they can dry. I'll grab one end if you want to get the other."

"Oh, that's a good idea, Greg." She purred, then picked up the opposite end. They draped a mat over the fence. Draping the rest of the mats atop the fence took a few more minutes; Greg was wet and dirty after they had drapped the last mat over the fence.

"Thanks for your help, Greg. I wish I had thought of using the fence earlier," Hannah said, squeezing the bottom of her T-shirt and wringing out some water. However, tightening her shirt against her chest only outlined her breasts even more, only succeeding in making her T-shirt transparent, which made things worse for Greg, trying not to notice.

He wrenched his head away, and to cover it, he made a show of arching his back as if it were stiff. "Don't worry about it, Hannah. I am happy to help." Greg said in a hoarse voice.

Hannah reached out and began rubbing Greg's back. Greg felt another shock and jumped away. "Your hands are cold, Hannah. Thanks, but I'm okay."

"I'm sorry."

"I need to get changed before Grace gets home. I promised to go with her to look for furniture for the new house." Greg took a few halting steps back, smiling weakly.

"Oh yes, that house over there," she pointed at the nearly completed house adjacent to the church. Fr. Ortiz told me about that. I hope you can give me a tour sometime."

"Sure, maybe next month. I hope the contractors finish building the house by then." Greg's voice had returned to normal.

"By the way, where is your wife?"

"She is at a doctor's appointment but should be back soon. It is just one of her checkups. Nothing to worry about."

"I see." Hannah turned to where they hung the mats and asked, "How long do you think I should leave them? They are pretty wet." She rubbed her hands over her wet shirt again, forcing Greg to look away once again.

"I think you can leave them there overnight. It's not supposed to rain. So, you can bring them back in the morning."

"That sounds good to me. I will take out the trash and lock the church doors before I leave. I need to shower after that," she said, rubbing her hands on the wet t-shirt again.

"I'll tell you what, I will take out the trash, and you can lock the doors before you go home. That will make it easier for you, and the dumpster will not be far from my RV."

"You don't have to, Greg."

Greg walked ahead of her so he would not have to look at the young woman's wet clothes again. "It's no big deal, Hannah."

Robert was walking to the church's front doors when Greg saw him, "Hey, pilgrim, the church is closing. Go pray somewhere else."

"Funny, dork. Do you know where the creepy groundskeeper is? I want to pray for him; he needs it." Robert said sarcastically. At first, he didn't notice Hannah because she was behind him, but then she came into view as they got closer.

Oh my. What is going on here? A wet t-shirt contest?

"You must be Hannah. I am this poor soul's only friend, Robert." He extended his hand. Hannah grasped it and held it longer than Robert expected.

Hannah seemed puzzled and stared at him, "Nice to meet you, Robert."

"What brings you here, Rob?" Greg said.

"Nothing. Can't a guy stop by and check in on a friend?"

"We were closing up the church. I was going in to take the trash bags to the dumpster while Hannah locked up. She lives across the street, "Greg said, pointing at the house.

"Don't let me stop you. I can supervise while you take out the trash." Robert grinned, "Nice to meet you, Hannah."

Hannah waved and closed the doors.

Robert followed Greg to the back of the church with the trash bags.

"I had heard that Fr. Ortiz got some help with the cleaning when the regulars went on vacation. Is she new to the parish?" Robert asked.

"I think so. That girl is a college student. Fr. Ortiz found her inside the church a few weeks back, and she said she was just curious. They seemed to hit it off, and you know, the padre, always the shepherd."

Robert's expression was blank, and Greg knew his friend well enough to know that it was his way of mulling over something on his mind. "What is it, Rob? I can tell something is bothering you."

"I'm not sure. Something about Hannah feels off. I don't have words for it."

"What do you mean?" Greg's replayed in his head the interactions he had with her, and he could see nothing unusual. Except that, he felt like a dirty old man staring at her wet clothes clinging to her young, shapely body.

"When I shook her hand, she did not let go at first, as if trying to get me to notice her."

"I'm glad it's not just me, then," Robert laughed. We are getting older; my friend and the girls are getting younger."

"Are you saying we are becoming dirty old men already?"

"Yep!"

"We will keep this between us and not tell our wives." Greg laughed.

Both men jumped at a voice behind them, "Keep what from your wives?"

Chapter 21

Uninvited Guest

Behind St. Rita's Church, there was an unused parcel of land. Over the decades, it was home to wild creatures and occasional wilder children playing among the trees. Dirt trails were created by people passing through on foot or dirt bikes, cutting deep ruts in the soil as they weaved around the trees. Graffiti and trash were scattered throughout. Near the back of the lot was a medium-sized pond connected to a creek that fed the James River. Occasionally, some locals would fish or swim to pass the time on a hot summer day. But all of it was gone now; the lot was now cleared, and a new house under construction sprang up in place of where there were trees and dirt trails. The house had a clear view of the church. A gravel road ran along one side of the church property that connected the home under construction to the main road. Today was Sunday, and the construction workers were off, so the job site was silent and empty.

Hannah had been curious about the house since Greg told her it was his new home. So, while Mass was underway, she decided to explore it. It was a good way to kill time and, more importantly, take her mind off her hunger.

I'm so hungry. James is late with bringing me someone.

The house was a modern two-story design with an attached two-car garage. Around the back was a large outdoor patio area with a nearly complete pergola and outdoor fireplace. From the outside, the house construction looked complete. Maybe there was still more work to be done inside the house. Then, a noise caught her attention from inside the home. Hannah moved closer and noticed that the patio door was slightly open. She heard more noise again from inside and the sound of someone breathing. A succubus's senses are keener than a human's; she heard the sound of a person trying to control their breathing and—a heart beating fast. A lot like her prey when it was scared. Hannah opened the door and took a deep breath. She could smell that there was a human here: male.

So hungry.

She pushed the sliding door open and quietly stepped inside. "I know you are here; I can smell you, darling; whoever you are, you may as well come out. I will find you." The breathing stopped, but the heart rate increased. She stood still, trying to locate her prey, waiting for the person to resume breathing. They couldn't hold their breath too much longer. Then, a loud gasp and quick inhalation of air.

Got you!

She moved into an adjoining room near the garage at a speed no human could match. Laundry room? Then she saw an old man crouched behind some trash stacked on one side of the room. Hannah smiled, "Don't worry, love. I will not hurt you. Come to me." She extended her hand and touched his face. The man stood up against his will, his eyes full of fear as if he sensed his impending doom. He was wearing dirty old clothes and worn-out shoes. An equally dirty and ragged backpack was on the floor next to him. "Come here, love, let me look at you. I will not tell anybody you are here, I promise. It will be our little secret."

The man shuffled over to Hannah, eyes blank, like a mouse mesmerized by the snake and powerless to resist. She put her hands on his shoulders and felt his life force pulsating under his skin. He smelled awful; he probably had not bathed in days or weeks, and his hair was greasy and unkempt. He was missing some teeth. These flaws did not matter to her; she was starving, and he was simply a meal. No one would miss another homeless man. Hannah's eyes turned black, and her fingers morphed into claws. She grabbed him, pulled his face to her waiting mouth, and kissed him. At first, the man did not struggle, and then suddenly, like a fish with a hook in his mouth, he began to flail, pushing away, but she was too strong. The man struggled as his strength was giving out, and his life was leaving him, but Hannah held on, greedily feeding on him, until there was nothing left for her to devour. She roughly dropped him to the floor, momentarily savoring her meal. Hannah breathed deeply, eyes closed, and her breath slowed as she licked her lips.

"Not the best I have had, but when a girl is starving…" she said aloud.

Voices were coming from the front of the house—at least two people. The front door opened, and the people talking with each other walked inside. Hannah crouched, reflexively listening. She thought she recognized one of the voices, Grace, the other she had never heard before. Grace was showing AM around the nearly completed interior when she felt the twins start to move.

"Are you ok?" AM said, concerned, and grabbed her friend's arm.

Hannah made it out of the house and ran into the woods. She took a circuitous route back home, hoping no one would see her.

Grace braced herself against a wall and took a few deep breaths. She was seven months pregnant, so physical exertion drained her energy fast. The long walk from the church was not as simple as it used to be, even a few weeks ago. "Give me a minute, AM. I'm ok." Ok, held up a hand. "Maybe the twins are happy with their new home."

"Ok, maybe we should have driven up here instead of walking, stubborn momma." Grace admonished.

"I was fine until we walked inside, but it's ok now. The babies have settled down." She rubbed her abdomen. "Let me show you the back of the house. I promise we will go slow."

"Okay, we should call Robert or Greg to pick us up in the car when we leave. Is that OK?"

"Sure."

They went to the back of the house after looking at the kitchen and all three bedrooms; next was the back patio and living room.

"This looks nice, Grace. I am a little jealous. You guys have lots of room. I guess it's good you went with three bedrooms before you knew you were having twins," AM said.

"Yes, but the third room was meant to be an office or guest room. But that is life." Grace smiled, thinking it was good for the kids to have their own rooms. Her smile faded when they entered the living room and saw the sliding glass door open.

AM noticed, too. "Did the contractors forget to close this door?" She looked at the floor and saw a trail of grass and leaves going off to one side. "What is over there?"

"The laundry room and garage," Grace answered.

"Wait here, Grace." Before Grace could protest, AM was in the laundry room doorway. "Oh shit!" AM went inside the room.

Grace walked in and saw AM crouched over a man lying on the floor. She ran her fingers over the man's neck and then stood up.

"He is dead. His body is still warm."

Grace lost color in her face, and AM rushed to her, "You, ok?"

"Yes."

"I wonder what happened. This man looks so gaunt as if something sucked him dry." AM said in horror; her face was pale.

"Funny, your description looks like what happened to him. I have only seen someone like this once before."

"You have? When?"

Grace turned her away from AM. "When I was young, and my mother and I were hiding, she had not fed in a long time. One night, I saw her with a strange man, and she was kissing him. I thought it was strange for her to do this while we were trying not to attract attention; the kiss seemed to take a long time, and then the man fell, and he looked like that one behind us."

"Do you think your mother...?"

"No, not her. Someone else just like her was here, and it looks like we got here right after whoever it was here."

Chapter 22

The Police & Press

"One of the patrol officers recognized the deceased as Herman Jones. He had been panhandling at several intersections across town. Mostly harmless, he was an Army vet known to ask for rides to the VA Medical Center in Hampton. Beyond that, we don't know where the man was from. We only know he was discharged from Fort Monroe two years ago." The detective closed his notebook. "We will keep in touch with you guys if we learn anything new. But the medical examiner recommended that we keep people out of the house until we know how he died. He wanted to rule out any contagion or harmful substances." he said, "Ms. Cassidy, he recommended that you and your friend Anna-Marie stay away from others until we know what happened."

Greg was about to protest when Grace grasped his arm and squeezed lightly. "Thank you, detective. We will follow your advice."

Greg asked the detective, "Can we please have the news trucks move away from the house?"

"I can ask them to leave the property, but I think they would just camp out on the street."

"He's right, honey. Once the press has moved across the street, I'll talk to them, just like the old days. Don't worry, I will not get too close to them," Grace winked.

Greg smiled. *No one was better with the News vultures than her.*

Once the police had cleared the press from the property, Grace met them at their new spot and answered some of their questions. She knew she was more skilled talking to them than Greg because of his notoriety and controversy last year during the governor's campaign. Plus, he could be a hothead sometimes.

The majority of police officers left the house, leaving two of them assigned to watch the house. It was a crime scene; the yellow tape circled the home. Most of the reputable press had left except for one or two tabloid reporters still sitting in their cars.

The couples regrouped inside the RV.

"Almost like old times," Robert said, sipping Grace's iced tea.

Greg scowled at his friend, but he knew that Robert did not mean anything by it, "if you mean we have another dead person associated with me, then yes."

"Robert did not mean it that way," AM said apologetically.

"I know, AM; he was only saying aloud what we all are thinking." Greg couldn't help but agree with Robert.

"I'm sorry, Greg, that was insensitive of me," Robert said.

"I've known you long enough to know you were just born with foot-in-mouth disease."

That broke the tension.

AM sat next to Grace. "Tell them what you told me in the house."

Grace fleetingly hoped she did not have to repeat what she had confided in AM in the laundry room.

"What did you say, babe?" Greg put down his glass.

"The condition of the body."

"What about it?"

"That man did not die a natural death. I have seen someone in that condition before." Grace said, her voice trailing when she said the word condition. "Our house is not on holy ground."

"Grace, are you trying to say someone from your mother's world is responsible?" Robert asked.

She nodded, "Yes. It looks like a demon may have killed that man. She recounted the story she told AM earlier about her mother when she fed on a man while on the run with young Grace.

"I see," Robert said. "Does she have to kill when she feeds?"

"No. Mother can control herself, but I think she was too hungry to stop herself then." Grace looked down, not wanting to look into her friend's eyes.

"Are you saying that there was another succubus in your house, Grace?" Robert's eyebrows raised, "If so, then our problems are just beginning. I was hoping that we could at least have a normal year. I was looking forward to being a tiyo (uncle)."

"I hate to ask this, Grace, "AM broke in. "You don't think it was your mother who did this?"

"She is many things, but she holds her family above all. She was very protective of me growing up, so much so that, at times, it was suffocating. She will be just as protective of the babies, though I think Greg and I can moderate some of her tendencies to go overboard. So, she would not do this in our home," Grace said.

"Sorry, I wanted to get that question out in the open," AM said.

"It's okay, AM. I understand. But that means there is someone else, like my mother, out there we don't know about," Grace said grimly. "I, too, had hoped that we had earned a break from the drama between my mother's people and your friend Raphael, Robert."

"Guess he and I need to chat to see if he knows anything," Robert said.

"Who would that be?" Greg asked.

"Greg, I suggest you talk to our new governor friend, Nicole. I know she may be busy, but you could tell her what happened here, and she could make discrete inquiries to law enforcement about any 'unusual' talk or activity." Robert said.

"Makes sense. I am sure Nicole would love to hear that there is more creepy shit going on again." Greg said.

Robert turned to Grace, "I think you know whom you should talk to."

"Yes. I'll talk to Mother about this; she has her sources, too."

"And I will talk to our favorite Archangel." Robert sighed, "AM, we still have those feathers from Ralphel?"

"Yes." She said.

The Archangel Raphael had given AM, Robert, and Fr. Ortiz one of his white feathers for protection last year when they had to defend themselves from two fallen angels. The feathers are not as good protection as the Ring of Solomon or the pendant Grace had, but they were better than nothing.

"AM, can you talk to Fr. Ortiz about what we suspect. He may want to keep those feathers close by. We owe him that."

"Sure."

"One more thing," Robert looked at his friend, "Greg, you may want to keep the Ring on you when you are not on holy ground."

All eyes were on Greg. "I understand why I should wear it, but it has a price. I can feel its power every time I put it on. Its personality presses on me, and I will drown if I wear it too long. I don't know how else to describe it."

"You have to think of Grace and the twins," AM said gently.

"I know, and I will do anything for them. You guys know that." He showed them the chain around his neck. "I always have it close." Greg put his hand on his wife's and smiled.

"I will do anything for you and us," she said, placing her other hand over her belly.

A heavy silence hung over the friends as they mentally prepared for the new fight. Robert broke the silence.

"Let's all go get something to eat. All this planning makes me hungry."

AM jabbed her husband on the stomach, "Sounds like an excuse for you to eat again."

He shrugged, "Yeah, so?"

"He's right, AM; the babies are hungry too, and I think so am I," Grace smiled.

"I know better than to argue with a hungry momma," Greg stood up, "Where should we go? You guys are welcome to eat here, but I don't think we have the room in the RV or the groceries right now."

"I want Mexican food," Grace said.

"Bueno!" Robert laughed.

Hannah pulled the curtain aside enough to see St. Rita's across the street. She could see Greg, his wife, and two other people get into a car and drive off. She saw one patrol car parked on the path to Greg's new house.

She said out loud, "Julius and Mr. Tan will be mad at me if they find out about this."

"Why would I be mad, my dear?"

Hannah nearly jumped out of her skin. Behind her were Mr. Tan and Julius. Tan went to the window, not so gently pushing Hannah aside. He saw the church and noticed the police car nearby, too.

"What am I looking at, Hannah?" He said in a low voice.

If she were physically capable, Hannah would have broken out in a cold sweat as Mr. Tan's icy gaze bore into her eyes.

"Nothing really, boss." Her trembling lips gave her nervousness away.

Julius looked over Mr. Tan's shoulder and saw the police car. "Nothing?"

Tan frowned and repeated, "Nothing?" He put his hands on her shoulders and said, "I think there is more you know than you are telling me, doúlos (slave)."

Hannah swallowed; this was the first time her boss called her a slave. "Please, boss, let me tell you what happened." She wanted to run but knew that she had no chance of escaping.

Julius was reading something aloud from his phone, "It seems a man was found dead in the home of the former Brother Greg. Police are uncertain as to the circumstances or cause of death. An interview with his wife, Grace Cassidy, only revealed that the couple does not know who the deceased is or how he got into their home, which is still under construction."

Tan stared at her for a moment and then walked away. "I am very disappointed in you, Hannah. You showed so much promise among all the recruits I talked to last year. Was my faith in you misplaced?"

Hannah slumped to the floor. "I'm sorry. I was so hungry, and it was just a homeless man." Her voice trailed off.

"I wonder if we let her out into the field too soon, Julius," Tan said.

"That is a possibility, sir. Do you think that some additional correction or training is required?"

Hannah understood what Julius was saying and shook her head nervously, "Boss...I..."

She was cut off abruptly by a hand around her throat, squeezing her words off.

"You will speak when spoken to, doúlos!" Tan spat. He effortlessly picked her up from the ground and held her up, his face red with rage. Hannah was suspended off the ground for what seemed to be an eternity for her, then roughly threw her to the ground. He reached into his pocket, pulled out a handkerchief, and wiped his hands. "I have some business to attend to, Julius. Stay here and dole out any retraining you think is appropriate."

“Yes sir,” Julus bowed as Tan dissolved away.

Julius turned to face the shaking succubus, “Now, my love, where do we begin.”

Chapter 23

Parking lot

The heat in the Walmart parking lot was oppressive. Heat waves rippled in front of the car, distorting the pavement, and giving it the illusion of being underwater. Grace was grateful for the AC in her car, even more so in the August heat. She picked up her phone.

"Mother ... yes, I am fine. Can you come to the usual spot? I need to talk to you."

Within seconds, her mother materialized in the passenger seat next to her.

"What is it, my dear?' Naamah asked.

She recounted the news about the man discovered in their unfinished new home; most concerning to her was the state of the body. Naamah's face is typically unreadable to humans unless it suits her needs, but never to Grace. Naamah remained silent, lost in thought.

"You think it is one of my kind?" Naamah's tone was rhetorical. Her normally impassive face changed; even a human would have seen the rage on her face.

"Yes, Mother, I do. It *felt* like a succubus had drained the man in my home. I don't know how I knew it, but something inside me told me it was true."

"That is interesting, my dear. I didn't know you had that ability." Her anger abated a little.

"What ability?"

"You could sense another succubus' prey after it was dead. I know you are limited, but this is something new for you." Her mother smiled, almost, proudly.

"Maybe, it is or could it be a maternal... I don't know. Ever since I've become pregnant, or I wonder if it has something to do with what The Morrigan said about the twins?" Grace said, frustration in her voice.

"I would not discount that, my child. Their blood is something new in this world. Who knows what they would be capable of?" her mother shrugged. "Did you tell your husband about this?"

"Yes."

"I hope he does not suspect me."

"He doesn't; he believes you would do nothing to jeopardize your relationship with the twins."

"That is good to hear. I can make some discrete inquiries about demons here in this area. However, they may be long gone by now. Ordinary succubi will stake out a territory until things get too "hot" to remain, so they are not discovered. But as long as you remain on holy ground, you and Greg are safe."

"I always wear the protection pendant that came with the Ring, Mother. So, for beings outside of humans, I should be ok. I think."

"Ironically, humans are more dangerous than my kind," Naamah said.

"Mother, I wish you were not so..." Grace stopped mid-sentence. She recognized another car parked a few lots ahead of them. Hannahs?

"You wish I were not, so what?" Naamah said, then saw Grace looking ahead at something.

Hannah opened the passenger door and stepped into a waiting Ford Escalade. While it was open, they could see a man dressed in a suit.

"I recognize that man." Naamah squinted as if trying to get a closer look.

"What, mother?" Grace was straining to see what her mother was talking about. All she saw was her neighbor getting into a black SUV, and then it drove away.

"Do you know that person?"

"The one who got into that SUV? Yes, she is my neighbor who lives across the street. I don't know her well, though; she mostly talks to Fr. Ortiz and Greg." Grace felt her mother would not ask unless she had a good reason. "Why?"

Naamah sat back in her seat. James Dolus is the man behind the wheel of the Escalade.

"Who is he?" Grace had a sick feeling in her stomach.

"He is a familiar and works for an Original, but still very dangerous."

An Original is a demon that came into being simultaneously with the Archangels and is just as powerful. Successive generations of demons are not as powerful as their parents. Some lesser demons are weaker because of a diluted bloodline with humans or other inferior beings. Human hybrids were not allowed to live. Grace would be considered a lesser demon to her mother's people. The dilution prejudice of demon blood was why Naamah had to hide Grace when she was younger.

"So why would Hannah get into his car?"

"Because she, whatever she is, is working for James's master." Naamah reached out and grabbed her daughter's hand. "Tell me everything you know about your neighbor."

"You are scaring me, mother; what did you see when you looked at Hannah?"

"Nothing." Her face was grim. "Grace, remember, I can see auras around living things. Demons, angels, and humans have a distinct aura around them. She has none. As if she doesn't exist."

"So, she is not human? Then what is she?" Grace said.

"I don't know, child. Tell me about her." Naamah acted like she did when hiding the young Grace from her kind—a combination of fear and anger.

"I have not had too much to do with her, but Fr. Ortiz helped her get a part-time job while attending school. I think she said she had a boyfriend when she first moved in. But I have not seen or heard anything about him in a while. Greg works a little with her when she volunteers at the church cleaning and other odd jobs." Grace was becoming alarmed because Hannah was unreadable to her mother. She took out her phone and looked up the name James Dolus. "It says here that he is a former Governor Tan of Virginia staffer and currently works for a PAC called the Freedom's Heros, whatever the hell that means. It reads like most of the political BS I have seen." Grace read a little more, "Governor Tan has been urged by a faction in his party to run for higher office ... US Senate and may be higher."

"It seems, Greg had only stopped one plan of the fallen angels and Tan to seize power. It looks like there is another one is still in the works." Naamah laughed.

Grace was surprised by her mother's laughter. "I don't see how this is funny, mother. We were in real danger taking on Kanker last year."

"No, my child, that was, as you would say, amateur hour. Unlike a few fallen angels, these beings are not alone; they have many demons who would come to their aid."

Chapter 24

Coup d'état

"Follow me, Hannah. The boss is expecting you." James ordered, escorting her into Mr. Tan's office. They two passed his secretary, Gloria, and went in without knocking. "The boss is not in at the moment but will be soon. Take a seat." He left the room and closed the door.

Hannah sat in one of the overstuffed chairs facing Mr. Tan's large desk. James did not inform her why the boss wanted to see her so abruptly. She was nervously fiddling with the medallion around her neck as she waited. This medallion made her nervous too, ever since Mr. Tan gave it to her, and after Hannah put it on, he told her not to remove it or die. Anxiety was getting the best of her, so she stood up and began pacing around the office. The young succubus peered out a window, hoping the view would provide a distraction from her racing thoughts, but the view was no help. She only saw an undeveloped land full of brambles and a few trees. The structure was recently completed, following plans drawn up by Mr. Tan —a large home with offices for the former governor. Hannah walked around looking at a table with what appeared to be binders—with what she did not know. Mr. Tan was not in the Office anymore, so they could not be official papers. Maybe, it has something to do with his law practice. That had to be it, she reasoned. Behind his large desk were two rows of bookshelves between a small table with a serving tray, water pitcher, and glasses. Something didn't look right, though. The wall appeared uneven to one side of a bookshelf; there was a gap behind it, and she thought she could see a faint light leaking out of that gap.

"Hello Hannah, I'm sorry you had to wait so long. Looking for a good book?" a female voice said from the office door.

Hannah jumped. "What?" She turned and saw a statuesque woman with long brown hair and exotic features. Her arms crossed across her chest, accenting her breasts. Hannah knew she was also a succubus because she felt her power even at this distance. Was she an Original?

"I'm sorry you waited so long, Hannah, for Mr. Tan. Unfortunately, he is unavailable due to an unforeseen complication from which he cannot break free. However, I am here in his place, and we can get to business." The woman stood facing Hannah much too close for her liking. She took a step back. "Please have a seat," she indicated, one of the chairs on the other side of the desk.

Hannah smiled weakly and sat.

"I want to know that Mr. Tan appreciates your efforts in working your way into the former Brother Greg's family and that priest. I am sure you know that any information you deliver to us is important, no matter how small."

"Thank you. I am here to serve our master."

The woman smiled oddly, but Hannah ignored it for now. "Excellent," she sat in the large chair behind the desk and seemed comfortable sitting there. Hannah knew she would not have the courage to sit in the boss's chair. "I don't think I introduced myself. My name is Lilith, and I work closely with Mr. Tan."

"Yes, I have heard so much about you, ma'am. I am honored to meet you," Hannah bowed her head, recognizing the name.

Lilith smiled at Hannah, which, for some reason, made the young succubus more uncomfortable somehow than Mr. Tan never did. "Please, you don't have to call me ma'am. Lilith is fine, after all we are on the same side."

Hannah smiled weakly and nodded.

"I am sure you are wondering why we sent for you, my dear." Lilith leaned back in the chair.

"Yes. Normally, James would stop by and ask for a report concerning my relationship with Greg and Fr. Ortiz. I have only seen Mr. Tan once." Hannah unconsciously fiddled with the medallion, feeling its weight. "Does he still want to see me? I can always come by again another time."

Lilith leaned back in the chair, sinking into the soft leather. "You can talk to me anytime, child, in place of Mr. Tan. We are close, and he has total trust in me."

"Yes, ma'am, I mean Lilith."

Hannah sensed a chill in the air between them, and instinct told her not to trust Lilith. She was unsure if she should tell her everything since Mr. Tan had previously instructed her to talk to James or Julius; he had never said anything about Lilith. But Hannah knew Lilith was an Original, and she dared not cross her.

Lilith leaned forward in the chair, resting her elbows on the desk. "I heard a report that a homeless man was found dead in Greg's home."

Hannah's blood froze.

"I understand that house is still under construction, and he and his mongrel wife have not moved in yet." Lilith's said, her tone sounding unconcerned. "Can you shed any light on this?"

"Mr. Tan and James are already aware of this, and I promised them it would never happen again." She could still feel hands around her neck choking her and what Julius did to her afterward. She shivered and was louder than she intended to be.

Lilith's face darkened, "I'm aware of that, doúlos (slave), but I want to hear with my own ears. All I know is you clean toilets at a church and are friends with a Catholic priest. Have you tried to get closer to Greg?" Lilith's voice was increasingly impatient.

Now visibly nervous, Hannah said, "Yes, I have, but it is a slow process. He seems immune—I have tried."

"Could it be you are just incompetent? Or worse, defective? You know what happens to defective demons."

Her face flushed angrily for the first time, almost ready to fight, "I do not doubt my commitment to the mission, Lilith! Do you?"

"So, you do have a spine after all." Lilith rose from the chair and moved behind her, leaning down to whisper, "But spines can be broken; even a subpar succubus like you can have accidents. You, Hannah, can be replaced with someone more competent to get the job done." She reached down with one hand and grabbed Hannah's medallion, her other hand on her shoulder. "Maybe I relive you of this artifact now and pass it on to someone else." Lilith pulled on the chain until it painfully dug into the skin on her throat; one finger of her other hand squeezing Hannah's shoulder pushed hard enough into her collarbone until there was an audible pop.

Hannah yelped and tried to squirm away at first, but fear gripped her, so she sat still. Mr. Tan had warned her that if she removed the medallion, she would die. Lilith let go and pushed her down to the floor. Straddling her, she grabbed the medallion again.

"Ordinarily, I love this position, my dear." Lilith laughed, her eyes burning into Hannah's, her free hand cupped one of her breasts. "We may need to change your strategy regarding the former Brother Greg."

After a few long, anxiety-laced moments for Hannah, Lilith let her go and went to the desk; she pressed the intercom button, "Gloria, ask Julian to come in."

A second later, Julian walked in, "You asked for me?"

"Yes, Julian. We may have to bring Hannah in on our secret."

"Is that wise?"

"At this rate, the twins will be born, and we will be out of options."

Hannah found her voice again, "What do the twins have to do with this?"

Lilith ignored her. Julian stood with his back to the office door, staring at the confused Hannah, then glanced back at Lilith. He exhaled, "She does seem to be making very little progress. But she is only a doúlos; that is why I hesitate to tell her more than a slave needs to know to do her job."

"You are right; she is a doúlos, but even some slaves have to be trusted sometimes to help their masters reach their goals," Lilith said, stroking Hannah's blond locks. Hannah recoiled from her touch.

"What do you have in mind, Lilith?" Hannah said, still with a tinge of anger.

Lilith walked to the back of the room, where Hannah had noticed a crack in the wall. "Come here, doúlos," she said harshly. Obey or die right here; it's your choice." She shouted. James was behind Hannah, his face unreadable. She knew she had no chance against two Originals. She stood up and made her way to Lilith.

"Good. You see this small crack in the wall. It was not supposed to be visible, but good craftsmen are hard to find when you want a secret room installed. I believe the worker was in a hurry to get to another job and did a sloppy job. No worries, he never did get to that other job anyway. We can't have a lowly worker who knows about a secret room, right?" She placed her hand on the wall and pushed. It slid back and moved to one side. There was a dim light on the far side of the small windowless room. As her eyes adjusted to the low light, inside, a small platform was in the middle of the room. On that platform was a long, lumpy shape. "Follow me, dear," Lilith said.

Hannah reluctantly followed, with James's right behind her.

Is that a body?

Lilith stood on one side of the platform and pulled an old-looking cloth off one side to reveal Mr. Tan's face. Did it look like he was asleep or dead?

"What is this?" Hannah said.

"This is why you will report to me now." Lilith grinned. "Our former boss is now incapacitated and no longer in charge. *I am.*" The features of Lilith's face melted as if made of wax melting in the heat. But instead of melting off, the flesh flowed and resettled into a new shape. The same happened to her body; the flesh rippled and shaped, and the clothing changed. The once voluptuous form of a woman grew and broadened until it took the shape of a male body. Lilith's face finally settled into a familiar face: Mr. Tan. "I am in command of Hell now."

Hannah gasped.

"Impressive, is it not?" said the person who was Lilith, who spoke in Mr. Tan's voice. He walked over to Hannah and touched her cheek, "You see what I was saying earlier. What you say to Lilith, me, you are saying to Mr. Tan. I will use his image for a little longer until I cement my command over hell."

Hannah glanced back at the body on the platform, "is he dead?"

James snickered behind her, and the person who looked like her boss laughed. "You can't kill an Original, but there are ways of incapacitating them. You, of course, will never learn how to do that. If you did, then how would demons maintain order in our ranks?"

"But you are Lilith?"

"Yes, my dear, and now I am more. I have absorbed the essence of the former Mr. Tan, along with his power and position. That is why he is in his current state." Lilith leaned in close, still wearing the false Mr. Tan's face until it was uncomfortably close to Hannah's. "If I can do this to Original, imagine what I can do to you."

Hannah swallowed. She was born as one of the weakest demons, a few generations removed from the Originals. She felt weaker still ever since she started wearing the medallion. She was more human than a demon now. Cursed with human weaknesses but still having a succubus's hunger for human life force. In this weakened state, she had no hope of ever disobeying Lilith.

"What will you have me do, master." Hannah knelt.

"You were initially sent there to keep an eye on and report what Greg and the mongrel were doing because we are not done with them yet."

Hannah knelt in silence.

"My main interest is not the mongrel but her unborn children. They can be powerful servants or maybe allies; their bloodlines are unique, and I think it would be to our advantage to bring them into the fold."

"What should I do? Every time I get close, she is in pain." Hannah asked.

"What do you mean in pain?"

"She says the babies begin to move when I get close, and it causes her great discomfort."

Lilith leaned in further, "Tell me everything."

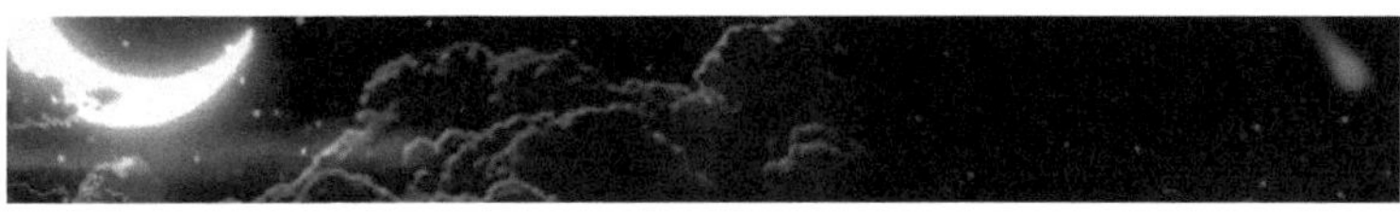

Chapter 25

Confrontation

AM parked the car close to the RV. She knocked, and Grace opened the door; she looked sleep deprived.

"You sure you want to go out today, Grace? You look, don't take this the wrong way, like shit," AM said.

"I guess we must be good friends if you can talk to me that way," Grace grimaced.

"I'm serious. We don't have to go out now; we can wait until you have more energy."

"That will be in about eighteen years when the kids are older." Grace groaned. She was not known for her sense of humor, but AM had to chuckle. "Besides, my OB said I need to keep moving. What else is there to do in this town besides go shopping?"

"If you say so, momma, but your doctor is not the one carrying twins," AM said, walking in. Did you sleep well last night?"

"Average. Give me a few more minutes, and I will be ready."

Grace went to the bedroom to finish dressing while AM sat on the couch.

"I am glad you called me, Grace, but why do you want to go out now? Any other time I called, you said that you were okay and could go alone." AM thumbed through a magazine she found on the table, not actually reading it.

Grace came out of the bedroom, struggling to put on her shirt. It was twisted behind the back between her shoulders. AM rushed over to help her untangle it.

"The doctor was concerned I was not getting enough exercise lately and suggested I go for more walks, but it has been so damn hot lately that it only leaves me with a shopping mall, which we don't have here in town." Grace exhaled loudly as she finally got the shirt untangled behind her."

AM smoothed out the last wrinkles, "Well, we are family, Grace; I hope we can help each other more often. I am sure you and Greg will need a few extra hands in another month or so. The babies are due next month, right?"

"Yes, to both questions. Hopefully, it will start to cool off in October, too. This heat is too much for me now," Grace said.

"Well, you can always count on Auntie AM. I can't vouch for Tiyo Rob, though. He means well, but I don't see him wanting to do the less glamorous part of helping with babies." She laughed.

"He may surprise you when you guys start a family."

Sadness flashed across AM's face, "It's not for lack of trying."

Grace heard the tone in her voice, "I'm sorry, AM. I did not mean to sound insensitive. Have you guys been trying?"

"Yes," AM sobbed, trying to cover it with a weak laugh.

Grace did not know what to say. She wrapped her arms around AM and said, "I'm sorry. I am still not very good at picking up what Greg calls body language."

AM hugged her back. "Don't worry, Grace. If we have no luck, we plan to talk to a doctor by the end of the year." She pushed back gently. "Well enough with me; maybe spending more time with you will expose me to the magic of pregnancy and rub it off on me." She laughed, rubbing a hand across her tummy.

Grace laughed, "You sure you want some of the magic? The bloating, nausea, and general can't fit into anything you own, kind of magic?"

Thirty minutes later, the two were shopping. They didn't have a shopping list; they were simply window shopping. Grace was getting tired but happy to have company during her "exercise" trips.

"I think, I need to rest a little AM. My feet are sore." Grace leaned on the shopping cart, trying not to sound whiny.

"I don't mind, and it is getting close to lunchtime. How about we grab a bite? There is a Panera outside. Want to eat there?" AM said.

"Sounds good. The restaurant is next door, right?"

"Yes." They had a few items in her cart. "Let's go to checkout and eat."

Marsha Harrison had placed the last of her items at the register belt when Grace and AM got in line. She was about to pay and noticed two women waiting with a cart behind her. One was pregnant, leaning on the cart, murmuring to another woman. An icy shiver ran down her spine as she recognized the pregnant woman as Grace Cassidy, formerly the assistant to the disgraced Brother Greg. Marsha used to work with her husband at Brother Greg's Christian Fellowship Center (CFS) in the donations office. The retirees supplemented their social security income with light work at the CFS donation office. Both were supporters of Rowan Kanker, and they were there that day when he came to the church to address the congregation. Her memories of that day were still fuzzy. From what she thought she saw from her seat, Brother Greg had started a special effects attack on the Senator, ending with a fight between them. In the struggle, someone pushed Brother Greg off the stage; there was a booming sound, and then a stampede of supporters tried to rush out of the church. Marsha and her husband were at a chokepoint near one of the exit doors. Marsha's husband was never physically healthy, to begin with. Still, he tried to protect his wife from being overrun by the rush of their fellow church members, who, in the end, only trampled him to death and left Marsha with several broken bones. She had heard that the now disgraced pastor was living at a Catholic Church with his mistress, now wife, and both were exonerated of any criminal wrongdoing as a result of the stampede at the CFS. There was a rumor that he had a golden parachute worth millions of dollars while her church struggled to survive and may have to go into bankruptcy protection in a few weeks. Attendance at the CFS was only a quarter of what it was when Brother Greg ran the church. The loss of her church, extra income, and mostly her husband of thirty years put her into a deep depression that she never healed from. Now, behind her was a person who seemed to have come out of the tragedy happier and better off than everyone else.

AM and Grace did not notice Marshia glaring at them until they saw the pistol she pulled out of her purse. She pointed at Grace and said, "Was this your reward for your sins, Ms. Grace?" Marsha's voice was low and dangerous.

Their smiles melted away like ice cream in the August heat. Grace recovered first, looking the woman in the eyes and asking, "Reward for what?"

"Killing my husband and my church. You and the so-called Brother Greg," she spat the name, "destroyed my life, and in exchange, it seems you two are doing alright. How does killing my husband and one hundred of God's faithful feel!?"

AM recovered her senses first. "Please, my friend is pregnant. I don't think you want to hurt someone about to be a mother. That is not what God would want." AM stood between Grace and the gun.

By then, the other shoppers around them had run away, except for the young cashier still in high school. She had tears running down her cheeks, and her body was frozen.

"What God wanted was for a pastor not to *fuck* his assistant! And then run away with all the money from his church, leaving it in danger of closing!" The gun in her hand was shaking as her voice grew louder.

"Ma'am, please..." AM only got out a few words when Marsha quickly struck her on one side of her face with the gun. AM fell to the floor, holding her hand to her cheek, blood quickly flowing between her fingers, looking at her assailant in shock.

Grace reached down to help her wounded friend.

"Not so fast, Jezebel. Don't move!" The gun waved up and down.

"What do you want from me?" Grace said, her voice steady; one thing she inherited from her mother was the ability to control her emotions.

For the first time, Marsha was silent, unsure of what to say next. AM managed to grab something from one of the racks at the checkout counter and put it on her face to slow the bleeding. It was a dish towel.

"What is your name?" Grace said. The gun was shaking in her hand. Grace was afraid it would go off anytime.

"Marsha Harrison. My husband and I worked in the donations office. He died when Brother Greg started that stampede in the church." Her hands shook more violently, and tears streamed down her face.

"I am sorry, Marsha. Brother Greg did not start the stampede. It was Kanker."

"Liar!" Marsha screamed hysterically, "I was there!" The tears stopped, and her face lost all expression. She lowered the gun to Grace's stomach. "You should suffer as I did that day. You carry his bastards. You both should feel my pain." Marsha's voice was low and dangerous.

This time, Grace's fear for her children overcame her ability to control her emotions. She did not know a way of preventing this woman from harming her and her babies. The Protection pendant she always wore was only for supernatural dangers, not human ones. Her heart was racing, and a cold sweat drenched her face. Suddenly, the twins inside began to move quickly and painfully; Grace fell to her knees. A surprised Marsha took a step back but lowered the gun more, her finger slowly squeezing the trigger. At that exact moment, a ball of orange-white light appeared between Grace and the weapon, which grew and moved to envelop Marsha. A bright flash of light blinded onlookers, and then, with a soft pop, she was gone.

AM recovered her vision and stood up, still holding the dish towel on her wounded face. "Let's get out of here before we have to answer questions we don't know how to answer," she said. The woman hurried out of the store and returned to their car. Grace seemed to be in pain, holding her belly.

"Are you OK?" AM said.

Grace was pale, but her breathing slowed. "I'm okay; I'm just a little out of breath." She pulled her cell out of her purse.

"Calling Greg?" AM asked.

"Later, I need to talk to someone about what happened, but I don't think he will have any answers."

Grace put the phone to her ear, "Mother, I need your help. I can meet you in the usual place." she hung up.

AM had never met Naamah. Grace saw the concern in her friend's face. She reached over and patted AM's hand, "It will be ok, I promise. Can you drive the car to the far end of the lot?" She pointed in the direction.

"Is that the usual place?"

"Yes."

"I'm not sure about this, but I understand sometimes a girl just needs her mother," AM said.

AM parked the car where Grace indicated. They saw an anxious-looking woman standing nearby.

"That's her?"

"That's my mother." Grace acknowledged.

"She does not look much older than you or me," AM said in a muffled voice.

"Guess you never met a succubus."

"Nope—first time."

AM stopped the car, and her mother went to Grace's side of the car. She waved at her to get in the back seat. Naamah looked irritated but complied.

"What happened, child, and who is this?" she said anxiously.

"Good to see you too, mother. This is AM, Robert's wife, and my friend."

"Nice to meet you... I'm sorry I don't know what to call you ma'am." AM said nervously.

Naamah could see Grace was okay, so she slowed down and looked at AM. "You can call me Naamah." She looked at Grace and then back at AM and quickly said, "Nice to meet you, too." Back to Grace, "Again, what happened, my child? You sounded scared. I have not heard that tone in your voice since you were a small child."

Grace recounted the events in the store and the confrontation with the church member who pointed a gun at her. Grace said a strange light came in between them, and the person with the gun disappeared.

Naamah leaned in closer to Grace and looked into her eyes. "I still can't sense you. But something does feel off." She reached down and touched her belly. Naamah's eyes at first looked puzzled, then opened wide. "ouáou (wow)."

"What do you mean, wow?" Grace said.

"Did anything happen before the light?" her mother asked, still holding her hand on her daughter's belly.

"No."

"You sure?"

"You looked like you were in pain, Grace; you grabbed your belly," AM interjected.

"Is that true? Were the children moving inside you at the time?" Naamah said.

Grace replayed the memory, "Yes, I thought I was having a contraction." She looked at her mother, "What does this mean?"

Naamah took her hand. "Daughter, I don't know, but I will find out. You don't have any power to speak of except for some minor things you got from me. For now, I am happy you are safe." She looked at AM and said, "And your friend is safe, too."

"So, where did Marsha go?" AM asked.

"I don't know, but I think I know someone who may have the answer. AM, please take Grace home; I will look into this and get back to you as soon as possible."

"Thank you, Mother. I know she pointed a gun at me, but you need to find her, I dont want to think of my children being dangerous."

"Yes, I know." Then Naamah melted away.

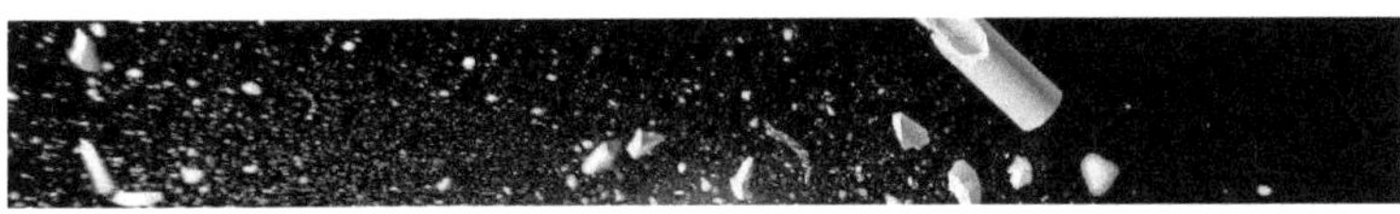

Chapter 26

Blown Cover

"You don't have to clean that room, Hannah, dear. I already got it." Jasmine leaned her broom against the wall; she was one of the regular cleaners for St. Rita's Church. She had been on vacation with her husband, Will, when Hannah filled in for them. Hannah asked Fr. Ortiz if she could keep helping out even when Jasmine and her husband returned. They were a retired couple in their sixties who wanted to stay busy, so they took the job of cleaning inside the church a few days a week, mostly on Mondays and Saturdays. The couple accepted Hannah and treated her like a daughter; they had no children of their own, and Hannah filled that role.

"Oh, ok, Jasmine," Hannah said.

"Fr. Ortiz told me you are a hard worker, and Will and I love the extra set of hands cleaning." Jasmine smiled. "I am sure your help will be needed mostly in the winter when the parishioners track more dirt and muck."

No one, especially humans, had ever complimented Hannah. Most of her existence was not in the human world but with others of her kind. Succubi are competitive and don't easily cooperate. They are solitary predators that would fight each other if prey were scarce, or it had been a long time between feedings.

Their prey is humans, male or female; it does not matter; a life force has no sex. She still had not gotten used to being treated with kindness, especially by the priest. A succubus's education brought out the worst in people to feed on them. When she gave her report, she dared not talk about this side of them if they thought she was getting soft. Hannah had changed since Mr. Tan, or rather Lilith, put this medallion around her neck. It suppressed her succubus nature enough to allow her to walk on holy ground, but she began to worry that it was making her weak. Hannah began to feel the strange emotion of affection toward Fr Ortiz, not in a sexual way, but in a way, humans call friendship. Hannah was confused; she enjoyed the friendships she was building and did not know if the strange emotions were authentic or a product of her weaker condition.

"I think it is time for lunch, my dear," Jasmine said. Come. Will made some excellent turkey chili."

The two women walked into the church's small cafeteria, which also doubled as a meeting room, where Will was stirring a large pot on an induction cooking plate. "You all are just in time; I think the chili is ready to eat." He said, tasting a small sample in a bowl.

"Smells great, sweetheart," Jasmine kissed her husband's forehead.

"You two have a seat, and I will bring you a bowl." Will picked one up and dipped a ladle in the pot. He brought a bowl for Hannah and his wife, and a few moments later, he sat down with his bowl.

"Do you want to say grace, Hannah?" Will said.

Hannah did not know what to say. Her mouth was open in a wordless expression.

"Don't worry about it, dear. I got it." Jasmine lightly elbowed her husband. "Don't put her on the spot, sweetheart." She began with the sign of the cross, followed by her husband, and said, Grace. Hannah just bowed her head, feeling out of place.

"Dig in, Hannah, eat it while it's still hot," Will smiled.

Jasmine noticed the medallion around Hannah's neck. "That's lovely, dear. Is it a gift from someone special?"

"You could say that, I guess," Hannah said, unconsciously covering it with her hand.

"Oh, I'm sorry, I didn't mean to embarrass you. Was it a gift from a boyfriend?"

"Hardly," she coughed. She saw the puzzled expression on Jasmine's face. "It was given to me by one of my relatives, and I promised not to take it off until she asked me to."

"That is a strange request. Is it maybe a family or cultural thing?"

"You could say that, yes," Hannah said, not meeting her gaze.

"Sorry, dear, I am making you uncomfortable again—change of subject. So, Hannah, we are done with the cleaning today. What are your plans for the rest of the day?" Jasmine asked.

"I thought I would try and see if Greg needed any help with his work."

Jasmine scrunched her face. "I'm not sure what he's doing today. Will, do you know?"

"I saw him get out some paint, and it looked like he was planning to tackle painting the large shed out back. He kept saying it was on his to-do list. Maybe today is the day?" Will said. "I'd give him a hand, but if you want to, Hannah..." He grinned.

Jasmine elbowed him again, "You just don't like to paint anyway."

"I cannot lie, especially at church; no, I don't." Will laughed.

"I don't mind helping him paint," Hannah said.

"Do you have some old clothes, dear? You don't want to ruin what you are wearing," Jasime tugged on one of her sleeves.

"These are old clothes anyway, so it does not matter."

Jasmine shrugged, "Well, you finish eating first, then go and see if Greg needs help."

Hannah finished lunch, said goodbye to the couple, and met Greg at the shed. He was standing on a ladder with a roller in one hand, trying to reach some of the higher spots. Greg had already painted one side of the structure bright white. He turned his back to her and did not see her standing under him.

"Hi, Greg!" She shouted below him.

Startled, a few drops of paint fell off his roller and splattered on her hair and clothes. She squealed in surprise, feeling paint in her hair and shirt. Greg looked down and saw Hannah pulling her v-neck shirt away, trying to keep the paint off her skin. He could not help noticing that she was not wearing a bra again and almost lost his footing.

"Hi Hannah, what are you doing here?" He said it a little louder than he meant to. "Oh, I am sorry. I didn't mean to get paint on you." Greg slid down the ladder.

She kept holding her shirt away from her chest. "It's my fault that I startled you." She could tell Greg was very interested in looking at her because a succubus attests to human desire. She could not resist teasing him even more, moving her shirt to reveal more cleavage than necessary. But he still seemed able to resist eye contact with her, so puzzling.

Greg put away the roller, "I think I can offer you a clean t-shirt, and you can soak that one in a basin inside the shed. At least the paint may not set in and ruin your shirt if you soak it now."

"That would be nice, Greg. But I am not worried about this old thing. That is why I wore it today to help with the cleaning." She tugged on it more, revealing her bare stomach in a way that is usually enticing to her target.

He is not my food target. I have to stay on track, or Lilith will have Julian—correct me.

She shook her head, trying to dispel the unpleasant thought.

Greg could not help but notice her slim, sexy waist when she pulled up on her shirt. He yanked his eyes away, "Follow me; I'll get you an old shirt and show you where the basin is."

Greg opened a metal locker inside the shed where he kept extra work clothes and pulled out an old T-shirt. “it’s clean and maybe a little big for you, but you can put it on so you can at least go home without a paint-spattered shirt.”

“Thanks,” Hannah began, taking off the soiled shirt.

“Wait! Let me leave first.”

Hannah smiled innocently. “Oh, sorry, Greg. “She had taken her shirt off already and stood before him, making a token effort to cover up.

He turned his head, holding out the t-shirt, “Please put this on.”

“Okay. “Hannah put on the shirt, but it was too large, so she gathered the bottom and tied it around her waist. “Done.”

If a woman could look sexier in an overly large shirt, Hannah managed to do it. Greg could not help but notice that tying the shirt at the bottom accentuated her breasts even more than her own shirt.

“Over here, Hannah,” he pointed, wrenching his eyes away again, “the sink is there.”

“Thanks, Greg,” she said, her voice an octave lower, lightly brushing him as she walked by.

“The soap is on the shelf above if you want it. I will go back and finish painting.” He said, turning to leave.

Hannah ran water over her shirt. “I can help Greg; that is why I went to see you in the first place.”

“No need. I am almost done, and I only have one roller and brush. But thank you.” He left before she could reply.

Hannah looked at her shirt under the running water and felt the medallion hanging on her neck.

What am I doing? I have been a failure since I put this thing on. I have no power over Greg, and hunting has become more difficult.

She was sure she would starve if Julian had not brought over men for her to feed on. Hannah took the shirt out of the sink and turned off the water. She had no interest in cleaning it now and threw it away in a trash can beside the basin.

"I must be losing my touch; I can't even get Greg to look interested in me," she said out loud, kicking the trash. *Mr.* Tan," she said with sarcasm dripping from her mouth, "will not be pleased with me. He would say I am an inferior demon."

"I think you should leave now," a woman's voice growled behind her.

Hannah turned to see Fr. Ortiz and Grace standing in the doorway. The person who spoke was Grace.

"Grace... ahh."

"If you work for Mr. Tan, you are not welcome here. I don't know what kind of demon you are or how you can step onto the holy ground, but you need to leave right now and not return. Especially if you mean to harm my husband!" Grace's face was flushed, and her hands clenched in fists.

Fr. Ortiz looked sad, but he also had a stern look in his eyes. "Are you a demon, child?"

Hannah could see Grace's anger and Fr. Ortiz's disappointment. For one moment, she felt an uncharacteristic emotion for a succubus: shame. "Father, I..."

"Are you deaf? Leave now!" Grace yelled.

"Please let me explain."

"Go!" Grace almost screamed the command.

"I can't, if I do, Julius will..." Hannah sputtered.

At that moment, Grace doubled over, clutching her stomach, and fell to her knees. Fr. Ortiz put his hands on her shoulders and said, "Grace!"

The priest looked at Hannah and said, "I think you should do as she says." He was harsh. The once kindly priest was no longer there.

Hannah moved closer, trying to squeeze past Grace, who still partially blocked the doorway, "Ok, I'll go." She was in the process of walking around the groaning mother when the air was still as if they were inside one of those soundproof rooms. The kind so quiet you hear your heartbeat. A ball of light appeared between Grace and Hannah, growing with blinding intensity, and then there was a slight popping noise. Hannah was not there when Grace and Fr. Ortiz's vision cleared.

The pain in her belly was gone, and Grace stood up. "You ok, Father?"

"That was going to be my question. What happened?" He said, rubbing his eyes, "Where is Hannah?"

"I don't know."

"Look," Fr. Ortiz pointed at the ground where Hannah had stood, "What is that?" He reached down and picked up a medallion on a silver chain.

Fr. Ortiz put it in her hand, and there was a slight sizzling sound, "Ouch!" she dropped it.

Fr. Ortiz picked it up again. He did not feel any pain like Grace. "Do you think this is her's?"

"It seems so, Father. Let's find Greg. Hannah was not what we thought she was."

Chapter 27

The Aughlish Stone Circles

Naamah was again back in Derry, Ireland, looking for an old friend. Well, maybe a friend was not the right word, but not an enemy, either. She had already passed Bishop's gate in the city wall expecting to be transported to The Morrigan's realm, but instead, she merely walked inside the city center.

"Where the hell is she? I spoke the password, and nothing!" She said grumbling. Naamah ensured she wore more conservative clothing to avoid drawing attention to herself. Such a thing a succubus would not care about. But she was on a mission and did not need any distractions or detours. A young man walked by and smiled at her.

Oh, he looks tasty. Naamah forced her head to look away. *Stay on task!*

A set of stairs led to the top of the stone wall surrounding the city; she hoped to find a clue as to why she had not been able to find The Morrigan. When she made it halfway around the wall, she faced the city hall building, feeling abandoned and frustrated.

"If you can hear me, my friend, I need your help again," she said out loud. A crowd of tourists with cameras excitedly chatting with each other moments ago turned to see who was shouting into the air. Naamah wanted to melt away and disappear; she disliked the stares of strangers.

"It's okay, everyone. My friend is just venting. Pay her no mind," said a blonde woman behind her. The crowd of people resumed their activities and walked away.

"I don't need your help to miss," Naamah snarled.

"Oh aye, Naamah, you just said you need help." the woman smiled.

Naamah squinted at the stranger. "Who are you? You are not The Morrigan. There is no mistaking her presence."

"Goodness no, I am not nearly as great as her; I am simply her servant. Fia."

Naamah remembered Grace telling her that Fia was a shapeshifter and could appear as anything or anyone she wished. "No, you are not nearly as great as her, but you have the gift of disguise."

Fia bowed. "Thank you."

"Can you help me get in touch with her? My need is urgent." Naamah controlled her voice well, even if she wanted to scream inside.

"Yes, I imagine it is. Your grandchildren have caused some trouble here for my mistress."

"Excuse me? I don't understand." Naamah is not easily surprised, but this statement from The Morrigan's servant was the last thing she expected.

"It is not my place to explain, so I will take you to her with your permission."

"Please do."

"Aye, mi lady, take hold of my hand, please." Fia extended her small, childlike hand.

Naamah grasped it, and the hand was cold and dry. Fia clenched her hand tightly. "Whatever you do, don't let go, ma'am."

Nothing happened for the first few moments; Fia looked like she was concentrating. Naamah saw perspiration on her brow as if she was trying to do something challenging. Maybe she had never had to transport a succubus before. Probably, never, Naamah thought. Just when it seemed like the pooka would not be able to take them anywhere, the city walls and surroundings blinked out, and they were in a dark space with the sound of a howling wind. She could see a pinpoint of light ahead that grew brighter and then a popping noise. Naamah felt grass under her feet, and in front of her was a lamb chewing a mouthful of the same grass they were standing on. It blankly stared at Naamah and walked away, still chewing. She felt Fia release her hand.

"We are here, ma'am."

"Where is here?"

"We are still in county Derry, just a wee bit west of the city. Fia pointed, The Morrigan can be found in the middle of there." Fia pointed at a part of the field with several old-looking stones arranged in a circle. "Just walk into the middle of that circle and say the words, and you will see her."

"Why is she not at the last place we met? I don't understand."

"That makes two of us. But I do not question my lady's instructions."

"Very well," Naamah said as she walked toward the stone circles. When she reached what she thought was the middle, she spoke the words that The Morrigan had given her—nothing. Now she was getting angry: "What the hell?" She turned to where Fia would have been, and the scenery changed.

"Welcome, Naamah." It was The Morrigan. She saw they were standing on a large grassy field surrounded by rolling hills. Behind The Morrigan, in the distance, was a grove of trees.

"Thank you for seeing me. But I don't understand your games?"

"Games?"

"Having your servant take me outside the city to a sheep field just to walk into another field without the sheep." She was trying to control her anger.

The Morrigan smiled and held up a hand, "Sorry if you see it that way, old friend, but there are no games about why I had you brought here in this manner. Follow me."

She led Naamah to the other side of the hill behind her, where the trees stood. At the top of the hill was the edge of a forest with large oak trees. "Please, this way."

The two walked over the hill and into the trees. They came upon a small clearing, where Naamah saw a small, thatched hut. Outside the front door, a woman was sitting on a rocking chair. She rocked back and forth, muttering to herself. She appeared to be a woman in her seventies, pale and sunken.

"Let me introduce you to Marsha. She is from your daughter's town and is here because of your grandchildren." The Morrigan said.

Naamah looked at The Morrigan with surprise, which is something she rarely does. "Excuse me?"

"I will explain in a moment." She turned her attention to Marsha and asked, "How are you doing today?"

Marsha's eyes were looking at something far away and did not acknowledge The Morrigan.

"You see Naamah, she is here in body, but she thinks this place is in her mind. I think the shock of being transported here was too much for her."

Marsha was mumbling again to herself; something about demons was all Naamah could make out.

"Remember, Marsha, if you need anything, touch the stone beside you, and one of Fia's sisters will be here." The Morrigan said.

Naamah noticed a short, weathered stone, similar to the ones she had seen in the stone circles earlier.

"The devil's tools!" Marsha screamed and rocked faster.

"I think we should leave her. We seemed to have made things worse, but I had to bring you here to show you what your grandchildren did."

The Morrigan led Naamah out of the clearing. "Are you not worried that she will run away?"

"She can't leave the clearing. There is a barrier between mortals and those I need to keep 'safe, 'so she is contained within."

"Are you going to explain what you mean about my grandchildren being responsible for this person in your realm?"

"Patience, my friend. Walk a little more with me. We have one more person for you to meet."

"Very well," Naamah said, trying to rein in her impatience.

They walked through the forest until they came upon another clearing with a thatched hut. This one's chimney had smoke coming out of it, indicating that someone was living there.

"Who is in this place?"

"One of yours, Naamah."

For the second time, Naamah felt surprised.

Once inside the clearing, the Morrigan called, "Hannah, come out! I want you to meet with someone!"

A petite blonde woman stepped out of the hut, wiping her hands on her pants. Naamah could see immediately she was a succubus; the woman recognized Naamah as an Original. The young succubus bowed.

"Who are you?" Naamah said in a tone that one uses on a subordinate.

"I am Hannah, mistress." she was still bowing.

"Stand up, look at me. You are a young one."

"Yes."

"What is your relationship with Greg and my daughter Grace? And don't try lying to me." Naamah's tone was ominous.

Hannah was visibly shaking. "It was not my fault I was following Lilith's orders."

Naamah's blood was starting to boil because The Morrigan said that her grandchildren were responsible for Hannah being here, so she must have somehow been a threat to them. "I thought you worked for Mr. Tan?"

Hannah swallowed, and she didn't stop shaking.

"Answer me, child!"

"I was warned never to reveal myself to humans. Julius will punish me again." A tear rolled down her cheek.

"You know I am an Original, just like Julius, and I can inflict the same or even more punishment on you. In fact, I am more motivated to punish you for personal reasons, so you better answer me, or Julius looks gentle by comparison! Why would Lilith give you an order if you work for Mr. Tan?"

Hannah swallowed, then blurted out, "Because Mr. Tan is not in charge anymore."

Naamah grabbed Hannah by the throat and lifted her up. Hannah struggled to breathe and grabbed Naamah's wrists, trying to break free. The hands on her throat may as well have been made of iron because they would not budge. Hannah looked at The Morrigan, pleading with her eyes for help.

"Don't look at me, child. I am not part of your world. I stay out of things that do not concern me." The Morrigan said.

Naamah cooled off enough to throw Hannah to the ground, "start talking and tell me everything about Mr. Tan and Lilith.

Hannah described seeing Mr. Tan lying on a table in a secret room behind his desk and that Lilith was responsible for that. Julius was also part of it, but she did not know how. Lilith is now in charge of all the demons, and she gives the orders for their realm. She did not know how or why Mr. Tan was deposed. But Lilith had ordered her to get close to Greg and try to seduce him.

"And did you?" Naamah said, her voice lower with an undertone of warning.

"No. I tried, but Greg was immune, or the medallion I wore around my neck that Mr. Tan, I mean Lilith, made me wear. It allowed me to walk on holy ground to get close to the priest and others in the church. For some reason, when I got close to Grace, she was having pains in her stomach."

"What medallion?" She looked at Hannah; nothing was around her neck.

Hannah made a face like she had inadvertently told a secret, "I was not supposed to tell anyone about it."

Naamah stepped closer again, menacing, "Too late, young one. Tell me about this medallion and where it is now."

"I don't know where it came from or what it is exactly, but when I wore it, like I said, I could enter holy ground. My succubus powers were diminished. It made me feel weak, like how it would be to be human. When I arrived here, it was gone."

"Any magic items from another realm will not be allowed here, so I expect it is still in the human world." The Morrigan said, anticipating Naamah's question.

"I see. I will talk to my daughter and ask her if she has it. What would you have me do with her?" Naamah pointed at Hannah.

"For the time being, she can stay here, my friend, and the human too. If I returned the human, it might cause trouble for your daughter, and if she, "indicating Hannah, "returned, she would die, which may make it harder for you to address your concerns about Lilith."

Naamah nodded, "I am not concerned with what happens to either of them. They both could die now for all I care, but you are right. It would make things more difficult for my daughter if they suddenly reappeared." She turned to Hannah, "Your luck has not run out yet, young one. Be grateful that your host has taken pity on you."

"I am grateful, thank you," Hannah bowed her head to The Morrigan.

Morrigan smiled. "You are only here and alive because of my friendship with Naamah. So, if you want to repay me, you will cooperate fully with my friend. Is that understood?"

"Yes, ma'am."

ground, got to her feet, and dusted herself off. Her interest [illegible] Ghent, [illegible]

"[illegible]." She looked at Hannah, [illegible]

[illegible] made a rule like she [illegible] said a secret. "I was not supposed to tell anyone about it."

Hannah stepped closer [illegible] "[illegible] tell [illegible] about the medallion and where it is now."

"I don't know where it came from or what it is exactly. But when I [illegible] [illegible] the medallion's powers [illegible]

Chapter 28

Stuck Between Realms

"Where the fuck is she!" Lilith screamed, throwing a glass at Gloria Báine, Mr. Tan's, or rather her, receptionist. Gloria was unaware of Tan's condition in a secret room behind his desk. But she was only a damned soul on 'parole' from hell. Lilith had been trying all morning to reach the young succubus on her phone because while she wears that medallion, her powers are limited, including the ability to come when summoned. Summoning powers are reserved for Originals and work on lower demons and not between Originals.

"I have tried calling Mr. Dolus and Mr. Laban, but all I get is their voicemails." She was cowering beside her desk; afraid Lilith would throw something else. She may be a damned soul, but she could feel pain even in this borrowed body that her boss obtained for her so she could work here on Earth.

Gloria may not be able to summon a familiar, but I can!

At that moment, James Dolus appeared in the office. "You need me, Mr. Ta...?" He saw it was not his boss but Lilith. She was a blur in his eyes as she suddenly stood before him; her eyes were the color of red coals. James was picked up and thrown to the other side of the office. He yelped in pain. Then Gloria opened the office door and went inside.

"I'm sorry, mistress, I..." She barely got out those words when she was thrown next to James. The human body she used was necessary for her to do work in the mortal realm, but it was fragile; her back and head had hit the floor, and Gloria, for a few moments, was stunned, laying on her back.

Lilith managed to cool off enough for rational thought to return to her brain. "Gloria, get your human carcass out of here before I turn it into a lump of lifeless flesh, and you will be back where Mr. Tan retrieved you from: hell. With a limp, Gloria painfully got up off the floor and left, closing the office door behind her.

James still sat on the floor. He was not in as much pain as Gloria, but it still hurt to be unexpectedly hurled across a room. "What can I do for you, mistress?"

"You know about the succubus Hannah tasked with watching the former Brother Greg?"

"Yes. I know Mr. Tan holds a grudge against him and is concerned that he may hinder future political ambitions."

"Does Mr. Tan still has political ambitions?" Lilith said, trying to sound unconcerned.

"I am not sure, ma'am. He has been away from the public spotlight for almost a year now. In politics, which is a lifetime." James was still sitting on the floor. "Come to think of it, I have not seen the master in a few weeks, and you, not him, summoned me here. I wonder how that is possible. I hope things are well with the master."

Lilith laughed, "Oh, he's okay now. You could say he left me in charge, which is how I summoned you."

"I see. Very well, I am nothing if not adaptable, as any good familiar is. I would not have been summoned here unless you had true power over me." He stood up and bowed. "Since I answered you now, what do you want from me?"

"Tell me what you know about Hannah's mission and any reports she may have given you or anyone else. She has gone missing, and I don't like underlings that disappear without permission."

"Aside from feeding on that homeless person in Greg Cassidy's house while it was still under construction, she has been quiet. The last time I talked to her was a few days ago when she told me she was still helping clean out that *church* even though the regular cleaners had returned from their vacation. She seems to have gained the trust of the priest and the other workers there. There was one puzzling thing she did say."

"And what was that?" Lilith said as she sat behind the desk.

"It was about the cambion."

"What about her?" Lilith sat forward in the chair; this got her attention.

"Well, I am sure you know she is pregnant with twins. That is what Hannah told me. She said that whenever she got close to her, she appeared to be sick, clutching her belly, and had to leave. It happened at least twice that she knows of; very strange. I mean, Hannah is wearing the medallion that masks her demon blood. I worry that maybe the cambion can sense her true nature. I should not give you my opinion, but the story seemed concerning."

Lilith did not respond, her face unreadable now since she had let her anger abated. She turned around in the office chair, her back to James. "Thank you. I think I know what I need to do. You can go now but come back here tomorrow morning." Lilith ordered.

"Yes, ma'am." He melted away and was gone.

Lilith opened the office door to see Gloria sitting at the desk, rubbing her head. She didn't care that she caused the damned soul pain; she did enjoy inflicting it on her, though, "Gloria."

She snapped to attention. "Yes, ma'am."

"Contact Mr. Laban and tell him we need to talk today."

"Right away, ma'am."

"When he arrives, I do not want any interruptions." Lilith's tone made it clear that she was deadly serious.

When her phone rang, Grace was looking at the financial spreadsheets on her computer for the church. At first, she ignored it, deep in thought about what was on the screen. But the phone kept ringing.

"Damn it!" She looked at the phone and saw it was her mother, "Mother?"

"Grace, do you know the girl known as Hannah?"

"Yes, why?" Grace swallowed, "I tried to call you earlier, but you did not answer your phone."

"I left it at my place and just returned from visiting The Morrigan."

"I see. Can you tell me what is happening, and why are you asking about Hannah?"

"Because I was just with her. She is a 'guest' of The Morrigan for now." Her voice had a slight tinge of anger, "I may still kill her once I hear what happened between you two."

Grace closed her eyes and exhaled, "Mother, can we meet at the usual place?"

"No. Let's pick a new one. I think that we will still be watched if we go there."

"Okay, how about another public place?" Grace scanned the local map. "I know. There is a Starbucks not far from here. Let's meet in an hour. I will text you, my location."

"Very well, child."

Grace parked her car in the Starbucks parking lot an hour later and texted her mother. Naamah typically took her time coming to Grace, but her mother melted into the passenger seat in less than a minute. Grace tried to reach over and kiss her, but her larger belly restricted her movement. "Sorry, Mother. I am getting too big to kiss you this way," she sighed.

Despite the seriousness of the meeting, Naamah smiled, "You owe me one later." The expression on her face changed, "what can you tell me about Hannah, the succubus?"

Grace shook her head, unsurprised, "That explains so many things about her and what happened at my house. But how was she able to walk on holy ground?"

"Did you notice that she wore a plain-looking necklace with a medallion?"

"Yes," Grace pulled a Ziplock bag out of her purse. Inside it was a plain-looking medallion. "She left this behind when she disappeared. I put it in this bag so I would not lose it. But another thing is if I touch it, it burns my skin."

Naamah took the bag from her. "If it is what I think it is, then the reason you can't handle it is your human blood. This medallion is for demons only. It is one of the 'cursed items' of our realm."

"I never heard about 'cursed items' from your mother."

"That is because I never told you about them anyway. I saw no need to discuss them with you. But never mind that child, I want you to tell me what happened when Hannah disappeared. Did she threaten you?"

"No, Mother. She was not threatening, and she seemed confused and scared. It was like what happened with that crazy person in Walmart. Fr. Ortiz and I were together when we heard her talking to herself about a person called Julius..."

Naamah stiffened, "you sure it was Julius?"

"Yes, and she said something about being a poor demon. I confronted her and told her to leave and not come back."

"And she did not go?"

"When I think about it now, Fr. Ortiz and I were blocking her way out. But I thought if she were a demon, she would melt away." Grace searched her memories, "she was trying to get past me and leave. I was just in her way. As she got closer, a light appeared between us. The babies were moving around painfully, so I could not focus on her anymore. The next thing I knew, I was on my knees, and I think she reached out to catch me, and the light got brighter, and then a flash. When my vision cleared, she was gone, and the medallion was on the ground." Grace looked back at her mother after replaying the memory in her mind. "What does this have to do with The Morrigan?"

Naamah's face scrunched a little. "She is not certain because no one ever enters her realm without her permission. But remember, she did call the children divine twins. That is something not of my realm but hers. It may have something to do with Greg's bloodline through his mother; at least, that is what she believes."

"I thought he was part of our realm, mother?"

"Only on his father's side. What do you know of his mother?"

"Almost nothing, except Greg commented that he had no living relatives. We were dealing with more pressing issues then, and I did not ask about it again." Grace said.

"I think we need to talk to Greg; his bloodline is more of a factor in what my grandchildren will turn out to be."

"I don't understand. I thought that divine twins were what The Morrigan's culture called fraternal twins."

"It is more than I am afraid. The twins have feet in both realms, which makes them powerful, more powerful than even Originals like me."

Grace did not like the sound of that. After the defeat of the fallen angels last year, she was hoping for a quiet life with Greg. When she discovered she was pregnant, they were both overjoyed that last year's nightmare was behind them. Naamah saw the sadness on Grace's face.

"What's wrong, Grace?" she put a hand on her daughter's shoulder.

A tear rolled down her cheek. "I don't know if I am strong enough for all of this, mother." Grace rarely, if ever, cried, even as a little girl. Naamah thought it was because Grace was like her in many ways, but her human side was coming through. Maybe, the pregnancy was making her more emotional, as it does to fully human women. Naamah did not know what to do except hold her and let her cry.

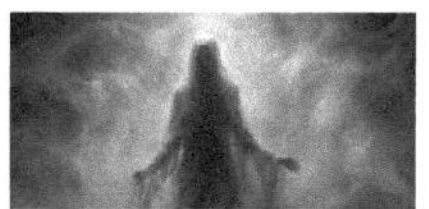

Chapter 29

House Guest

"Were the police just here?" Greg asked. He had left a meeting with the contractors at their home and then joined Grace at their RV for lunch when he saw the squad car leave the church parking lot.

"Yes. The police asked about a missing person from where we used to work." They hardly talked about their old jobs anymore, probably because the past was too painful and weird. "The police are at a dead end on the missing woman at Walmart, you know, the one that threatened AM and I. They are talking to anyone who has ever worked or known her on where she may have gone."

"Even if you told them where she was, they would not believe you, babe," Greg said, washing his hands before they ate.

"Mother did say that The Morrigan was going to send her back by the end of the month with or without relatives to send her back to. AM is still hoping she can find a long-lost cousin or something.

"True, but what makes you think she can find relatives if the police can't?"

Grace shrugged, "she wants to give it a try."

"AM is too kind like her husband. I can't think about it right now when I am hungry anyway. What are we having?"

"I made some refried rice and chicken." Grace scooped some rice onto two plates, and the chicken was already on the small table.

Greg went to the refrigerator and grabbed two sodas. Grace placed the plates on the table and sat at the small table.

"Here, babe," he kissed her on the top of her head, handing her a drink.

They ate in silence. Greg had worked up an appetite fixing some of the fencing around the back of the church earlier before the meeting, and Grace was craving rice. Later today, he will have another meeting with the county inspector for the house. It was nearly completed, and the couple should be able to move in before the end of the month, if not sooner, if all goes well. Grace had already informed Greg that she was moving in by mid-month (October), ready or not. She did not want to bring home twins to live in an RV. Greg didn't like that either; he felt claustrophobic after nearly a year of living there.

"What time is your meeting with the contractor, honey?"

Greg looked at his watch, "in an hour from now. Even if everything is not done, we should be able to move in when you want. All the major things are done. All that is left is cosmetic work. The gravel for the driveway to the street arrives tomorrow, the paved part at the house is ready for us to park our cars, but we don't have to rush moving them, Fr. Ortiz told me don't worry about moving them out of the church parking lot until we are ready.

"He just wants to be supportive of the parents of his adopted grandchildren." Grace smiled. "If you think about it, our kids will have interesting grandparents."

"Holidays and family gatherings will be interesting." Greg laughed.

After they finished eating, Greg collected the dishes and took them to the sink when they heard a knock at their door. "I'll get it, babe," Greg said. He opened the door to see a young woman with pale skin dressed in a robe—at least. He thought it was a robe because it seemed to move like a breeze blew. The one disturbing thing was her pale red eyes. She could not have albinism because of her hair color and brown eyebrows.

"Hello, what can I do for you?" Greg said.

"Oh my, what a nice way to greet a being like me and offer me help! "She had a thick Irish accent and a pleasant smile. "My name is Fia, and The Morrigan sent me to see Lady Grace. You must be Master Greg."

"Yes, I am just Greg, Fia; one moment, please."

Fia curtsied, her dress, if that is what it was rustled like mist as she moved. "As you wish."

"Grace... it's for you. I think it is one of your mother's— friends." He said in a bemused tone of voice.

"You could have just let whoever it is in, silly." She saw who it was and smiled, "Fia! Please come in."

"Thank you, mi lady."

Fia came inside. Greg noted that her moving dress made it look like she was gliding across the floor because the misty dress hid her feet if she had any.

"It is good to see you, Fia, but why are you here?" Grace said.

"Has your mother not told you yet?" The pooka said.

Grace exchanged looks with Greg, "No, I did talk to her a few days ago."

"Oh my, I am afraid I may have overstepped my bounds. I was under the impression you have already talked to your mother."

"I can contact her now, Fia. We need to find a new place to meet now because she fears I am being watched, even if Hannah is not here anymore," Grace said.

"Do you think that she can see you at our house?" Greg asked, "If we are still being watched, they can see either of us come and go."

"Oh, that is no problem, Master, Greg," Fia smiled, "I have the gift of shapeshifting and can temporarily alter the form of Lady Grace to make her unrecognizable to human and non-human eyes."

"Is that safe... I mean, for the babies?" Grace said.

"Oh yes, milady. In essence, I extend my mist," Fia indicated her dress with a hand, and part of it grew to cancel her hand. Around you, and all anyone can see is what I want them to see. The only one who will not be fooled is The Morrigan."

"I'm not sure," Greg looked doubtful.

"Please let me demonstrate," Fia said. What animal would go unnoticed on the grounds?"

"There are a few feral cats around the woods here," Grace said after a few moments of thought.

Before their eyes, the mist that was Fia's dress grew to envelop her body and shrunk into a small cloud shape that reformed into a small black cat. An extension reached out from the cat to a chair next to it, enveloped it, and then shrunk down to another cat. The cat, that was Fia, sat down and looked at them. The other cat that was the chair just stood motionless as a chair would.

"Wow, which is impressive," Greg said.

"Thank you, Master Greg," the cat replied. "You see, I can move, but the chair looks like a cat; of course, chairs don't move as you would expect. If I were with Lady Grace, she would only look like a cat on the outside, not changed inside."

"That sounds kind of fun, Greg," Grace said.

"You have a strange definition of fun, babe."

Grace tried to slink over to him like a cat, but she did not look very feline in her movements. Pregnancy has its limits; she mused to herself. Greg could not suppress a snicker and was rewarded with a light slap on his shoulder.

"Just wait until the babies are born. I'll be my bad old self, Honey." Her smile reminded him of a cat, though. "Fia, I'm ready."

The chair resumed its normal appearance, and a new extension of mist extended out from Fia and enveloped Grace. The mist shrank to cat size, and another black cat stood alongside the first.

"How do I look, honey?" the second cat said.

"I feel like I am watching a Disney movie with talking cats." Greg said, "It's funny and a little creepy all at the same time."

The cat that was Grace looked at Fia, "Follow me to my new home." The cat turned toward Greg, "Honey, can you grab my cell phone and bring it to the house? We will meet you there in a few minutes."

Greg opened the door, and two cats jumped out and walked across the parking lot. One was walking slower than the other, so it must have been Grace.

She is due in a few weeks, so she is entitled to be a little slow.

Greg picked up his wife's phone and waited ten minutes to give them a head start. Hopefully, leaving alone would not draw as much attention as if they had gone together.

Greg unlocked and opened the house's front door and turned off the new alarm system. He had left the door open because he was unsure how this camouflage or transformation worked or if Grace, as a cat, would be able to open it. A few moments later, two cats walked in. One walked by Greg and let out a very human-sounding meow. The cats kept walking toward an interior room, so Greg closed the door and followed. He caught up to the cats inside.

This is some weird shit, and I have seen weird shit before, and this has to be in the top five. Greg shook his head.

The cats both became a shapeless mist and grew taller. The mist dissipated, and Grace and Fia stood side by side. Grace looked a little out of breath but smiled.

"Thank you, Fia. That was fun, even if I was a little winded," she said. Honey, please hand me my phone."

Grace took the phone and called her mother. "Mother, can you please meet Greg and me at our new house?"

Within moments, Naamah melted into the room. She hugged her daughter, "How are you, child?"

"Mother, you should start calling me by my name. After all, I will be having my children soon. Also, I'm over thirty." Grace sounded tired, and it was not just because she was nearing the end of her pregnancy.

Naamah smirked. Except for Fia here, you and Greg are very young compared to someone like me who has been on this earth for millennia." She sighed. "But I will respect your wishes, Grace; you are about to be a mother yourself." She reached over to her daughter and embraced her; Greg could see a tear in his wife's eye.

"Let's get to business," Grace had recovered enough to be her usual self and get to the point. "Fia, now that Mother is here, what must you say to us?"

"Aye. Yes, right to business. The Morrigan wants me to stay with you for a while, after the babies are born. She thinks that because they are responsible for sending the succubus and human to her realm, their powers come from the Celtic realm rather than Naamah's." The pooka said.

"I don't understand Fia, Grace and I are descendants of Naamah's realm. I don't understand how that could be possible." Greg said.

"Ahh, but that is not entirely correct, Greg. Your grandmother on your mother's side was from Donegal, near where you, Naamah, met with my mistress. Her servants are tracking down exactly who and possibly what, your grandmother was, Greg."

"Fia, what does your mistress think this grandmother could have been? Not a normal human, I imagine." Grace asked.

"True, lady Grace. The Morrigan wants to talk to Leanan sídhe, a powerful being known as a fairy to modern humans. But not to be confused with the fanciful and harmless image that today's humans think about that race. She is far from harmless and powerful, not as powerful as my mistress, but I would not wish to cross her."

What else could happen? Greg thought.

"What is this being, and why do you think I need your help with the twins?" Grace said.

Fia sighed, "to tell you everything I know of her would take some time."

"Is she dangerous to them?" Naamah indicated Grace and Greg.

"Yes, but they are not her 'type.' But if threatened, she is formidable. I don't think she would travel all this way for people she has no interest in any way, milady." Fia replied. "The Morrigan wants me to assist Lady Grace because she may need my help with the Celtic magic they seem to possess. She is certain I would be more qualified to advise her if the twins exhibit that magic."

Greg turned his back and walked to the other side of the room. Concerned, Grace approached him and placed a hand on his shoulder.

"What is wrong, honey?"

Greg's shoulder moved up and down. *Is he crying?* "Greg?" She heard a few giggles escape, and Greg was laughing.

"What is so funny?" she lightly slapped him on the shoulder.

"It's just Robert." Greg laughed louder. "Lately, I was teasing him about his Archangel friends; now wait until he hears that we have Celtic magical beings in our house."

She lightly pushed him, "You and Robert can be so immature."

Chapter 30

Leanan Sídhe

Naamah was in Derry again, this time at The Morrigan's request. There, she uncovered vital information regarding Greg's bloodline that would directly impact her soon-to-be-born grandchildren.

She believes my grandchildren are the divine twins of legend in her realm.

Fia told her that the entrance was again at the Bishop's gate on Derry's city walls. She hoped it was true Naamah was not in the mood for Celtic goddess games so soon to the birth of her grandchildren. She was concerned for her daughter's safety and wished she still lived on holy ground instead of in her new house. At least she would be safe from those of her realm who want to harm her. She approached Bishop's Gate at the city walls, walked through it, and came out the other side into the same grassy field she had been previously.

"Welcome, my friend," a pleasant voice said.

"Hello." Naamah nodded and saw it was The Morrigan.

"Thank you for coming here on short notice. I see Fia gave you, my message."

"Yes. I am grateful you sent Fia there to watch my daughter when I cannot."

"You are quite welcome, but she is not good at offensive magic, only concealment and distraction. But she is very loyal and tenacious with her assigned tasks."

"Still, I am grateful for the assistance."

The Morrigan smiled, "shall we get to business?"

"Yes, please."

The grass around her feet was moving. It grew taller behind and in front of them until a small table and chairs formed. "Please have a seat." Naamah noticed a third chair between her and her host at the table.

"Who is that for?"

"That's for Leanan Sídhe. She will be joining us soon. I thought it best to talk directly with her since it involves your son-in-law and grandchildren."

Several small creatures emerged from the grass carrying trays containing an amber-colored liquid pitcher and small bowls containing what looked like biscuits. They placed the trays on the table, bowed to The Morrigan, and vanished.

"Please have some mead and biscuits while we wait for her, Naamah." The Morrigan was already pouring the drink into cups.

"When do you expect her?"

"Anytime now, my friend. I know you are concerned about your daughter, which is astonishing for a demon, so you must genuinely love her. There is nothing stronger than a mother's love for her children."

Naamah was about to respond when there was movement in the grass that got her attention. The grass thickened and grew as tall as a person and formed into the shape of a woman that moved towards them. As she got closer, Naamah noticed that she was dressed like The Morrigan's servant Fia, in a dress that looked like moving mist or cloud around her tall, shapely body. Her hair was long and black. But her face had no features—no eyes, nose, or mouth. Her face was blank. Naamah has seen strange creatures in her long life, but one without a face *that* made her feel uneasy.

"Naamah, let me introduce you to one of the great fairies here in the realm, Leanan sídhe." The Morrigan said.

Leanan sídhe bowed slightly, "I am always pleased to meet new friends and even more intrigued to meet other beings from other realms." Her voice was clear and melodic.

"It is good to meet you, too. I hope this does not offend you, but why do you have no face?" Naamah asked.

The fairy giggled, "Oh, I am sorry, let me fix that." Her blank face shimmered slightly, and then the form of eyes, nose, and mouth slowly appeared. Her eyes were cobalt blue, her eyebrows the same vivid black color as her hair, a narrow nose that flared delicately out, and full lips that displayed perfect white teeth when she smiled at Nammah. "I had forgotten that you are not mortal and do not influence my appearance. With mortal men, I can appear as their ideal of beauty."

"That is a fascinating talent that I can appreciate."

"Thank you, Naamah. We are similar in that we feed off a lover's life force. In return for their energy, you give sexual satisfaction, whereas I give artistic inspiration. We both are deadly to our hosts eventually." the fairy said, smiling, her perfect teeth framed by full lips.

Naamah shrugged, sipping mead, "It is what I am, and I cannot change my nature any more than you can."

"Are you sure about that?"

She put her drink down, "What are you getting at? You are not an expert on the beings of my realm, and I admit I know only a little about yours. We coexist in this world with mortals who can interact with either realm. It is their energy that sustains us; if they were to become extinct, I don't think you and I would exist anymore. Humans can change their beliefs. Things that once terrified them no longer do so. There may come a time when they terrify us. Humans have evolved from creatures afraid of everything to fearsome ones, feared by all of nature."

"That is a fascinating theory, my friend," she leaned back in her chair and then glanced at The Morrigan. "Do you agree with that assessment?"

"Yes," The Morrigan nodded.

Naamah felt she was missing something. Was it something lost in translation? "What are you talking about?"

The Morrigan smiled. "We are saying that something is changing in the world. They used to fear us, and that gave us power and life. I think, a time is coming when they stop believing in beings like you and me, and we will cease to exist and be replaced by them as the higher beings."

"You have lost me. How can we be replaced?"

"Naamah, you said it yourself: we feed off them to survive and live. But to do that, it required them to give in to us by fear, lust, or some other strong emotion."

"So?"

"We can't feed off them unless they fear or want something from us." The Morrigan paused, letting Naamah digest her words. "It will not happen anytime soon; humans are still weak and immature, but they will eventually 'evolve' out of their infantile state and achieve an equilibrium with beings like you and me. They are still developing their type of magic, whether from science or something yet to be discovered."

"We think it is already happening. A hundred years ago, I gave birth to a child from a human man, and you have too. In the past, those children born of being like you were seen as defective and dangerous. Most did not live long or not at all. These children were supposed to be impossible to conceive, or at least we thought so. Even in your realm, the demons and angels try to kill such children."

Naamah felt a chill over her body. "Grace."

"Yes, Grace, your daughter is a being that is not supposed to be, but here she is and about to give birth to twins from both bloodlines. Greg is similar, but he never manifested some of the 'gifts' his soon-to-be-born twins already have."

"How is Greg similar? His father is a descendant of the Nephilim, not the Celtic realm."

"His father, yes, but his mother is a descendant of my daughter," Leanan Sídhe said. Naamah thought she heard a slight catch in Leanan's voice as if she were recounting something painful. "I had to give her up to a human woman to raise during a time of turmoil here on the island of Erie. Revolution was in the air, but I had no choice because her life was in danger from others here within this realm.

Naamah felt a kinship with this woman sitting across from her. "I see. We have similar experiences, but what do you need from me?"

"This intersection of realms is not new, but now individuals are manifesting their gifts to a higher degree," Morrigan answered, "Your son-in-law Greg never manifested his gifts, so he stayed, as some humans say, 'under the radar.' Others, like him in the past, had manifested minor gifts such as strong resistance to disease or unusually long lives. One or two individuals in the past were famous for being able to escape from traps or gain renown for being clairvoyants. Most were dismissed as mere tricks, but a few used genuine 'gifts' from one or both realms. They were small enough not to be a threat to bad actors in any of the magic realms."

Naamah remained quiet. She had heard rumors like this amongst her people but was unaware that this happened outside her world. "And you think that my grandchildren have 'gifts'?"

"We don't think they do. We *know* they do, Naamah. After interacting with Grace, you see that a succubus and a human have been deposited into the Celtic Otherworld. We learned that the mortal was angry with Grace and ended up there, and the succubus tells me that Grace seemed upset finding out that she was a demon before the twins sent her here."

"The human threatened my daughter?" Naamah sat up. Her anger is always quick to flare up when it concerns her daughter's safety.

"Yes, it seems so, but when I release her back into the mortal world, her rantings will most likely get her ignored as a mentally unstable person who is not to be believed. What you decide to do in your daughter's defense is not my concern." The Morrigan said flatly.

"When do you plan to send her back?"

"After you leave here my friend."

"Just tell me where you plan to send her, and I will deal with her."

"Of course."

"Getting back to your grandchildren's *gifts*," Leanan changed the subject. We can agree that they are extraordinary even before birth, simply because one or both sent two individuals to our Otherworld. I believe, they are the divine twins because if they were this powerful, they could have easily killed them outright or sent them into the ocean, not have been found."

"What makes you believe that?" Naamah said.

"In our world, divine twins are such that one is a healer, and the other is a warrior. You can imagine the one who is the warrior would probably just kill any threat to their mother right away. The healer may have mitigated its sibling's impulse to kill and sent the threat to a place where they are no longer a threat."

"But why here?"

"Instinct, maybe," the fairy shrugged. "I think you know that children do things oftentimes on impulse without thinking; they act on instincts and not any particular reasons until they learn from their mothers what is acceptable behavior, right and wrong, etc."

"I see. So, what kind of 'gifts' do divine twins have?"

"Each set of twins is different, but yours may be extra special, Naamah. In the past, previous divine twins had talents such as telepathy, not just between themselves but the ability to read other people's minds, not just humans but beings like us. There are reports of the ability to heal wounds and illnesses and kill and maim enemies." Leanan said.

"They sound much like the powers of the saints and some higher angels or demons in my realm. But what happened to the divine twins of the past?"

"They were destroyed."

"By your kind? Out of fear?" Naamah said.

"Yes, regrettably," Leanan said, her head bowed.

Naamah sensed shame in her voice and would not press for further details. There are some things in her own life that she now regrets, too. It is better to let some sins stay in the past and not dwell on them, or they will eat you alive. "So now you wish to correct that error from the past when the early twins were destroyed?"

"Exactly. I have asked Fia to watch your daughter for her safety and that of the children. Fia is most useful in hopefully mitigating any unpleasant issues that could occur." The Morrigan took another sip of mead.

Naamah was not sure she liked where this conversation was going. She could not shake the feeling that The Morrigan wanted control over her grandchildren. The Morrigan seemed to pick up on this, studying Naamah's face.

"Please, my friend, I want you to be at ease. I have no intention of interfering in your daughter's life, but you have to understand that if the children had not sent a demon and a human to the Otherworld, we would not care what happens in the human world. I hope you can appreciate our concern."

Naamah stood up from the table and walked behind her chair; her face was impassive. That was a trait that Grace inherited and excelled at when she needed it. "My friend, I do understand your concern, and if it were not for my family, we would not be having this conversation. You and I are from different worlds, and we almost always stay out of each other's business. Equally matched, I think, in power so that a confrontation would be futile." Naamah gazed intently at The Morrigan's eyes and changed into her true form as an Original to the two fairies sitting at the table. She was taller with large black wings and wicked-looking horns on her head nestled in her long black hair that moved slightly as if in a breeze. The nails on her hands became claws, and fangs jutted between her lips.

A serpent-like tail was whipping behind her. "This is my true form. Even my daughter has never seen me like this. I will not threaten an ally, especially one so gracious to one of my kind and who treats my daughter with kindness. However, I must impress upon you my commitment to my family—*all of them*."

The Morrigan smiled, put her cup down, and stood up. "I am happy we understand each other, my friend, and you are impressive in your Original form." She walked over to Nammah, and the two faced each other. "I give you my word that I have no intention to harm anyone in your family. The twins, including you and their parents, will be welcome any time in our realm if they choose. I have no desire to fight you, and I hope we can become friends as we watch these young lives unfold. You, Naamah, are always their blood, their grandmother. I hope I can be a trusted family friend one day."

Naamah laughed, and in her current form, the laugh did not sound joyful but ominous, so much so that Leanan shrunk back in her chair.

Chapter 31

Hathor

Naamah walked in the hot and dusty streets of the Khan El Khalili bazaar in Cairo. Vendor stalls were set up to sell everything from fresh and cooked food to clothing and modern electronics such as cell phones. The noise of the vendors, animals, and people would make it hard to hear anything clearly unless you were close to the source.

It has been a long time since I walked these streets. Maybe... a thousand years?

The streets were less crowded mid-afternoon, but there were significantly more people in the evening. The majority of the shoppers are dressed in modern clothing like jeans and t-shirts; there was a sprinkling of others dressed in traditional clothing such as the abaya, a loose robe-type garment that covers everything except hands and feet for women, and gallibaya, a long shirt, and pants for men. Naamah wanted to blend in and wore an abaya with a face mask that some wore to keep out dust. She could sense there were other beings besides humans in the area, so she moved quickly to the rendezvous spot they had agreed to earlier. She was here to meet with someone she had known for more years, more accurately, centuries, to get information about the medallion that Hannah had been wearing. The medallion was found where she was standing when the twins sent her to the Celtic Otherworld. A barrier prevented magical items from a different realm from entering there. The younger succubus was told that if the medallion were removed improperly, she would die; that did not happen when she entered the Celtic Otherworld, where only their magic and rules applied. Naamah could have cared less about Hannah, but she wanted to learn more about a medallion that could mask a demon's presence on the holy ground, which also had the side effect of reducing its powers. Also, her contact always seems to know things before other demons or angels do; it must be a perk of not being either one. Time was getting short, and Naamah was feeling on edge.

Where is that bitch?

"Looking for me, Naamah?" A voice said above her. A black crow was perched on one of the many telephone and communications wires strung all along the bazaar. One of its large black eyes was looking intently at her. The crow cackled and flew toward an alleyway nearby. Naamah followed. In the alley, a woman stood there waiting for the succubus. The woman appeared to be in her late twenties or maybe thirties, but Naamah knew better how ancient she was. Maybe older than her, she had almond-shaped, light brown eyes framed with black eyelashes and brows. Mortal women today paid money for those lashes. Her hair was dark brown, fell to her shoulders, and glistened slightly even in the dim light of the alley. She looked Middle Eastern, with almond completion and complete but not extremely full lips. She had the body of a model by today's standards and stood at the same height as Naamah, though she could adjust her stature to match whoever or whatever she was with. Naamah stood before her and smiled. She loved the old magic and missed those days when it was not so hidden from the world as it is today.

"Hello, my old friend," Naamah smiled.

The two embraced each other.

"Good to see you again, my friend. It has been a long time since we met. I think the last time we saw each other was after the death of your lover. You were looking to find a place to hide your daughter."

The memory of that time made Naamah's heart ache for a moment. Hathor, the Egyptian goddess of love, had known Naamah for more than a millennium, and they had become friends even though they belonged to different realms. "I am grateful to you for your support and help back then. You helped me find my daughter afterward as well."

Hathor bowed her head, "I am happy to help a friend and her now expanding family."

When Naamah reached out to her, she told her about Grace's pregnancy. But the real reason she contacted an old friend was she needed to know if she knew anything about a medallion that masks and suppresses the powers of a demon. Hathor sent her a message and said she may have useful information. She asked if they could meet. "I will always be in your debt when my daughter needs help, and you offered to help even though it was not the business of your realm."

The woman shrugged, "We both exist in parts of the same places on Earth, so I never had a problem with beings from other realms. As some humans are fond of saying, 'Live and let live,' or something like that. I am a goddess of love and other pleasant things." She moved sensuously to Naamah, cradling her face in her hands and giving her a light kiss on the lips. Naamah did not push back. She returned the kiss and wondered if this was what kissing was like between humans because she had no power over this Egyptian goddess, and Hathor had no control over her. They were equal in every way; both were from different realms, able to interact but unable to use their 'gifts' to gain an advantage over the other. Naamah would have loved to spend more time like this with an old friend, but she was on the mortal time scale, at least where Grace was concerned.

"Pragma (my love). I would want nothing more than to continue this, but now, I must think of my daughter and her children. Our sense of time is much more generous than hers now. I can promise you that I will thank you properly another time." Naamah kissed Hathor again, looking into her dark eyes earnestly while trying not to get lost in them.

Hathor gently pushed her away, closing her eyes. "Yes, my love, another time." She turned her back to Naamah, her posture slumped momentarily, then she straightened her back and shoulders, and held her head up. "Your family needs you first, and we immortals have time." She turned around, her face emotionless. "You asked about a medallion that could suppress one of your kind's powers and make them appear as if they were only human."

"Yes."

"One such medallion did exist and was thought to be lost millennia ago."

"Where did it come from? Who made it?" Naamah asked.

"I could not find the answer to either question. But I learned it did not come from my realm or yours."

Naamah saw her old friend was genuinely puzzled, and knowing her, it did not sit well with her; Hathor was always so sure of herself and one of the wisest beings on Earth. "Don't beat yourself up if you don't have all the answers my love, we will learn the truth someday. The young demon Hannah said she would die if she took the medallion off without the proper procedure. She is only alive now because she is the guest of another realm as a favor to me from an old friend."

Hathor crossed her arms, "is there something about this 'old friend' I need to know about?"

"Don't get jealous, pragma." Naamah laughed, stroking her face. She is just what I told you: a friend."

"Very well, Omri (my darling)." She smiled.

"So, we know less about that medallion than when we started."

"Not entirely; I did learn one thing, though." Hathor then smiled and went silent.

Naamah stood with her hands on her hips. "Yes?"

Hathor laughed, "I am terrible with secrets, Omri. One of my counterparts here remembers a medallion used at the time of the pharaohs to subjugate one of his servants. That servant burst into flame when her master removed it, and that servant was reduced to ash."

"What kind of servant?"

"One that was supposed to be immortal." She answered, "But the servant hinted that it came from someplace south or maybe west of Egypt."

"What happened to the medallion after the servant died?

"Unknown. Maybe a mortal took it because when the medallion was removed, it was in the middle of a marketplace. The fire caused panic, and in the confusion, my counterpart did not think of looking for the medallion."

"Somehow, it got around a young succubus' neck, and she did not wear it willingly. I think a senior demon must have ordered her, maybe even an Original." Naamah said.

"Whoever it was went to a lot of trouble for it, my love. Why do you think she was wearing it?"

"My daughter says that she was on holy ground, and I guess the medallion had something to do with that. Even I cannot walk on holy ground, so the young demon should have been unable to."

Hathor moved closer, wrapping one arm around Naamah's waist. "All this talk has made me hungry. Why don't we go to the Duat (the realm of Egyptian gods) for something to eat? Or could we see what humans have in the market? If we stayed in the mortal realm, we might attract attention, but if we went to the Duat, we could relax away from mortals."

"I don't have much time, but I think I could squeeze in a few moments in the Duat for you, my love." Naamah smiled.

"How long has it been since you visited?"

"The centuries are all a blur; but yes, it has been too long."

Chapter 32

Incubus vs. Pooka

Julian was at Hannah's place in a chair, looking out a window that allowed him a full view of St. Rita's across the street. Being a demon, this was as close to holy ground as he could be or ever wanted to be. Lilith had ordered him to watch the church if Greg or Grace left for the hospital. Grace was due anytime now, and that would be their only chance of intercepting them off church grounds. He was fuming that Lilith had assigned this task to him instead of a lesser demon like Hannah. *Hannah!* When he thought of her, it made his blood boil; she was always difficult to work with, and he considered her unintelligent and lacking conviction. She needed another century in hell to be ready for assignments in the human world. But Julian knew better than to disobey Lilith now. Even though they were both Originals, she was now the boss, the new Satan. She had the human world scoured to find the AWOL demon, but to no avail. They could not understand how a demon could simply disappear. The only thing they could come up with is that she is somehow allied with Greg and his family and hiding out on holy ground; the medallion gave her the power to do that.

"Where is that bitch!" He hit the arm of his chair in frustration; it broke easily under his clenched fist. The last report from Hannah was that the couple were still living in the RV parked behind the church while a new house in an adjacent lot was under construction. Julian could barely see the new house through some trees; from the home that faced St. Rita's, he hadn't noticed any new activity at the church aside from that old pastor walking into the church and returning out again early in the morning—no sign of Greg nor the pregnant half-breed. He could feel his patience starting to wear out just sitting here like an underling watching a human church. Lilith promised he would not be there all day, and James, her assistant, would take over for him in a few hours. At the time, James was finishing a task for his mistress. He stood up, his patience at an end, and was about to walk away from the window when a car pulled up onto a gravel road leading to the house still under construction. Demons have excellent vision, much like a hawk, and he could see inside the car and the half-breed driving.

She is not going to the church... not to holy ground.

He was waiting for this chance to confront them off the church grounds where they were safe and end this game now that Lilith was playing by getting rid of both of them. Within minutes, he stood at the edge of the trees, looking at his prey exiting their car and walking inside the house. The daylight was starting to dim as the sun hid behind the trees, a perfect time to strike. Julian moved around the house's perimeter, sticking to the trees to get a view of the entire property. Julian stopped where he had a view of the back of the house; lights were on inside, and he could see a figure of what he assumed was Grace in front of the window.

There you are...

Julian stepped out of the trees, taking a few steps on the freshly laid grass sod. He kept his eye on the figure in the window, reveling at his luck; the figure suddenly vanished when he was a few steps from the window.

Did she walk away? No, he saw it was there and abruptly gone.

"Are you looking for something?" said a woman's lilting voice behind him.

He spun around, startled, and angry that he did not even sense someone behind him. Julian studied the small figure of a woman standing there with an impassive face.

She is not human.

"I am, but it does not concern you. So, leave, whatever you are, and I will allow you to live."

"So confident in your words, demon, but I don't think you are as strong or clever as you think you are," the small woman smiled. Julian already knew she was not human; it disturbed him that he didn't understand *what* she was, but she knew what he was. More concerning is how to fight a being he knew nothing about. "I know what you are because my mistress warned me that you may attack the one I protect."

"Protect?" Julian was surprised.

"Aye," the woman said, her voice transitioning to a menacing tone, "I have sworn an oath to protect the mother of the divine twins." Fia could move faster than human eyesight was capable of tracking, but not for an incubus. Julian saw that she had transformed into the shape of a large black horse. Its red eyes blazing as she charged the demon, knocking him off his feet and ripping up the fresh sod.

Julian stood up in full demon form, black leathery wings outstretched. He had grown taller, savage horns jutting out of his skull. Rage distorted his previously handsome face, displaying rows of dangerous carnivorous teeth. "σκύλα (skýla = bitch)," Julian growled, lunging at the grinning pooka, who faded into a mist as Julian passed through her, painfully landing on the ground. Roaring like an angry lion, he spun around and saw she had rematerialized, laughing at him, which only further enraged him as he lunged again and ended back on the ground, creating a large crater in the new grass. When he stood up, he heard the sound of hooves running on the ground toward him, followed by a violent push from behind his back into the trees.

What the hell is she?

Julian was not angry anymore. Instead, he was impressed that someone or something had gotten the better of him for the first time in centuries. Only other Originals and, of course, his master had ever bested him in a fight. An incubus' power is not just his physical strength but, in his voice, and eyes.

I need to focus and be smarter than my enemy.

This time, he stood up slowly and turned to face his opponent. The strange woman was no longer there. In her place was a large black mare with flaming red eyes. Its coat shimmered like ripples in an angry sea. The horse stood its ground, not going near the trees.

"I am impressed that you are just as fast and agile as I am."

"I think I am faster." The mare stamped with one of its front hooves.

Julian kept his anger in check, trying not to take the bait again. He shrugged and smiled, showing perfect teeth that you only see in actors on television. "You are. To deny that you bested me a few times is silly." He was again back in his human form, looking like a male model. Moving out of the tree line and onto the grass, he kept his gaze on the horse's red eyes.

"I think I bested you three times, demon."

He almost exploded in anger again but instead smiled, "You know what I am, so tell me, what are you?"

"Just a servant carrying out the wishes of her mistress."

"Who may that be?"

"Sorry, demon, but I cannot tell you."

Julian was inching closer to the being, restraining the urge to rush at her again. "Very well. Then, can you tell me who these divine twins are? I have never heard of them, and where are they from?" He was within arm's length of her, his eyes still locked on hers.

"Again, I can..." Fia felt weak, and she melted back into the form of a woman, her eyes unable to break free of his.

Julian touched her shoulders; she was solid this time. Good. "Are you sure you can't answer my question?" His grip tightened.

"My mistress..." Fia didn't finish.

Julian brought his hands higher around her neck and tightened further. "I have no interest in what your mistress wants. You need to answer my question!" He had returned to his demon form, lifting her off the ground. Fia's eyes widened in panic; her hands were uselessly trying to pull his off her throat while her legs were kicking in vain. He was just too strong. Fia's struggles were weakening, and Julian sensed victory. "I guess you will have failed your mistress. Soon, I will go inside the house and take care of that mongrel woman and the children you swore to protect and failed."

At that moment, spotlights illuminated the yard, temporarily blinding Julian and forcing him to break eye contact with Fia. He felt his grip on her neck slip away into a mist, and she was gone.

Inside the house, Grace looked outside the window after telling the home assistant to turn on the spotlights. She had a sudden feeling of dread and, without thinking, had the lights outside turned on. There was a demon in its full form holding up Fia by her neck for a moment, and then she quickly turned into a mist and was gone.

"Lady Grace! We have to go now!" It was Fia standing behind her, her eyes full of fear. At nine months pregnant, Grace could not move quickly, but she surprised herself that they made it to the front door. The front of the house faced the back of the church. Greg said that holy ground was about the distance from home plate in baseball to second base. It is an easy distance for a person to cover quickly, not so much if they feel like they are hauling around a medicine ball in their abdomen. Fia opened the door and saw the demon Julian standing there as if he were a guest waiting at the door.

"Thank you for getting the door," he said in a pleasant voice that did not match his smile and rows of teeth.

Fia put her back to Julian and grabbed Grace by the shoulders. "I beg your pardon for doing this without your permission." Grace felt her body change along with her vision. Suddenly, she saw the ground before she, and her night vision had dramatically improved. She reached out a hand, and it was a cat's paw. Fia had used her magic again to transform her into a feline, still pregnant but a smaller target and maybe a little nimbler. Grace, the cat, dashed between the demon's feet and ran as fast as four paws could carry her; what she didn't see was that Fia had changed again and attacked Julian as a large cat clawed at his face, distracting him long enough for her charge to get a head start. Grace could hear Julian's cry of pain, the cry of a cat in pain, and another demon's roar. Grace saw a dark figure fly past her and land far before her. Grace was out of breath and still not close enough to holy ground when her perception changed again to that of a human. She had gotten to the equivalent of first base in her husband's analogy. In front of her was Fia, naked; the mist that was her clothing was gone, and she looked broken and vulnerable. One of her arms and a leg were bent at unnatural angles. Grace hesitated a moment, giving the demon enough time to stand before her with a smile of satisfaction.

"Cambion bitch!"

"Stay away!"

"Or what? Your mother is not here to defend you like when you were a child!" He moved closer, walking around her like a predator circling its prey. "I have many questions, and I am sure Lilith would want me to take you to her."

"Aunt Lilith?" she said in disbelief.

"Just because your mother and her are sisters doesn't mean she will not harm you. Wherever did you get that idea?" he sneered. "She is too weak or timid or maybe both!" He stopped circling and moved close enough for Grace to feel his breath on her face.

"Too weak to do what? Kill me?"

"Well, you are not as dumb as I thought a mongrel could be! Yes. Look around you now. This patch of earth is the last thing you will ever see; I should give you a proper burial right here. Before I kill you, do you have a message for your auntie?" Julian said.

Grace's mind panicked, feeling her abdomen. *Of all times, to be quiet, guys!* Were they powerless against an Original? Hannah was no original, and she was easy to deal with. She steadied herself and looked defiantly into the demon's eyes, "Yes, I have a message for her."

"Please go ahead." He smirked.

"I never trusted Aunt Lilith, but I do not think she approves of hurting her sister by killing me. But tell her when my mother comes after you and her that I am grateful for the life and love she gave me."

"Is that intended to scare me or make me feel sorry for you?"

"No, just a fact. One other warning: my husband will not rest until he does to you what he did to the fallen angels."

"How could a weak mortal harm them? I think you are just doing, as humans say these days, 'mind fucking' with me."

Julian reached up with one of his clawed hands, intending to deliver a murderous slash across her throat. The hand raced down, and before the claws impacted her exposed neck, a blinding red light flashed, and Julian was thrown back, his hand mangled. Grace recovered first and moved as quickly as she could toward the church, followed by Julian's howls of pain and anger. When she finally made it to the church grounds, Grace had the luxury of looking behind her and could see that the demon was gone, as was Fia.

I hope she is ok.

Grace slowly reached the small cottage where Fathers Oritz and O'Brian lived. She pounded on the door, crying; she was now safe enough to let the tears flow.

Chapter 33

Defending the family

Father O'Brian opened the door of the Pastor's cottage to see a crying pregnant woman. For a moment, he did not recognize Grace; her clothing was dirty, with leaves and grass covering her pants and shirt. Her hair was unkempt, and her face contorted with a deep sadness among the tears.

"Oh my lord, child, come in," he said as he grabbed her arm and brought her inside. He then sat her on a chair in the nearby living room, where Fr. Ortiz was sitting a moment before, reading a book. Lucas, it's Grace!"

Despite being seventy, Fr. Ortiz bolted up from his chair like a man, years younger. The book he was holding tumbled to the ground. "¡Vaya!" He rushed to her side. "Grace, what happened?" He could see her clothing was in tatters, and she was out of breath. She clearly was in distress. She shook her head, still unable to speak between labored breaths. Finally, she held up her hand. "I am... okay, Father."

"What happened?"

Fr. O'Brian returned with a wet washcloth and handed it to Grace, saying, "Here, child. It's not much, but it may help." She took the washcloth from him and began wiping her face; she didn't even notice he had left.

"Thank you." She looked at the formerly white cloth, now a dirty grey color.

"Where is Greg?" Fr. Ortiz asked.

"He is out with Robert but promised not to be too long."

"We should give him a call..."

"Ahead of you, Lucus." Fr. O'Brian already had his phone to his ear. "Greg, can you please come to the parish house... It's Grace. No, she is okay, but I think you need to be here... OK, see you soon." He put down his phone. "He is on his way."

"Thank you, Father," Grace said, her breathing more normal now.

"Can you tell us what happened now?" Fr. Ortiz looked at her neck and saw the protection pendant still around it. He pointed at it and said, "Help?"

"Yes, it did." Grace had not told the two priests about Fia the Pooka. Grace had decided not to tell them about her 'protector' from another realm. It would make things more complicated for the couple right now. Fia did stay close to Grace, but whenever one of the two priests was around, she changed into her cat form; they just assumed that the couple had gotten a new pet. Grace was worried about Fia. The last time she saw her, she was lying on the ground, and Grace did not have time to see if she was ok.

Fr. Ortiz saw her brow furrowed, "What is it, Grace? You seem distracted."

"Nothing, Father. Just worried about my... cat."

The elderly man touched her shoulder and said, "I'm sure she is okay; cats are resilient creatures."

Grace hoped that Fia was, as Father had said, resilient like a cat. She had recovered enough to stand up. Both priests rushed toward her, "My dear, what are you doing?" Fr. O'Brien said, putting a hand on her shoulder.

"It's ok, Father, I'm fine; I just want to use your bathroom." Grace entered the small room and looked into the simple medicine cabinet mirror. Her hair is ordinarily neat and brushed, with tangled pine needles and leaves. “Great,” she whispered. There was no time to take care of her hair right now. The twins were pressing on her bladder, and she needed to empty it before she embarrassed herself. Sitting on the toilet, she relieved herself, wishing that Greg would arrive soon. She hoped he would not do anything stupid like speeding and get caught by the police. How would he explain that a demon attacked his wife, and he was rushing to her to protect her with a magic ring he kept around his neck? Wait, Father would not know that a demon attacked her because she did not tell him.

Or did I?

She was not thinking straight. Grace never felt this helpless before.

Where are the twins, ok? Why didn’t they fight back?

She put her hands on her stomach, unconsciously rubbing it. “You guys, ok?” She imagined she felt a little flutter over her hand.

Greg pulled into the church parking lot a little too fast, the back end of his old truck fishtailing.

“Easy, Greg; as long as she is on the holy ground, she is safe.” Robert held tight to the dashboard and the door handle as his body slid around in his seat. He had his seatbelt on, but still.

Greg did not answer, driving too fast for a church parking lot to the Pastor’s house at the back of the property, where he stopped abruptly, not even bothering to turn off the ignition when he bolted out of the car, rushing to the front door. Robert reached over, turned the keys, and brought them to the Pastor’s house. Inside, he saw his friend hugging Grace and checking her for injuries.

"Greg! I'm okay, really! It looks worse than it is, honey." She gently pushed him away. Greg did not let go of her hands; she could tell he had the Ring on; she felt its power around Greg. She did not know how she would react if she were not wearing the protection pendant.

"Please, babe, sit down at least." He half pushed; half guided her back to the chair she had been sitting in earlier. Grace did not fight back, and she had no energy to resist. She felt his hands on her swollen belly as if he could tell if the twins were okay.

"They are okay, too, honey. "She put her hands on top of Greg's, and he seemed to calm down.

"Can you tell me what happened?"

Grace described Fia encountering one of the Originals on their property earlier today. She was able to slow him down but did not know what happened to her. "Fia was lying on the ground, hurt, when she told me to run. I almost reached the church grounds when he blocked my way."

"Who, Grace? Do you know him?" Greg asked.

"I am not sure, but he is an Original. I could feel his power. He managed to hurt poor Fia."

"Who is Fia?" Fr. Ortiz said, sounding worried.

Grace and Greg exchanged looks, and Greg said, "She is not human, Father, so I am sure she will be ok."

"Oh my," Fr. O'Brian did the sign of the cross. "When you told me what happened here earlier, I admit it is hard to believe. But I have never known you to tell tall tales, my friend. What can we do to help?" He said to Greg.

Greg opened his mouth to answer when Fr. Ortiz interrupted, "Who is Fia? Or the better question is, what is Fia?"

"Fia is a Pooka; she was assigned to watch me over me on orders from The Morrigan."

"The Morrigan!" Fr. O'Brian exclaimed, "I thought she and Pookas were old Irish tales."

"It seems there is more between heaven and earth than we first thought, Father," Greg said with a wiry smile.

"I'll go look for Fia," said a voice near the front door. It was Robert. Greg had almost forgotten his friend, whom he had left in the car. Robert still walked with a limp, so he could not get to the cottage as fast as his friend.

"I don't think that is a good idea. What if the demon is still there?" Greg said. "I'll go instead," he held up his hand with the Ring and then looked at his worried wife. "I'll find her, babe." Grace nodded her agreement with pursed lips, "Guys, watch over her, please." He ran out the door.

Greg followed his wife's path, running from the demon. It looked like Grace had turned on the floodlights mounted outside the home; at least he could see the grounds around it. He made his way to the front door by walking around the periphery of the trees. It was too dark to see anything, and the Ring did not give him night vision.

That would have been a nice bonus.

Nothing seemed unusual until he got closer to the house itself. He saw several deep tears in the newly laid sod; not only was the grass pulled up, but several gouges in the ground were evident. It looks like the Pooka put up a fight. Greg looked as far as the floodlights from the house could penetrate the darkness for any signs of Fia. Greg went inside his home and did a heart-pounding survey of all the rooms inside. Nothing seemed out of place, no evidence of… demon activity. Whatever that was.

"See anything, Greg?"

"Shit!" he almost screamed. "Why are you here, Robert? You don't have any defense against a demon."

Robert grinned, pulled an envelope from his jacket, and waved it, "Raphael's feather is not good enough?"

"But Grace…"

"Is fine. She is on holy ground with two priests."

Greg was about to protest.

"What about Fia? Any sign of her? I saw a lot of damage to your yard. It looks like a hell of a fight." Robert said, looking around.

"I have not found her." Greg did not know the Pooka well, but she genuinely cared about Grace, which was good enough for him. "Let's go, Robert; I should take Grace to the hospital to check up."

"Her due date is any day now, right? Is it safe for her to leave the church?"

"Yes, and I don't know."

Greg locked the house, and they started walking back to the church grounds.

"Hello, Brother Greg, or I guess I should just call you janitor Greg these days." Julian stood a few yards away from them in his full demon form, with black wings like a large bat, twisted horns from his skull, and claws instead of fingers.

Greg did not blink. "Are you the one responsible for attacking my wife?"

Julian's once perfect mouth was a snarl, "So you are the one married to that mongrel? I pity you. Guess you can't find anyone of your own kind to knock up?"

Greg bristled. Robert's hand was on his shoulder. "Be careful, bud. We have not dealt with one of the Originals before. They don't go down as easily as fallen angels."

Greg kept his eyes on the demon, "What is an Original?— Never mind, we will talk about what you know later." Julian was still outside the range of the Ring, but Greg could feel it was reacting to this powerful demon even at this distance. The sensation was similar to what he had with Naamah.

"Listen to your friend, Greg." The demon said mockingly. "Though he did say something interesting. How did you 'deal' with the fallen angels? Do you care to enlighten me?"

"Wouldn't you like to know," Greg said, keeping his eyes on him.

"Not particularly, I could care less about those lesser beings. Angels always thought they were superior to demons, but if they were superior, then why would they want to be like demons?" Julian smiled, his mouth full of dangerous teeth toward Greg and Robert, "They are maybe one notch above humans. Because all you are to an incubus is a food source, male or female."

Why is he not getting closer? Greg was puzzled. *I guess he needs a push.*

"You will find this food source bites back, especially when you threaten my family." Greg did not look away but nudged Robert behind him. "He looks scared of us. Maybe original means weak or scared to fight anyone not pregnant." His tone was flat, trying to show that he did not fear the demon before him.

Julian did not take the bait; he stood there staring at humans; it was his turn to be puzzled. "What do you think you could do to me? You have no power that I can see, but I can tell you want something. What is it? You can't possibly hurt me, let alone kill me."

Greg was afraid that if he did not act soon, Julian would leave and be free to attack them again anytime in the future. He had to deal with him now. Greg took a few steps forward, getting closer. The demon stood his ground, unconcerned. Greg walked closer, and the Ring on his finger felt alive. It seemed to be pulling him further. The smile on Julian's face melted away, and for the first time, Greg saw a hint of concern that a mere human would stupidly move closer to an Original. Closer to his death. Julian took a small step back.

"Stand still, demon!" said a voice from behind him. It was Fr. Ortiz, and he was holding a white feather with a black tip in one hand and a coffee cup in the other. Julian turned around to see the old priest holding the ridiculous items in his hands, and he smiled.

"Oh, this is my lucky night! I get to feed on a priest, too." Julian moved closer to Fr. Ortiz, and the priest flung the contents of the coffee cup to the surprised demon. The liquid hit the demon's face, and he felt like someone had turned on a blowtorch; the searing pain made the demon howl. The sound made Robert and Greg shiver involuntarily. All three humans felt weak at the sound, as if it had drained their life force. Greg recovered enough to bolt ahead and stand a few feet from the howling demon.

"Hear me, demon! Do not move from this spot!"

Julian felt it immediately as if his body was encased in cement, restricting his movements. The more he tried to struggle, the tighter whatever it was became around, straining arms and legs trying to move and get free. The worst part was he was unable to move his head. The demon tried to speak, but his mouth could not move. The only thing unimpaired was his eyes and ears because he saw and heard the human move in front of him with a satisfied look. The priest blessed himself, and the other human moved next to Greg. The more he struggled the angrier he became; he had not felt this much rage in eons. *Is he human?*

"Demon, tell me why you attacked my wife?" Greg said in a steady tone, laced with seething anger.

"Do I need a reason to attack a mongrel?"

Greg punched him and instantly regretted it. It was like punching a brick wall. He was sure he would have broken his hand if he wasn't wearing the Ring.

"Touchy, are you not human?" Julian laughed. "I told you you could not hurt me."

"But I can hold you can I, not, your shit!"

"Temporarily, but not forever. Once I am free, your mongrel wife, this priest, and your friend are all dead. I may just kill everyone close to them until my anger is sated." His smile sent a chill down Greg's back.

"You are not going to kill anyone. Is that understood?"

Julian felt something different now; the force holding his body was inside his mind, this time forcing him to obey. For the first time in his existence, he felt fear and helplessness. His mouth opened against his will. "Yess," he said in a strained voice.

"I have another question for you, and you will answer it. Who sent you?"

Again, Julian spoke against his will as if someone inside him was pulling the strings, "Lilith."

Robert and Greg exchanged looks of surprise, "So she is real and not a myth?" He shook his head, "I guess after the past few years, I should not be surprised at anything now. Why is she giving orders instead of Lucifer—he's real, too. Right?"

The demon smirked, "Both are very real, human. Lucifer is no longer in charge. Lilith has taken his place. She is in charge of hell now."

Chapter 34

Auntie Lilith

Fr. Ortiz spoke first, "Lilith? What happened to Satan?" Julian stared definitely at him.

"I have no obligation to tell you—priest," the demon spat.

"But you have to answer my questions. Why is Satan no longer in charge?" Greg commanded.

"Because Lilith took his power away from him, she is now in charge of hell." The Ring was forcing him to divulge that Lucifer, the leader of demons, had been toppled in a 'coup.'

"How is that possible? How do you take Satan's power away from him?"

"Satan is just the name of a demon ranked in the hierarchy, human. Lucifer became lazy and complacent; he was happy with the status quo, and when that happened, he lost power and then the will to rule."

Greg and Robert exchanged puzzled glances. Fr. Ortiz spoke up, "What you are saying is the power of the 'office' of Satan is held by a demon's willpower, and Lucifer had let that lapse?"

"Go to the head of the class, priest. I guess you did learn something in your seminary training." Julian said mockingly.

"The willpower of demons was not on the curriculum." Fr. Ortiz replied. "So, Lilith is now in charge because her willpower overcame Lucifer? That is interesting and frightening, too."

Greg stepped closer, "What does she want with Grace, then? Why hurt her?"

"Because she, like I abhor beings like your mongle wife, cambions should not exist. Her sister Naamah fell in love with a human, and she was born."

"Sister? The head of the demons is Grace's aunt?" Fr. Ortiz exclaimed, then blessed himself.

"Any other reason besides her prejudice against my wife?" Greg said.

He could see the demon was still trying to evade the question but soon relented. "The children are another reason. Their unique bloodline makes them a wild card that she is concerned would hinder her power."

"Explain!"

Julius squirmed again, "They contain the blood from at least four different realms. The realm of angels and demons, humans, the gods of the Celtic realm, and Naamah's lover, Grace's father. The Aztec realm. I don't know if they have manifested any power or abilities yet, but Lilith is convinced they will soon, which concerns her."

Greg thought about Hannah and how she disappeared during a confrontation with Grace. *It was too late; their powers had already started to manifest.* "I think I have learned enough from you." Still not taking his eyes off Julian, Greg addressed Fr. Ortiz and Robert. "You guys need to know anything before I send him to hell?" Both men answered no. "OK, we are all done with you. First, tell me your name."

"Julian."

"Julian, I am ordering you to leave here and go straight to hell, never to hurt my wife or my children and their descendants. Also, you are never to hurt the family or descendants of Robert, Frs. Ortiz and O'Brian. Do you understand your orders?"

The demon's face flushed with anger, and in a strangled voice, he answered, "Yes."

"Good. Now go, I never want to see your ugly face again!" Greg said clearly and forcefully.

Julian, still red-faced, melted away and left them standing on the fresh sod, now able to breathe again. Greg fell to his knees.

"My boy are you okay?" the priest asked.

"Yes, I am fine. I did not realize how draining it is to send an Original to hell." After a moment, he stood back up. "I want to check on Grace. We need to talk about her aunt." The three rushed back to the church grounds; they did not hear the faint mewing of a wounded cat.

When the trio returned to the cottage, Grace was still sitting in the same chair when they had left. She looked uncomfortable but smiled brightly when her husband kneeled and held her hand. "How are you babe?"

"Uncomfortable. Grace said, rubbing her stomach. She then looked at him and slapped him on the shoulder, "What the hell were you thinking running out after a demon!" She gently rubbed the same shoulder, "I don't know what I would do without you." A tear ran down her cheek.

"Greg did find the demon, and then he used the ring to command him to go back to hell," Robert said.

"He did what?" exclaimed Fr. O'Brian.

Fr. Ortiz gently ushered his co-pastor out of the room, "Think I should tell you the full story about what happened last year..."

"I guess it was a matter of time before we would have to share our secret with Fr. O'Brian," Robert said.

Greg nodded in agreement and sat down. Grace sensed that there was more to what had happened at their house. She looked at Robert, who did not meet her gaze, and finally returned to her husband. "OK, guys, you are keeping something from me. That's dangerous to a cranky pregnant woman. What is it you are not telling me?"

"We are not keeping anything from you, babe. I am not sure how to word this." Greg finally looked up, looking into her eyes. *She is stunning even when she is pissed.* "What do you know about..."

There was an urgent knock on the door. Fr. O'Brian answered, and AM quickly approached Grace, pushing past Robert, who, despite the circumstances, had an amused expression.

"How are you, Grace? Robert told me someone attacked you." Without thinking, her hands were on Grace's belly.

Grace placed her hands on top of her friends. "We are okay, tita AM," she smiled.

"So what happened? Robert told me most of it when he called me, but I am sure there is more."

"Yes, there is more, AM," Greg said, "We need to discuss Lilith."

"Lilith?" Grace sounded startled.

"More correctly, your Aunt Lilith, Grace," Robert added.

"What about her," her voice sounded small.

"The demon Julian said that she holds the office of Satan and is after you and the twins," Greg said gently. "I remember that Naamah had obliquely said something about a sister, but I didn't think it was her actual sister. Also, I was not aware that Satan was an office and not an actual being."

Grace nodded, "It's complicated... my mother's world. Lilith, yes, she is my aunt. I have only met her a handful of times, and Lilith was less than kind to me each time. Mother had told me she was more ambitious than she was, wanting power and influence in the world of demons. She never completely trusted her, especially since my father died."

"Do you think your mother knows about this?" Robert said.

"I don't think so, but I don't know for sure, to be honest. But if my aunt tries to kill me, I don't think I will be able to convince her not to go after her."

"When was the last time you spoke to her, babe?" Greg asked.

"Well, you know we are overdue to meet for lunch; it's past time to meet. I am surprised Mother did not try to call me or even show up at the house. I hope she is okay. "She looked up with sudden concern. "Greg, what if Lilith already did something to her?"

"Your mom is not one who is easily deceived. I will go to the house and get your phone so you can call her." Grace nodded, and a tear made its way down her cheek.

Greg went to her side. "It's ok, babe."

Robert accompanied Greg on the way to the house. The damage to the lawn from last night was starker in the morning light. They walked in the front door. Grace, because she was running from Julian, did not have time to lock the house up.

"Where does she keep her phone?" Robert said.

"There are many places, but the last room she was in last night was the living room. Rob, check there; I will look in the bedroom and bathroom."

"Sure."

After a few minutes, Robert yelled out, "Found it!" Greg met him and took the phone. "Looks like she missed a call from her mother, he said, indicating the missed call on its screen."

"Ok, let's get this to Grace. I wonder why she called. Grace says she normally calls her first."

"That's because she is in danger, and I had to warn her," Naamah said, materializing in front of them. Her ordinarily beautiful but impassive face had a small crease of worry on her forehead. Greg chose not to get upset that she appeared in the house without warning.

"She was attacked by a demon called Julian, and Grace is ok." Greg said flatly, "I ordered him back to hell."

A few more worried wrinkles appeared on her face, "The children? They are ok too?"

"Yes."

The furrows on her face disappeared, and she went from concern to anger. "Julian! It is more serious than I thought. I need to talk to Grace. Can you bring her here? Don't worry. It is safe for a while because the demons will not know so soon about his fate."

"You sure?"

"Yes, please bring her, Greg." That was the first time he had heard her call him by name, let alone say "please." Greg was still wearing the ring. He was sure she could feel its presence but knew that her tone was not because of the Ring but because she was concerned for her daughter.

"Ok. We'll be back." Greg motioned for Robert to follow.

"You will be faster than having me slow you down. I will keep Naamah company until you and Grace get here."

Greg was too distracted to think about leaving his best friend with a demon; his mind was on his wife. "OK, I am getting the car, so she does not have to walk back home." Greg left his best friend and demon alone in his house.

"You are not concerned about being left alone with me, a demon, an Original?" Naamah asked.

"Not really. Besides, I have a message for you from Raphael."

"You have my attention."

Thirty years earlier:

"Why, sister? Why did you betray me?" Naamah cried, clutching baby Grace in her arms. The body of a man lay crumpled behind her, blood forming a pool underneath his head. Another demon that Naamah did not recognize stood beside her sister, his hands stained with the same blood from that man on the ground. *Who was that man?* She recognized who the demon was by his bloody hands and face. The same one that threatened her—*Julian!* Anger flared up, and she wanted to kill him. She screamed in rage...

The present:

She felt someone's hands on her shoulders shaking her, the concerned voice from far away yelling her name. "Grace! Babe, wake up!"

Grace opened her eyes to see her husband hovering over her in bed. His hands were still on her shoulders, but he was fully awake and staring intently into her eyes.

"You were having a nightmare. It's ok." She rolled to her side and sat up on the bed.

It felt so real—like I was there.

"I'm ok, honey, just a bad dream."

"Babe, we don't believe in things like a *just* a nightmare anymore, do we? What did you see?"

She rubbed her eyes, feeling the last tendrils of sleep fall away, "I saw a mother holding a baby... I think it was me." He walked to the other side of the bed and sat beside her, resting a hand on her back. "There was a man behind her. It was my father; he was lying on the floor, and I think he was dead... so much blood. I also saw Aunt Lilith with the demon that attacked me, Julian, his hands had blood on them." Grace turned to her head, tears beginning to flow, "he killed my father, and I think he tried to kill me too." She hit a fist on the bed, "I hate feeling helpless."

For a moment, Greg thought that his wife's eyes had changed, resembling Julian's when he was in demon form. He reached across and hugged her, "Well, he is gone now. I banished him to hell. According to Raphael, Robert told me he could not get out for thirty-three years. We will come up with a plan on what to do before that. At least the kids will be adults by then and can defend themselves. Besides, you are not defenseless," he lifted the pendant slightly that she wore around her neck, "didn't you tell me that when Julian tried to strike you, he was repelled by the pendant you wear, and that is how you were able to make it to the parish?"

"Yes, that is true, and I had forgotten I was wearing it. It hurt Julian when he tried to strike me." She managed a weak smile.

"We never did discover where this pendant came from or who made it," his fingers still holding it up.

"That is the least of our concerns now, honey." Grace seemed to be herself again. She smiled and rested a hand on his face, pulling him in for a kiss. "First things first this morning," she stood up.

"What is that?"

"What else have I been doing nonstop since becoming pregnant going to the bathroom."

"Ok, I'll see you in the kitchen. I will start breakfast." He laughed.

The couple was finishing up in the kitchen when the doorbell rang, followed by, "Grace! I'm here, child!" It was Naamah. Greg told her she was welcome to visit anytime, but he asked that she ring the doorbell first before entering the house. She made a face but agreed to it for the sake of her daughter.

"We are in the kitchen, mother!" She called out.

Naamah dressed more conservatively than usual in simple jeans and a shapeless hoodie. She still exuded an aura of sexiness even when dressed like that, which was one of the properties of the kind of demon she was. "Good morning, child, and good morning, Greg." She hugged her daughter and sat down in the chair beside her. "I got your message last night about coming by. So tell me, what is happening?"

Greg and Grace exchanged glances. "Mother, it's about Lilith."

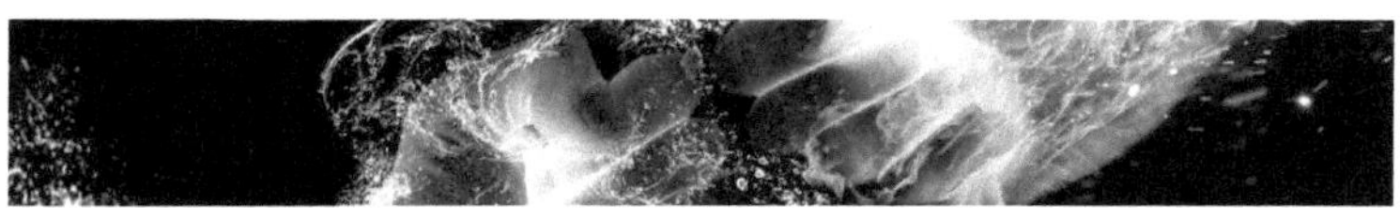

Chapter 35

Gathering Storm

Halloween was a few days away, but Greg did not feel much like putting up any decorations. He made a token effort by putting out a carved pumpkin and some blowup ghost figures. Grace was already past her due date, but the obstetrician had assured them that first babies may take a little longer than subsequent pregnancies, so they should not worry too much. He heard a car coming up the driveway and recognized his friend Robert's van. Through the windshield, he saw that AM was next to him in the passenger seat; she was waving at Greg.

"Hi Greg, how are you and momma?" she asked as she bounced out of the van and hugged him.

"Good, AM. How is Lola and Mrs. Diaz?" Greg smiled.

"About the same, except they both keep asking why Grace has not had the babies yet."

"I think Grace is more impatient than they are to have them, especially since it is past the due date."

AM looked at her watch, "Yeah, it's already October 22nd; she was due last week."

"Come inside, guys; she would like the distraction."

They found Grace standing on the back patio; she was walking slowly, her hand on her swollen belly, with an expression of discomfort clearly on her face. AM rushed to her first, "Everything ok, Grace?"

"I'm ok. I need to move around some more. I can only sit so long in that chair," Grace indicated the rocker Greg had placed on the patio for her earlier that day; her voice had an irritated tone.

"I understand... even if I don't. What can I do for you?"

"Give birth for me." Grace said a little too angrily, then she softened, "Sorry, AM."

"No worries, friend, I will walk with you. Maybe walk around the house?"

"Sure."

AM hooked an arm around Grace, and they left the patio.

"You still want to have a cookout?" Robert said, and the girls left.

"I don't think Grace will eat much, but she would enjoy the company at least."

"Can I help?" They turned around to see Naamah, accompanied by Fia, standing behind them.

Fia looked the same as before, with no evidence of injury from her fight with Julian. "How are you, Fia?"

"Grand, thank you. Naamah found me in the woods injured and took me to my mistress, who attended to my wounds."

"I am glad you are well," he says, looking at his mother-in-law. It is good to see you, Naamah. Grace is with AM walking around the house, and she is a little cranky and uncomfortable."

"I see. Well, I do need to talk with you too about when the time comes for my daughter to give birth."

"Oh? What is there to talk about?"

"Much, Master Greg," Fia said. We are concerned not only about the twin's safety but also about Lady Grace's."

"Greg, I do not intend to overstep my bounds, but you will need all the protection you can get from me and Fia's kin," Naamah said.

"They will not be wholly unprotected, Naamah," Robert interjected. One of the reasons I came here was not just a free dinner from my friend, "He lightly elbowed Greg, "but I have been talking to Raphael, who also, with his kin, be protecting Grace and the twins when they are ready to be born."

Greg groaned. "Jesus! When were you guys going to tell me about all this shit?"

Robert laughed, "No promises from any deities, my friend. But seriously, we had just ironed things out, and I planned to discuss this with both of you tonight. I guess, this birth is a much bigger event than anyone thought."

"This 'event' is the birth of my children and not some spectacle for magical beings to observe," Greg said hotly, walking off the patio onto the lawn. He stood there and dropped his head. After a moment, he returned to the group, "Thank you all, I mean it. I never liked asking for or receiving help, but I will welcome it this time as long as my family is safe."

At that moment, the girls had walked off the lawn. "Mother, Fia! It is good to see you both. Fia, are you ok?" She hugged them both, "what brings you here?"

"Sit down, babe; this may take some explaining for both of us," Greg said.

"AM and I will take care of the dishes. You guys still need to talk," Robert said after everyone had eaten. Despite the serious nature of the dinner conversation, everyone ate their fill except Grace, who only nibbled at her food.

"Thanks, guys, but you don't have to leave. You guys are part of this, too." Grace said.

"We won't take long." AM cleared the rest of the dishes and followed Robert inside.

Greg sat beside Grace, holding her hand. "Okay, so let me make sure we understand what will happen when it is time for Grace to give birth. You, Naamah, and Fia will work with Ralpheal to ensure Lilith, and her demons do not even get close to Grace and the twins. You all will do your best not to reveal yourselves to other humans. How will that be possible?"

"I never said it would be. I said we will try not to be seen by anyone except you all." Naamah said gently, more for Grace's sake than to alleviate Greg's concerns.

"Effort...?" Greg said in a disbelieving voice.

"Honey, I think you know she will make an effort. Remember last year in Richmond? Many people saw what happened, and the press played it off as fake, not a real exorcism with the Ring."

"People want to believe what they want," Naamah said.

"I seem to remember a fallen angel telling me that." Greg replied, "You are right, though."

"Greg, you still wear the Ring on a chain around your neck. I am glad you choose not to wear it always, as it could be bad for you in the long run."

"It does drain me the longer I wear it, and my heightened senses can be overwhelming to the point of headaches."

AM and Robert returned from the kitchen. "We loaded the dishwasher and put the food away. We are going to our car to get our things," Robert said. At dinner, they decided that AM and Robert would spend the night in the guest room due to the late hour and because they had had a few beers at dinner. "We will turn, guys. Good night."

Greg wakes up to the sound of retching noises in the bathroom. Grace's side of the bed is empty. "Sweetheart, are you ok?" He sprang out of bed and stood at the bathroom door. "Babe?" He heard the toilet flush and then running water; after a moment, a pale Grace opened the door.

"I'm ok. I threw up a little bit."

He was helping her back to bed again when she suddenly stopped and moved quickly for a nine-month pregnant woman back to the bathroom. Greg followed to see his wife hovering, kneeling in front of the toilet, dry heaving. He felt helpless, and all he could do was rest his hand on her back, gently rubbing it. She waved him off, "Stop." After a few more moments, she said, "Well, any dinner left in my stomach is now gone."

"Do you want me to call the doctor or get you something?"

"No, honey, but I think the time may be here."

"Time for what?"

Grace looked at him in disbelief and put a cold hand on his cheek. "It's good that you are cute but can be so dumb sometimes." As she said this, water splashing onto the bathroom floor explained things to Greg.

"Oh shit!" He froze, then snapped out of it, "I will get your bag, put it in the car, then I will come for you." Greg rushed to the bedroom door, and Naamah opened it before he could get there.

"Everyone stays in the house! They are here."

Greg didn't have to be told who the 'they' were; he took the Ring off the chain around his neck and put it on; instantly, the world changed, and his senses were heightened; he heard noises outside on the lawn, noises he had not heard in many years. He went over to the bedroom window that overlooked the front yard. At first glance, he saw nothing; dew glistened on the grass, still undisturbed. His enhanced vision at the edge of the lawn near the woods just beyond the property allowed him to see dark figures with black wings moving closer. In the sky above, he saw other figures hovering. "Shit."

"What do you see, honey?" Grace said in a pained voice. She was holding her abdomen; she was in the middle of a contraction.

"Nothing good."

AM appeared at the door, "Fia has alerted her mistress." She rushed over to Grace, noticed her discomfort, and ran to the bathroom, returning with a wet washcloth for her forehead. Part of the battle plans was for Fia to reach out to her mistress when Grace went into labor or if there was a threat to her and the twins. "I hope she gets here soon."

Last night, they decided on plans A and B when Grace went into labor. The hospital was out of the question; the couple had agreed on that weeks ago, and the attack on Grace earlier showed the wisdom of that option. Going there would have been too dangerous not only for Grace but for innocent people in the hospital if Lilith and her demons attacked them there. Greg had paid a midwife an exorbitant sum to be on call and come to the church property, the parish priest's home, to assist Grace with birth. The second and worst option would be giving birth at home if they could not make it onto holy ground. Naamah and AM would stay close to Grace, and AM had one of Rapheal's feathers for protection. Greg and Robert would defend the home; Greg with the Ring of Solomon, and Robert still had the protection of Ralpheal's feather. Raphael had stationed angels around the house and in the sky; for the moment, neither side made a move. Below on the lawn, Greg heard voices in an unfamiliar language. Several creatures of assorted sizes and shapes, he assumed, were beings like Fia, who moved out on the lawn holding what looked like weapons. They were gesturing to each other, organizing a defensive line. The demons at the edge of the trees were no longer hiding and stepped out; they were brandishing weapons in full demon form. Their leathery wings moved in rhythm to another demon who looked like the leader chanting something in a language Greg could not identify.

Grace, in the middle of a stronger contraction, "Where is Mother!"

"I am here, my child," Naamah said, walking in. I spoke to one of the angels, and they recommended that I stay close to you until we can get you to holy ground. They are afraid that in the heat of the battle, some of the angels may be unable to tell the difference between me and Lilith's demons."

"But what about you? I want you by my side." Grace was crying, "I don't want to lose you mother. The demons will not go easy on you, and if they catch you, they will take you to hell, and I don't know if I will ever see you again."

Cradling her daughter's face, "I will not let that happen. Remember, we have Greg and the Ring."

Grace nodded but would not stop crying.

Fr. O'Brian was in the sacristy tidying up, humming to himself. His habit was getting ahead while preparing for this morning's mass. It was his turn while Fr. Ortiz was back at the cottage cleaning up after breakfast. He planned to work with his co-pastor in the church office while Grace took a medical leave last week when it became more difficult for her to make it to the office from her new home easily.

"Good morning, Father," a voice outside the sacristy said.

"Mass is not for another hour, but you are welcome to stay and pray," he answered as he walked out to meet the person who greeted him. Standing near the altar was a tall man in simple jeans and a T-shirt. He looked different, Fr. O'Brian could not put his finger on it, but something *felt* different. "Good morning, son. Can I do anything for you?"

"Thank you, Father, but I am here to introduce myself to you. I am a friend of your co-pastor, Fr. Ortiz."

"Oh, I see."

"My name is Raphael."

"Not *the* Rapheal? The one Fr. Ortiz told me about from last year when I was on retreat?"

He bowed slightly, "The same."

"Raphael, I am a man of faith, but I must admit that I have doubts about last year's events. There is no doubt about the political events then, but I am human and ashamed to say that I struggle with the whole story."

"Of course, you are just a person that, like your kind, needs evidence sometimes to deal with the conflicts in logic and reasoning. Rapheal said, I would normally love to chat with you and get to know you better before I go 'full angel' as it were on you, but here it goes." At that moment, a set of large white wings with black tips appeared from his back and the hilt of a gold-handled sword over one shoulder.

Fr. O'Brian blessed himself, not scared but smiling, "Call me Thomas, I am convinced."

Raphael laughed, "Fr. Ortiz assured me you have a sense of humor; I am glad he was correct." The angel settled down on the ground and said, "Shall we both go to see Fr. Ortiz? I have something important I need to discuss with you both."

"Of course, follow me, please."

The angel and priest left the church and went to the cottage. Fr. O'Brian heard screams and violent noises coming from the direction of Greg and Grace's home. "Oh my God, what is that?" he exclaimed.

"The gathering storm, and it is only beginning."

They quickened their pace to the cottage.

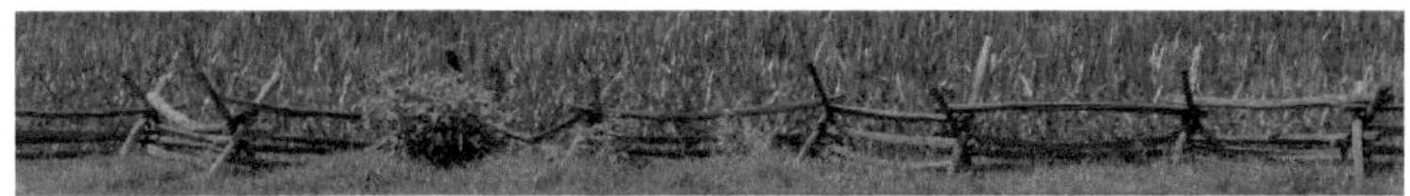

Chapter 36

The Battle comes Home

Raphael and Fr. O'Brian entered the cottage as an alarmed Fr. Ortiz reached the door on his way out.

"Oh, Lucas! We were coming to see you."

The priest saw Raphael accompanying his co-pastor. "What is going on? Have you not heard the commotion coming from Greg's house?"

"That is why I am here, my friend," the angel answered, "may I come in?"

Fr. Ortiz motioned for him to come in, and the trio sat in the nearby living room. Raphael was the calmest of the three. "There is a battle going on next door, and for the new mother's safety, she will have to be there where she will have better protection while she is in labor."

"Grace is in labor now?" Fr. Ortiz said.

"Yes, but for now, the demonic forces have surrounded the house. Archangel Micheal is there with other angels to repel the demons. That is the noise you are hearing."

"How do you plan to get Grace here safely?"

"We have allies from another realm whose powers are 'different' than ours, and they will get her here, hopefully in a short time."

"Other realm?" Fr. O'Brian said.

The angel smiled despite the seriousness of the situation. "Beings from your part of the world, I believe their leader is called The Morrigan."

"Oh dear," the Irish priest blessed himself.

"Who is that, Ian?"

"Another time, Lucas."

"Yes, I agree, we have work to do," Raphael said.

"What will you have us do, Raphael?" Fr. Ortiz asked.

"I will join the battle, so can you two prepare a place for Grace to give birth here?"

The pastors nodded their agreement, and the angel left.

"We can use the small room near the kitchen. It has no windows and would be easy to defend." Fr. Ortiz said. Both the priest rooms had windows that would be harder to defend if an enemy somehow made it on holy ground. "We can clear out most of the furniture except for the chaise lounge chair; that should do well for Grace." The men managed to clear out most of the smaller things in a room that generally functioned as an office when one of the priests needed to take care of personal or church matters. The only things left were the chaise and a desk, which was too large to move easily, so they agreed to let it be. The ground shook once they finished the work, sounding like an explosion.

"Dear God, I hope she gets here soon." Fr. O'Brien said he looked at his watch. The time was 10:00 am, October 23.

"What the hell was that!" Grace screamed. Naamah sat next to her, stroking her forehead. When she looked at her daughter, she had a gentle expression; looking away and out a nearby window, her face was one of murderous intent. It was clear she wanted to be in the battle.

"I think you are going to need a new garage door," Robert said, looking out the window. From what he could see, several demons had charged the line of The Morrigans people near the house. The clash of their weapons created an explosive reaction that injured combatants on both sides and the demons withdrew. Robert could not see the fighting because things moved too quickly for the human eye to see clearly, but the sounds of battle were distinctive. Blue flashes seemed the most violent, and one appeared to destroy the garage door.

"Where is that damned angel!" Naamah yelled, primarily to herself.

Greg was wondering that, too, although he did not say it aloud. "Rob, how long?" he whispered to his friend.

Robert closed his eyes and said, "Soon, he is with the priests and will be here in a moment; he said to get ready to move Grace."

The couple had a hammock on the back patio, and earlier AM managed to take the hammock portion off. Using the oars of Greg's canoe to loop through the ends, they decided to carry Grace toward the churchyard and onto holy ground with several of Fia's kin and angels above to fight their way to the church. It was a risky plan, but they did not anticipate that Grace would go into labor this early and at home. Initially, she was to meet the midwife at the church, and she would assist Grace there. This idea was a by-the-seat-of-their-pants plan. Naamah would not be able to accompany her daughter, but that was ok with her because she told Greg she wanted to fight if she could not be with Grace. There were several louder clashes outside, accompanied by otherworldly screams. AM was helping Grace into the hammock while Greg and Robert grabbed each end.

"Ready, Rob?" Greg said over his shoulder.

"Yep, let's get to the door."

"We will help carry Grace," Raphael said. The angel materialized into the bedroom with another angel beside him. "No offense, guys, but I think we are stronger than two humans and can move faster."

Greg put his end down, "Can't argue with that, and I was concerned that Robert, even with AM's help, may not be up to the trip." Robert did not need a cane anymore to walk, but he still was not as strong as he once was. "Ok then, let's go; I don't know how long Fia, and her friends can keep the demons at bay, even with your help."

The angels picked up Grace in the hammock and followed Greg to the back of the house and the patio doors. Before them, a fierce fight between angels and demons was taking place on the lawn. The church grounds were visible in the distance. Robert was next to Greg, AM was on one side of Grace, and her mother was on the other.

"How do we get across with so many demons out there?" AM shouted.

"Ready guys?" Raphael shouted.

"Let's go!" Greg responded and opened the door. At that moment, a demon appeared in front of him. "Go to hell!" he ordered. The demon was within the range of the Ring and immediately evaporated on its way to hell. At that moment, loud trumpets sounded, and a host of angels swarmed in front of them.

"I love you, my daughter," Naamah said as she kissed her and flew out into the fight. Naamah was in her full demon form, and anyway, she could not follow her daughter onto holy ground. She also had a score to settle with Lilith anyway.

"Run!" Raphael shouted, holding his sword high over his head. The group made it halfway to their goal when Grace cried out in pain; she was having a strong contraction.

Greg held her hand. *I hope she does not give birth while we are running.* "Hang in, babe, almost there." She turned her head to look at him and opened her eyes. He almost let go of her hand. Her eyes had changed. The ordinarily white portion of her eyes had changed to deep yellow, and her pupils were slits like a demon when they were in their true form. As he watched, her skin slowly changed from its typical olive hue to blue green like her mother when she was in demon form. "Grace!" he shouted, squeezing her hand. She turned to him, clearly in pain, but did not respond. "Rob!"

Robert saw what happened to Grace, "Raphael! Stop!" The angels carrying Grace in the hammock stopped. "Look!"

Grace's transformation was complete; her hair was longer and darker, and poking out of her hair was a set of horns, not as large as her mother's but unmistakably horns. Grace would not be able to come to holy ground in her current state. She was a demon like her mother. At that moment, a large explosion directly in front of the group stirred up a large cloud of dirt and dust that rained down on them. They could not see what caused it; in the middle of the dust, they heard what sounded like the hiss of a large snake. The fight shifted from the house to the group surrounding Grace. A large group of angels rushed in to cut off the advancing demons on one side, while on the other side, Fia, with her kind, took the other.

"Stop!" A commanding voice boomed from within the settling dust in front of them. Greg could make out the shape of a female demon. At first, he thought it was Naamah until he saw her serpent-like tail.

Raphael lowered his sword in front of him, "Lilith..."

"I am happy you recognize me, angel," her voice was taunting. "You know why I am here. Hand over the cambion, and I will direct my demons to stand down."

"Why should we believe you?" Greg said as he walked toward her. He could not understand what he was seeing. She did not look like the other demons when Greg wore the ring. Ordinary demons looked not only evil in appearance, but he also could feel their malevolence as if he had a sixth sense. A sense that the human mind did not have the tools to comprehend. Lilith's aura was at a magnitude many times than any he had seen. What was worse was the feeling he had for her that began to make him physically sick the closer he got. He wanted to retch from sensory overload, but he kept moving forward. He wanted to be close enough to use the Ring's influence on her.

"Brother Greg, it's nice to meet you finally." She smiled, displaying rows of razor-sharp teeth. Oh, that's right. You are now the janitor or groundskeeper,

Greg. That was a lovely house you had. I know you could not afford something like that these days now that you don't have a flock giving you their retirement money. I applaud you for fleecing your former flock once more before you left them to worship in a much poorer church. Well done," she taunted.

Greg knew better than to take the bait; most of the money he had was from a large life insurance payment when his first wife, Mila, was killed by a fallen angel. The church fell out of prominence due to the deaths when Azâzêl caused panic inside a crowded church, where many died. No one wanted to go to a place associated with that tragedy. "If you know me so well, then you know I will never hand over to you, my wife."

"Have you seen her lately? She is more of a demon than a human now, which means she is **mine.** If you cooperate, I may allow conjugal visits."

"What did you do to her?" Greg kept talking, moving closer.

Just a little closer.

Lilith laughed, "I can assure you I have nothing to do with your wife's change in appearance. She is finally showing what she is on the inside on the outside now."

"And what about my children? What do you intend to do with them? you can't raise them in hell." He was within the Ring's range now. He could feel it vibrating so much he thought it would shake him apart.

She shrugged, "Maybe I will finally find out the fascination you humans have for your pet dogs. Yes. I like that idea; I will make them my lap dogs—you know, kick them around a little. The mongrel will be my plaything; you can have her when I am tired of her if she still wants you. I would enjoy that so much because it would hurt my poor sister Naamah the most."

Greg's blood was boiling, "I don't think so, you bitch!" He held up a fist, wearing the Ring, "Lilith! Go to hell!"

Nothing.

"Performance issues? Oh dear, you are too young for that, my boy." She laughed. "The Ring of Solomon has no effect on the demon holding the office of Satan. So run away, little boy. I have a prize to collect." Lilith took several steps forward, shoving Greg hard to one side. Then, a loud war-like scream came from overhead, followed by the blur of a person pouncing on Lilith. Naamah attacked, but Lilith easily swatted her away with a single swipe. "Dear sister, this is no way to greet me."

Naamah lay on her back next to an unconscious Greg. She sprung up and lunged at Lilith again and was quickly repelled. Blood from a wound on her face and one arm looked deformed, broken. She got up again with less energy, only to be rebuffed again. Naamah landed only a few feet from her daughter, not moving.

Oh shit, this is not good. Greg tried again, "Go to hell, Satan!" He felt the Ring vibrate again at his command. But Lilith only sneered at him.

"The Ring does not work on Satan! The only thing it affords you is protection from me while you wear it. It does not, however, protect your friends and even these angels from me if I choose to harm them and, in those human's case, kill them." She was looking at Robert and AM. "Hand over the mongel, and I will spare all here." She extended her arms. Lilith was not smiling, her eyes showing her deadly intent.

Since she arrived, the battle had stopped, and the area was silent. A few heartbeats later, the sound of sirens in the distance reached his ears. Not now!

"You hear that too, former Brother Greg. Soon, we will have more uninvited guests at our little party. I promise I will make your home run red with innocent blood! Hand her over now, and we will go. No one else need be hurt or killed."

"Greg, you can't," AM said, holding Grace's hand, which looked like a child in her friend's transformed one.

"Honey," Grace said. Greg moved over to his wife. She cupped his face with a hand, hands that now were larger with claws on her fingers. "You have no choice. I don't want anyone to die because of me. Mother will find a way someday to get the children at least."

He put his hand on top of hers, "You don't believe that do you?"

Tears flowed from her demon eyes, "I have to. Remember, I love you always."

The sounds of emergency vehicles got closer. Greg could not think. His heart felt like a stone in his chest. Underneath Grace, a fog appeared. He looked up, and it grew until it covered the whole lawn and reached Lilith. Lilith looked confused and then annoyed for the first time, but this was not her doing. Overhead, the screeching of a giant crow made the humans cover their ears. Both angels and demons hunched down, looking for the source of the sound. Suddenly, a strong and forceful wind from above almost knocked Greg and his friends to the ground, kicking up dust and some of the newly laid sod a few away, forcing him to close his eyes. When he opened them up again, he could see a large crow landing between his party and Lilith. It was no ordinary bird; it was a large crow that he guessed must have been a dozen feet tall or taller; it was folding its gigantic wings and let out another deafening caw. It turned its massive head in Greg's direction. *Did it wink at me?* The crow turned its attention to Lilith; a fog enveloped it, and when it dissipated, the figure of a tall woman with raven black hair took its place. She wore green robes that a queen could have worn.

Greg felt a tug on his sleeve. It was Fia. "Master Greg, I have no time to explain, so please do what I ask. Give the Ring to your friend Robert now and ask your angel friends to allow us to carry Lady Grace instead." Fia cried, "Please trust me, there is no time."

Greg hesitated for a moment, then nodded yes. The angels also agreed.

"Rob, take this and keep it safe. The box for it is with Fr. Ortiz; put it in there for me. "He looked at Fia next to him and then back at his friend. "Trust me." Robert took the ring.

"Who are you, and what is your business here!" Lilith said, irritated.

The woman smiled and bowed slightly, "I am known as The Morrigan, and my business here is not with you but with the divine twins and their mother.

I will not let you interfere with my duties to them. So you may go now." She waved dismissively.

Enraged that someone would talk to her in that manner, Lilith lunged, fangs and claws bared, at the interloper. She passed through The Morrigan as if she was nothing but mist. Lilith rolled on the ground tearing up more of the freshly laid sod, leaving ugly scars on the ground.

While Lilith was distracted by her mistress, Fia took Greg and Grace each by the hand, saying, "Here we go. Traveling may be a little disorienting." More of Fia's kin surrounded them, and a thick fog enveloped them. Fia was not kidding about the feeling of disorientation; he wanted to vomit. Lilith noticed what was happening and flung herself at the mist, passing through nothing.

"I would love to stay and enjoy the craic (conversation) with you, Lilith, but I am needed at home now." With that, the Morrigan winked and became a giant crow again, then flew away with a loud caw. Naamah, whom Lilith had forgotten about while dealing with the intruder, had already evaporated from the lawn. The angels scooped up Robert and AM and flew them to the church grounds.

Fr. Ortiz and O'Brian heard Lilith's scream of rage inside the parish house.

Chapter 37

Birth

Greg fell to his knees, fighting waves of nausea. He had let go of Fia's hand when they arrived wherever it was. He kept his eyes closed to control a stomach that wanted to empty his breakfast. "Where are we, Fia?"

"I'm sorry, Master Greg, that you feel sick; mortals always have this reaction when we travel here."

Greg opened his eyes, trying to get them back in focus, "and where is here?"

"It has many names; Master Greg, the realm of the dead, is one of them. But I assure you you are alive." Fia laughed, standing next to Grace. She was still in demon form but asleep, lying on a raised bed made of grass. Greg walked over to her and stroked her forehead.

"Is she alright?"

"Oh, aye. Your wife is just asleep. The trip exhausted her, but the next contraction will wake her soon."

"And the children; are they ok too?"

Fia patted his hand, "aye."

"Why did you ask me to give the Ring to Robert?"

"Because sacred items from other realms are not allowed here. It would have simply fallen on the ground where you had stood. We did not want anyone to find it, and then the human world may have another problem."

Just like the medallion Hannah was wearing.

A chair grew up from the ground behind him, and it was of the same construction as the bed Grace was on grass. He sat down and held her hand; this was the first time he had been able to look at her closely and the changes to her outward physical appearance. He wondered if this form was permanent. "Fia, where is your mistress?"

"She will be along soon. Lilith has no power over her, and my master could only distract her and allow us to escape."

"What about my friends? They are still in danger!"

"My kin and the angels safely escorted them to the church grounds where the demons cannot enter; my mistress distracted the demons." A table grew up from the ground next to Greg. It was fascinating to watch, almost like watching plants grow in one of those time-lapse videos, except cups and a pitcher grew instead of flowers or stems. The pitcher had water in it. Fia picked it up, poured some into the cup, and offered it to Greg. "Water?"

"Thank you." Greg drank it, surprised that it was cold as if it were out of a refrigerator from home. He resumed inspecting the changes in Grace. Her hair had turned jet black, and she had horns not as large as Naamah's when she was in demon form, but horns poking out of her hair. He touched them, and Grace opened her eyes.

"Greg, I must look hideous." She lifted her hands, looking at them, flexing her fingers, and instead of fingernails, there were claws. "I was always afraid that this would happen someday."

He stroked her head, "You are not ugly; you are my wife."

"I am glad to see you awake, mistress Grace. I agree with Master Greg; you are not ugly."

"You are not ugly, child," Naamah said as she stood beside The Morrigan. She was in her 'normal' human form and ran to Grace. "How are you, daughter?"

"Better, but I think this is just intermission before the next contraction." she smiled weakly, "I am already tired, mother."

"You are safe here. Lilith has no power in this realm."

Grace glanced over to The Morrigan, "Thank you. I don't know how to pay you for the kindness you have shown us."

"You are welcome, but I am not doing this out of pure kindness. The twins are the divine twins we had been waiting for, and I had sworn to protect them until they come of age." She could see the concern in her face and held up a hand, "only an offer of protection. I have no desire to be a parent." She pointed at Grace and Greg. "I also heard your concern about staying in demon form. I don't know much about your mother's realm, but I think you will return to your human form once you give birth and leave here."

"Oh, that is a relief," Greg said. Grace gave him a hurt expression, "Well, it will be hard to explain your change in appearance to Fr. Ortiz and O'Brian, never mind if we ever wanted to go out on a date." Greg winked. Grace didn't think that was very funny, so she hit him. What she thought was lightly on his arm, "Ouch! You are stronger in this form, babe, be careful!" Greg rubbed his arm.

"You deserve it," and she stuck out a forked tongue and then smiled. "I am glad you can still tease me, honey." her face went still. Shit!"

"What?"

"Contractions are back, and they feel **stronger** in this form." Grace almost yelled.

Naamah held her hand. "Yes, they are, but Momma is here. You can squeeze my hand but be careful not to break your husband's. He is much weaker than you, demon or human." She could not repress a smile.

"Mother!"

"You know I am kidding," she patted her hand.

"Yeah, right..." she breathed as the contraction eased.

Greg turned to face his hostess, "I want to thank you too for helping us. What do I call you? The Morrigan?"

She smiled, "some of the humans before had called me Gentle Annie, but you can simply call me Annie. That is good of a name as any Greg."

"Annie, it is then. Can I ask you a question?"

"Of course."

"This may sound silly, but what day is it here? Is time different in your realm?"

"Not silly at all. Time is the same here if I want it to be if that makes sense. For example, there are parts of my realm where time moves slower, which was useful in the past if I needed to train a mortal in an important task in the human world. They had more time to learn, and when they returned home, it was as if no time had elapsed. Does that make sense?"

"I think so. Is time the same as in the mortal world?"

"Yes. To answer your question, October 23 is the date on your calendar, and the local time is 8 p.m."

"Where are Grace and Greg?" Fr. Ortiz said. He had followed Robert and AM to the church's property line to witness the police and fire trucks at the Cassidy home, combing over the damage. The lawn looked like someone with a tractor had torn up the newly laid sod. The house was damaged, with windows blown out and the garage almost destroyed.

"I think they are safe, but I could not tell you exactly where they went. I bet even Raphael does not know where they are." Robert said.

Robert and AM showed up at the Pastor's cottage after the angels picked them up and carried them faster than a human could run onto holy ground, where the couple would be safe from demons. They had to cover their ears at Lilith's scream of rage while they made their way to tell Fr. Ortiz and O'Brian did not expect Grace and Greg. After nearly twenty minutes of halting conversation and explanation of what a pooka was and The Morrigan, primarily to Fr. Ortiz, Fr. O'Brian explained that he learned tales of the beings growing up in Ireland. But he never believed they were anything more than folk tales.

"I expect we will have a visit by the police soon. What do we say? "AM said aloud.

"I am sure they will not believe you if you told them, you were in a battle between supernatural beings. Let me talk to the police, at least for now. It will not be lying to say you were visiting me, and Fr. O'Brian and I were in the cottage when we heard the awful noises coming from the house and did not know what was happening." Fr. Ortiz said.

"Let's get back to the cottage; it looks like the police are on their way here," Fr. O'Brien said, peeking out the window, pointing to the road alongside the church.

Grace screamed; the contractions were getting stronger, and even her mother could not hold her hand very long. She was sweating so much her black hair was soaking wet. Fia brought cool water-soaked cloths to wipe her face and forehead. "It's almost time, mistress Grace. Just a little longer."

All Greg could do safely was wipe her head with the wet cloths. "You can do it, babe; I love you." He felt helpless.

Grace looked at him with love and anger, "You did this to me!" In her demon voice, it sounded very menacing.

"Don't worry, Greg, that's the contractions talking, not her," Naamah laughed.

"Very funny."

She laughed again. Grace looked at her mother, fire in her eyes. Naamah reached out and gently stroked her cheek. Grace closed her eyes, taking a break between contractions. They were coming closer and faster than Greg thought. What little education he received from the midwife told him they can vary in timing but will get closer together and stronger until birth. That may be true of human females, but Grace? Who knows? Naamah was not sure either when he asked her about what to expect. He took this time to walk away and stretch his legs. Greg marveled at the fact he was not in the mortal realm anymore, but one Fia called the Otherworld. It did not look much different from the mortal one; it was even night here. The Morrigan said that time at this part of her world flowed like his. The Otherworld seemed no different than what he was used to, except it felt *off* to him, but not in a bad way, just different.

"Master Greg, are you hungry?" Fia asked, approaching him.

He had not eaten anything since breakfast this morning, and during the conflict with Lilith, he guessed it was around lunch or later; he did not realize it until the pooka mentioned it. At that moment, his stomach audibly growled. "there's your answer, my friend." he blushed.

"Then please follow me. I have prepared something simple for you: a sandwich and a pint of ale. I learned about making sandwiches from Lady Grace," she smiled. She is a good teacher about the mortal realm, food, and other things."

"I am happy you and she get along so well, Fia. I worried she would be bored and cooped up at the church while pregnant. Thank you for being a friend."

"It was my pleasure, Master Greg; she is a good person, no matter what those awful demons said. She is a lovely soul, human or demon."

Greg took a bite of his sandwich and finished it quickly; he was hungrier than he thought, and the ale was the best he had ever tasted. He sat at the table savoring the last drops of the drink when he heard Grace stir again. Greg gulped the last of the ale and hurried back to his wife. Naamah was wiping her head with another wet cloth, talking to her in what sounded like Greek. The Morrigan sat on a large, almost throne-like chair next to Naamah. Greg grabbed her hand despite the danger that she could break it and stroked her arm.

"I'm here babe. I love you."

She half smiled and nodded, lightly squeezing his hand back. "Honey, let go of my hand now. I can feel a big one coming." Greg did as she said, and she grimaced again as another wave passed through her.

Fia took up a position at the end of the table, "I see a head, mistress! Another push, and I think you will have the first one out."

Greg saw the head crowning, mesmerized at not only the sight of birth but, more strangely—a Celtic faerie for a midwife. No one would believe that part of the story. Grace let out a loud cry, and the first of the twins was out. She exhaled exhaustively. Fia held the child, and, without any tools, Greg could see, had the umbilical cord cut and then wrapped the child in a blanket, handing it to Greg.

"It's a girl!" she smiled.

Greg held his daughter, who looked like a normal human girl, "Hello, little one. I am your dad." Tears welled in his eyes, and he lowered his daughter to Grace, "And this is your mom." Grace reached up, and he put the tiny being on her chest; she was crying, too.

"She is beautiful." Grace looked at her mother and said, "Little one, this is your γιαγιά (giagiá—grandmother)." Naamah reached over to touch her granddaughter's forehead, her lips pursed. Grace smiled and nodded.

"Welcome, my granddaughter."

Greg looked at his watch and accounted for the time difference. His daughter was born at 1135PM local time, October 23. The new family huddled around its latest member. The baby girl did not cry, but her eyes were open, moving around the room as if studying the new faces around her. Even though she was still wet, the child had what looked like red hair and grey eyes; her skin had the same olive skin as her mother's. To Greg, he saw some of his facial features, like the shape of his eyes and a nose. But that may be how they look now, shortly after birth.

"She is lovely, my friend," the Morrigan said to Naamah, "I am happy for you and you too, mother and father."

Grace laughed, or was it a cry? Then, the smile melted away as another contraction moved across her body. "Shit!"

Naamah held her hand again.

"Almost done, my lady," Fia said, "I can see another head."

A second head was crowning. Grace was breathing haltingly. Greg reached out with one hand on her shoulder, the other holding the girl. Time seemed slower than before. Grace let out a pained cry, her head lifting, and exhaled as the second child was delivered. Fia attended to the new baby and wrapped it up in another blanket.

"It's a boy!" He had jet-black hair, olive skin, and the same grey eyes.

Grace exhaled noisily and smiled.

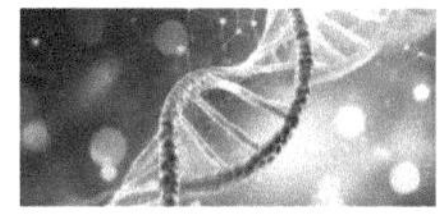

Chapter 38

Demonic Ties

"What shall we call them?" Greg said, holding his son as he slept in his arms. His daughter was sleeping in the crib that had grown out of the ground in the Celtic Otherworld, just like the rest of the furniture in this realm. The new parents had discussed several names since they knew Grace was pregnant with twins. The twins were just a few hours old, and both mother and father barely got much sleep after the last one was born. Greg checked his watch when his son was born; the date was October 24th, just after midnight. The twins were born on separate days.

That will make birthday parties easier, as children can have their own parties instead of having joint ones.

"I like the Irish names we talked about a few weeks ago. They seem appropriate, considering where they were born." She smiled, holding the sleeping girl in her arms.

Greg had gotten used to his wife's appearance and found it strangely appealing. Since giving birth, she still looked like a demon. The Morrigan believed Grace would return to her human form once she left the Celtic Otherworld, but she could not say for sure. Naamah did not know if her daughter would be stuck in this form either.

Her expression seemed sad. "Do you still love me even if I a— like this?"

"Remember our vows, in sickness and health... etc?"

"There was no line in those vows about one of us turning into a demon, honey."

Greg gently puts his son down in the bassinet, takes his daughter from Grace, and puts her next to her brother. "Sweetheart, I married you for what you are inside and out, just as you married me for what I am. I accept you for your past and love you in the present, and I am looking forward to our future. No matter if you look like a human or a sexy demon." Greg winked.

"You had to ruin such a lovely speech. You are such a boy!"

"So, you don't love me for who I am anymore?" Greg feigned a pout.

"Stupid question," she reached out, kissed him, and held him warmly.

"Easy babe, ouch! You don't know your own strength in this form," Greg pushed away, patting his chest.

She laughed, "Oh, sorry."

"Do you think they are coming back?" Fr. Ortiz said. He was having breakfast with Fr. O'Brian in the cottage kitchen. Yesterday was exhausting for the co-pastors, answering questions from local and state police for hours following the incident at the former Brother Greg's new home near the church. The press wanted to interview them, and they promised to talk to them sometime today. Their dilemma was what to say without lying or sounding crazy. The bishop called late yesterday, and they discussed with him what happened, leaving out most of the unbelievable things for now. The pastors feared they might have to go to the diocese's offices soon for a more thorough discussion. They agreed to cross that bridge when they got to it; for now, it was important to talk to Robert and AM, and hopefully, they had spoken to Raphael.

"You mean Greg and Grace?" Fr. O'Brian said. "I hope so; I am fond of them almost as much as you are, Lucas. Also, I am concerned about the welfare of the wee ones. I wonder if they have been born yet."

Fr. Ortiz nodded, and then the front doorbell rang. He answered the door to see Robert and AM standing there. "Good morning, Father. Can we come in?" Robert said.

"You two are always welcome; please come in."

Fr. O'Brian joined them in the living room, "Can I get you anything?"

"No, thank you, Father," Robert answered.

"AM and I stopped by to ask if you have heard anything from Greg or Grace."

"We were just talking about the same thing, and no, we have not. Since you are here with the same question, I gather you have not either." Fr. Ortiz said.

"Raphael told me that he had lost track of them when they disappeared. The Morrigan vanished shortly after that; we assume we hope she has them in a safe place."

"I imagine the twins were already born by now." AM said, sounding sad, "I was looking forward to meeting them and being their auntie."

Fr. Ortiz smiled, "I doubt that will change. Have faith that they will return. After all, the press and police are still at their house trying to determine what happened. I am certain the last thing they want right now is to answer questions from the police, especially the press."

"I have a few questions about the Morrigan for you, Fr. O'Brian. What can you tell me about her?" Robert said.

The ordinarily reserved priest blushed a little. "I am afraid, not much, and what I know is just more Celtic mythology. Truth be told, nobody took those tales seriously. I grew up reading or hearing them more for entertainment than anything else. They are akin to what I think you call here in the States 'campfire' stories. I will ask a few people I know back home if they have any books regarding her that I may see."

The four sat quietly in the room, lost in their thoughts, when Robert's phone rang. He looked at the caller ID on the screen, which only said 'unknown.'

"Answer it, Rob," AM nudged.

"Hello?..." At first, he had a puzzled expression, then one of recognition. "Yes, maam, we will be there... yes maam." He hung up.

"Well?" AM asked impatiently.

"I never answered a call from a demon before. That was Naamah. She says everyone is fine but wants to see AM and me at some Starbucks in the Walmart where Grace would meet her mother." Robert looked puzzled.

"Oh, I know the one; Grace had told me about it," AM said excitedly. "When?"

"An hour from now. Oh, AM, we must also bring the protection pendant with us."

Fr. Ortiz stood up, "Then you should go now and tell them that we here are praying and thinking of them."

"Yes. Ready, hun?" Robert said.

AM was already walking toward the door. "Already ahead of you. Thank you, Fathers." She opened the front door and almost ran into someone standing on the stoop. "Fia!"

"Hello, Lady AM. On your way, I see?"

"Excellent. The twins are just lovely, and I am sure they would love to meet their Antaidh and Uncail (aunt and uncle). I will wait here until they return."

"Were you able to reach him?"

"Yes, child, he and his wife have agreed to meet me at our usual place," Naamah answered Grace. How are you feeling, my new mother?"

"More normal now that I am back as myself." Grace had returned to her human form when they left the Celtic Otherworld. To avoid unnecessary questions, they went to Naamah's San Francisco apartment. The Morrigan was right that she would return to normal in the human realm.

They returned a few hours ago when Grace recovered enough after giving birth and was strong enough to travel. She did not look like a woman who had recently given birth; it must be one of the benefits of having demon genes. The twins were healthy and did not tire of the constant attention of some of Fia's kin, who just wanted to meet the 'divine twins.' The Morrigan had one request of them: when the twins were old enough, she wished to educate them in the ways of her realm. The new parents agreed, provided the twins wanted that when they were old enough. Fair enough was her reply, but they will not need to make any decisions for at least twenty years from now. The twins were asleep in their grandmother's bedroom for now. Greg was tired and lay down with them, taking advantage of the free time to rest; Grace did not seem to need any sleep.

Naamah, for the first time in a long time, seemed content despite having a target on her back by her sister Lilith, the new Satan. Right now, her sister was probably licking her wounds and contending with the politics within demons in light of her failure to obtain the twins for hell. One last gift the Morrigan gave the twins was pendants that would mask what they are from supernatural creatures; at least, it should work. The pendant's chain would grow with them as they grew.

"You seem happy, mother."

"I am because you and my grandchildren are safe...and, of course, Greg too." she smiled.

"Thank you, mother."

"What about you child? Anything on your mind since we are alone now?"

"Yeah, this is the first time I have been able to process the changes in my life. Before Greg, it was just you and me, and then I went away to university and relied only on myself. I enjoyed that, but it was a lonely existence sometimes because if I got too close to other men, I was not sure if they were interested in me or because of what I was. Then I met Greg and learned he was immune and loved me for me as a person. It is sinking in now that my life is not my own anymore. I am responsible for two lives that I love with all my heart. I am nervous and excited all at the same time. I know I am not alone; I have Greg." She looked at her mother and clasped her hands, "and I have you too."

"I am happy to hear that. I may enjoy this new role of grandmother more than being a mother. I hope the twins accept me for what I am when they are old enough to understand our world."

"Mother, they are part of your world too; the demonic ties of blood are unbreakable. They will learn to love their γιαγιά (grandmother). We still have time before you have to meet my friends. Should we order food delivery? Since we are in your home, I would love some seafood?"

Chapter 39

One Year Later...

"Aiden... Saoirse, it's time to come in for lunch," Fia said as she picked the twins up from the playpen. Your mother and grandmother made you something yummy to eat. "Despite her small stature, Fia is strong and easily picked up the children in each arm, taking them to the small table in the kitchen. "I hope you weans (slang for wee or little ones) are hungry." She sat them in their highchairs and playfully tousled the hair on their heads. Aiden had thick black hair in contrast to his sister's copper red. Aiden made a face and rubbed his hair; Saoirse giggled. She was the easiest to amuse compared to her brother, and she got along with everyone. The little girl had a knack for getting along with anyone. Aiden was harder to amuse and rougher than his sister; only his father or grandmother could control him. He will have an interesting teenage year when the time comes. His parents thought The Morrigan might help him learn to control himself in adolescence.

"Honey, lunch is ready!" Grace called out.

Greg walked in, rubbing his bloodshot eyes. Every time he cuts the grass, his eyes get irritated, "Smells good, sweetheart. What are we having?" He had come in early from inspecting their garden, which had become a new passion for Greg the year after the twins were born. Earlier today, he cut the grounds at St. Rita's; he still worked there primarily because he enjoyed the 'honest work' as Robert's mother would praise him for doing. He also liked spending time with the pastors there, who had become an extension of his family. They did not know the details of Naamah's true nature; they thought she was eccentric, consistently declining an invitation to visit the church, etc. The twins just called her Nam, and anytime she was around the pastors, she appeared to be the appropriate age to be a grandmother, so as not to complicate things outside the home. The couple reasoned that divulging information about the true nature of their family would be too much. The family sat down together for lunch. Nam was between the twins, she nibbled on a burger Grace had prepared at lunch for the grownups.

"Are we still planning on going to the park after their nap?" Greg said.

"Yes, I think we have been cooped up inside for too long enough, and after a year, the press has given up following us." Grace smiled.

"I'm glad. I guess being a boring family is paying off, and we may have some peace for at least a little while."

"Nothing is boring about this family, Greg," Naamah said flatly. She was not in the 'grandmother' disguise she used with the outside world; her outward appearance ordinarily was as a young woman. The twins were not confused about the changes in her outward appearance; they seemed amused, like it was a game from their Nam, as they called her.

"For once, we agree, Naamah." Greg laughed.

They finished lunch. The twins went to bed for their naps while Greg and Grace cleaned the dishes.

Later that afternoon, the new parents pushed twin strollers with the children, who were babbling to each other as they walked along one of the trails winding through the trees in the local park. They were not the only parents in the park on a fall afternoon. Some were in strollers like them, while others were on the playground equipment, screaming excitedly. Some children played soccer on the newly cut grass in the nearby field.

Grace looped an arm in Greg's, "This is nice; I can hear myself think when I am outside."

"Agreed, babe. We deserve some quiet time like this now. I have an idea: Why don't I call Rob to see if they are doing anything this weekend? We could get away for a few hours and have your mom or Fia watch the kids?"

"I would love that, but I feel a little guilty taking advantage of Mother and Fia that way."

"It's not like we go out all the time lately. You know we are stuck with Fia as a bodyguard and nanny for the twins."

Grace nodded in agreement. Keeping Fia around was one of the Morrigan's requests before they returned home. The new parents were happy to have an extra hand. Naamah was persona non grata in the demon world, but that did not bother her. She enjoys being a grandmother now. They were halfway on the park trail in the section that passed through a wooded area. A slight breeze blew off some of the remaining leaves from the trees. Grace froze, and the children stopped babbling.

"What is it, babe?"

"Something is here."

"I see you still have the ability to sense demons. No matter, it will not change anything. And you, human, don't try and put that Ring on and keep your hands visible, or I will kill them now." The man stood in front of them, holding a gun at the twins.

"Why do you need mortal weapons?"

He shrugged, "They are effective, and they will injure or kill all of you or at least hurt you enough so I can finish you off myself."

"Who are you, and what do you want from us?" Greg said in a low voice, not wanting to startle the children.

"I guess it will not hurt to tell you because you both will be dead soon. I am James Dolus; I am, or was, Mr. Tan's aide. Since he is gone, Lilith will not allow me to resume my old duties for that office. So, I thought that if I got rid of the ones that embarrassed her so much, she might even make me a demon. You see, I am just a lowly familiar, Mr. Tan promised me that he would promote me after a century of service. But that promise is gone along with him. So, you must understand I need to kill all of you to impress the new Satan."

"You have thought this out, haven't you, James?" Grace said sarcastically. Her anger swelled inside, and her body felt hot.

"What I have thought out is defending the honor of my kind, and I must punish those who would defy our leader and master. Beings like you muddy the bloodline of demons and cannot be allowed to live." He raised the gun slightly: "Who goes first, the human or the mongrel? When you are gone, the twins belong to their aunt. Their power will be hers."

Grace lept at the familiar; she had turned into her demon form, claws for fingernails extended, razor-sharp teeth bared. It happened too fast for Greg to react. She was on top of James when the gun went off, and a scream escaped her lips. Grace rolled on the ground, her hands on her chest; snarling, she sat up. A bleeding wound could be seen just above where her heart should be. James pointed the gun at Greg, "Goodbye, Brother Greg."

The twins began crying, looking at their mother on the ground, bleeding. Another shot rang out; Greg fell on the other side of the twins, not moving. A silence hung over the small section of the trail; the wind had stopped, and it felt like, for a moment, everything stood still.

Still holding the gun, James smiled. "I did it!" At that moment, all sounds of the outside world ceased, and an eerie silence hung in the air. There were no cries of children running and playing or parents calling to them—just stillness. He looked at the twins; they had stopped crying and held hands directly at him. A brilliant flash of light blinded James.

"How are you, Lady Grace?" a familiar voice said. She opened her eyes to see Fia hovering over her, smiling. Above her, she could see the branches of a large oak tree.

"Fia?"

"Yes, don't worry you, Master Greg and the twins are all fine. I can't say the same thing about the bastard that attacked you, however."

Grace had never heard the pooka swear before. It seemed so out of character for her gentle nature, even if she had witnessed her savagery when fighting demons. "Where are we?"

"The Otherworld."

"How did I get here, and where are Greg and the twins?' She sat up quickly and felt a dull pain in her chest. She looked down at where the bullet had hit her to see no visible wound. Her hands looked normal for a human, not a demon.

"The Morrigan attended to you and your husband. He is fine, just recovering now over there," she said, pointing at another bed beside her. Greg looked asleep and peaceful.

"Aiden and Saoirse?"

"Over there, my lady," Fia indicated to the other side of Grace. The children were with a blond woman, sitting on a blanket in the grass, playing with some toys. The woman laughed with them as she handed them snacks from a basket.

"Thank you, Fia, for helping us." She looked back at the blond woman again, her eyes opening in recognition. "Is that Hannah?"

"Aye."

"But why is she with the children?"

"My mistress struck a deal with her in that if she stayed here, she would have to assist in the education of the children in the ways of her realm and be responsible for their care when needed."

"I guess Hannah did not have too many choices: stay here and live, return to the human world, and die," Grace smiled.

"True," the pooka said.

"How long have we been here," Grace said, pulling her eyes away from the succubus nanny.

"You have only been here for a day. Getting you here was not my doing."

"The Morrigan?"

"No, my lady."

"The who?"

"It was Aiden and Saoirse, Grace." A familiar voice said from behind. It was The Morrigan.

"How do you know that?"

"No one has the power to enter my domain without my permission except for some reason, these two little ones," she pointed at the children. I knew they were powerful, but even this surprised me. After that familiar attacked you, they brought you and Greg here. I believe it was out of defense or instinct. The attacker is gone."

"Gone?"

"Dead. We got rid of the body. We left it in Lilith's office. Hopefully, she will take it as a message to leave Aiden and Saoirse alone."

Grace stood up and discovered that she was not wearing what she had on at the park. Instead, she wore a long, flowing green dress that looked soft and well-made.

"Looks good on you, babe," Greg said. He was sitting up on the bed, smiling.

She ran over to him, kissed him, and hugged him. Grace ran her hands over him, looking for wounds, but she found none. Greg was dressed in the same clothes he wore during their walk in the park. "I see you are still wearing the same clothing. What happened to what I was wearing?"

"He flashed a toothy smile on his face. The kind Grace was familiar with when he was going to say something NSFW. Well?"

He laughed, "Well when you went all 'she-hulk' in your demon form, you tore your clothes. You were naked, babe!"

Grace blushed, "What?"

"I have to say now that everyone is safe; you did look damn sexy, if you pardon the pun." Greg hunched over, expecting a slap from her, but instead, she kissed him on the head.

"I am glad you are still your normal naughty self. I love you, bad boy."

The Morrigan was pleased: "It is always good to see a couple in love. It makes a healthy environment for the children."

"What can we do to thank you?" Greg asked.

"I know you will be anxious to return home but at least allow me to prepare dinner before you go home."

"That sounds nice, but we need to contact our friends Robert and AM. They were expecting us yesterday for dinner. They must be worried," Grace said.

The Morrigan held up a hand, "We already took care of that. Fia went to see them and told them what happened and that you are alright. We offered to bring them here..."

"And we could not turn down the invitation." AM's voice said.

Robert and AM stood peeked from behind the tree. Robert grinning.

"How long were you guys there?" Grace said.

"Don't 'hulk out' on me, Grace, but long enough."

Grace blushed again; this time, she slapped Greg on the shoulder.

Robert looked at the Morrigan, "My wife and I would be honored to have a meal with you."

Robert felt AM push him, "I don't recall receiving an invitation, rude boy!"

The Morrigan laughed this time, "You three are always welcome."

"Three?" Robert said, puzzled.

"Oh, sorry, I overstepped my bounds. You have not told your husband yet?"

Grace ran over to AM, placing a hand on her abdomen. "Are you?" she asked. She nodded yes.

"Then we have more than one thing to celebrate with our meal." The Morrigan declared.

End of Book III

Cast of Characters

- **Atlatonin Quinn** – Grandmother of Grace's father. She is of Aztec ancestry.
- **Aiden Cassidy**- youngest twin of Grace and Greg. One of the divine twins.
- **Ash S. Tan**- Ash-Shaytān Muslim name for the devil. Former Virginia governor.
- **AM(Anna-Marie) Diaz**- wife of Robert Diaz, a childhood friend of Greg Cassidy.
- **Ellen Cruz**- grandmother to Robert Diaz and surrogate grandmother to Greg Cassidy.
- **Fia**– an Irish pooka that works for the Morrigan; she is a shapeshifter/fairy.
- **Father Lucas Ortiz**- co-pastor at St. Rita's Catholic Church.
- **Father Ian O'Brian**- co-pastor at St. Rita's Catholic Church.

- **Gloria Cope**- not human but a soul from hell working in Mr. Tan's office.
- **Grace Cassidy**- married to Greg. Mother is Naamah, the demon, and father is human.
- **Greg Cassidy**- former pastor of the CFC. Now lives a quiet life with his wife, Grace, as a groundskeeper at St. Rita's Catholic Church.
- **Hannah**– A spy for Mr. Tan. She is watching Greg and Grace. Low-ranking succubus.
- **Hathor**- the Egyptian goddess of love, music, and dance. In Thebes, she protected the dead—an old lover of Naamah.
- **James Dolus**- Mr. Tan's assistant, not human, a familiar.
- **Julius Laban**- Mr. Tan's Chief of Staff and an incubus. An Original demon.
- **Lilith**- an original demon, and a succubus who works closely with Mr. Tan.
- **Lisa Diaz**- mother of Robert Diaz.
- **Naamah**- an original demon, mother of Grace Cassidy.
- An **Original** – a being that was there at the beginning of the world. They are more powerful than lesser demons.
- **Robert Diaz**- Greg Cassidy's childhood best friend.
- **Ms. Rebekah Lot**- Party chairperson, handles party finances.
- **Saoirse Cassidy**- oldest twin of Greg and Grace. One of the divine

twins.

- **Yolotli Conner Quinn**- Grace's father. He went by his middle name, Connor.

MERCI 8)

Acknowledgements

First, I would like to express my appreciation to the members of my family who supported my work. This includes, of course, my wife, Eloisa. My daughter, Jeanette-Maria C Blackledge, never hesitated to boost my book announcements on social media and to anyone who would listen. Also, my extended (and blended) family for all their support and kind words. A thank you to my beta readers, who gave me valuable feedback on the first book in the Brother Greg series: The Rose of St. Rita. I want to give a special thank you to my beta readers for Demonic Ties; Lex and Nancy for their invaluable help in making this one of my best (hopefully) books out so far.

Lastly, I can't forget my co-workers (***at my real job***) who encouraged me with their kind words of support. This is not a complete list of all the influences in and around my life that have inspired me to put my ideas on paper (and digital, of course).

I hope those who read this enjoy the tale keep reading my new books yet to come.

Thank you
Gerard F Dunn

Other Books:

The Ring of Solomon
(Book II)

The Rose of St. Rita
(Book I)

Shylah

Canvas & Sunrise

About the Author

This book is Gerard F. Dunn's fifth book to date. He is a nuclear medicine professional with certifications in computed tomography and X-ray. In this capacity, he has seen people at their best, worst, and, unfortunately, also their lowest.

He published his first book, Canvas & Sunrise, which contained several short stories in 2009. Today, his books mix mystery and fantasy in the modern world.

You can always connect with me at my website:

gerardfdunn.com

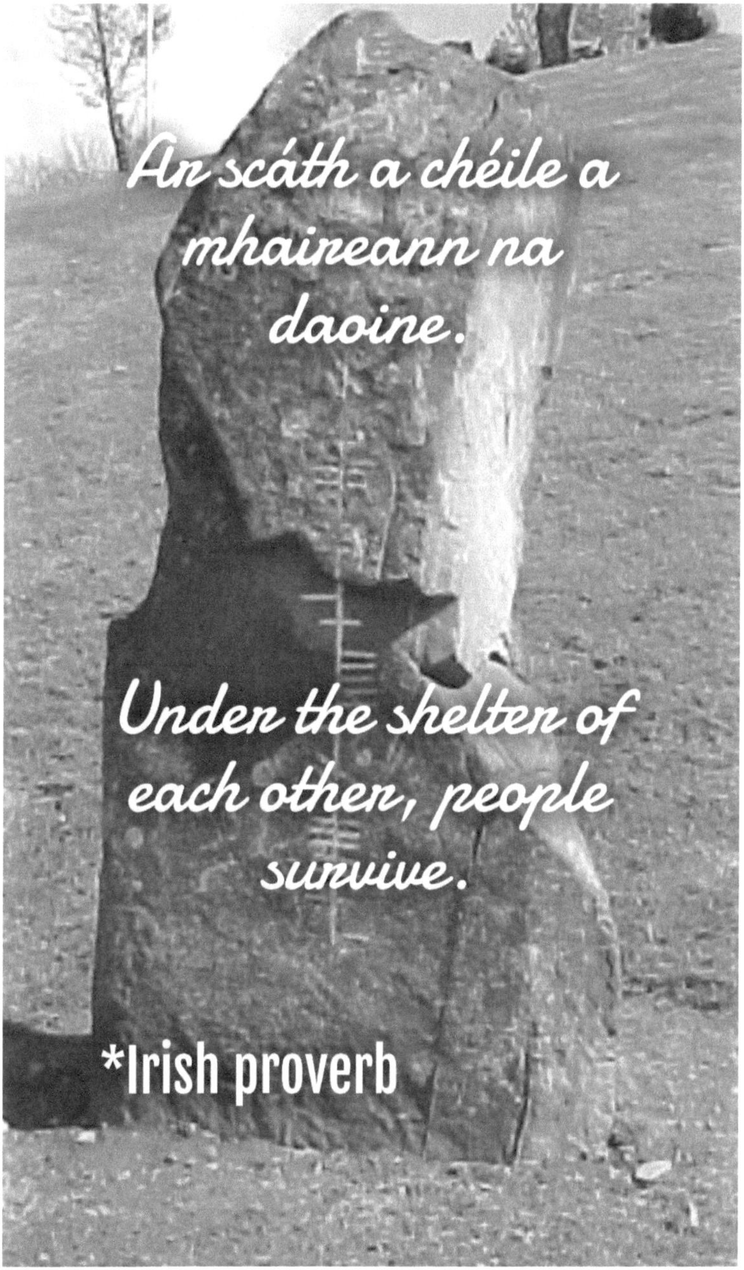

Ar scáth a chéile a mhaireann na daoine.

Under the shelter of each other, people survive.

*Irish proverb

This book has been produced in line with the EU GPSR guidelines about the safety of products.

The General Product Safety Regulation is the European Union's updated framework for ensuring that all consumer products, including books, are safe for consumers.

This book has been printed by Libri Plureos GmbH. The printer has issued safety certificates for the materials - like ink, paper and glue - being used.

The product identifier is: 9798990745834

The author is responsible for the content of the book and had it produced by Bookmundo.

Should there be any questions in regard to the safety of the product, please contact us.

Bookmundo
Delftsestraat 33
3013AE Rotterdam
The Netherlands
info@bookmundo.com